# NOTWITHSTANDING

Louis de Bernières is the bestselling author of *Captain Corelli's Mandolin*. His most recent novels are *A Partisan's Daughter* and *Birds Without Wings*.

ALSO BY LOUIS DE BERNIÈRES

*The War of Don Emmanuel's Nether Parts*
*Señor Vivo and the Coca Lord*
*The Troublesome Offspring of Cardinal Guzman*
*Captain Corelli's Mandolin*
*Sunday Morning at the Centre of the World*
*Red Dog*
*Birds Without Wings*
*A Partisan's Daughter*

LOUIS DE BERNIÈRES

# Notwithstanding

Stories from an English Village

VINTAGE BOOKS
London

Published by Vintage 2010

8 10 9

First published in Great Britain in 2009 by
Harvill Secker

Vintage
Random House, 20 Vauxhall Bridge Road,
London SW1V 2SA

www.vintage-books.co.uk

Addresses for companies within The Random House Group
Limited can be found at: www.randomhouse.co.uk/offices.htm

The Random House Group Limited Reg. No. 954009

A CIP catalogue record for this book
is available from the British Library

ISBN 9780099542025

The Random House Group Limited supports The Forest
Stewardship Council (FSC), the leading international forest
certification organisation. All our titles that are printed on
Greenpeace approved FSC certified paper carry the FSC logo.
Our paper procurement policy can be found at
www.rbooks.co.uk/environment

**Mixed Sources**
Product group from well-managed
forests and other controlled sources
www.fsc.org  Cert no. TT-COC-2139
© 1996 Forest Stewardship Council
FSC

Typeset in Adobe Garamond by Palimpsest Book Production Limited,
Grangemouth, Stirlingshire

Printed and bound in Great Britain by
CPI Bookmarque, Croydon CR0 4TD

This book is dedicated to my children, Robin and Sophie.
May they take their village with them wherever they go.

# Wilderness

There is a wilderness where once I lived
Whose every inch I knew and loved.
I roamed there as a dreaming boy
Before reality began;
I walked there still, remembering,
As I grew up beyond a man.

Sweet little in that wilderness I knew
Of God's indifference and of lovers' pain.
Too young to suffer, I remember
Longer summers, deeper slumbers,
Better laughter, warmer rain.

# CONTENTS

# ARCHIE AND THE
# BIRDS

'I'm not in. Over,' I told my mother, sighing as I held the walkie-talkie in my right hand and with my left continued painstakingly to stick small seeds to the outside of my living-room window.

'When will you be back? Over,' she asked.

'Oh, I don't know. Over,' I replied.

'Well, I hope you're back soon,' she said, reprovingly. 'This is the third time I've walkie-talked and you haven't been there. How am I supposed to talk with my own son if he's never there? Over.'

'But, Mother, I was here. I was busy. And now we are talking. Over.'

'What's keeping you so occupied, anyway? Over.'

'I'm sticking seeds to the living-room window, Mother. Over.'

There was a pause for thought, and then my

mother said, 'Well, at least you're keeping out of mischief. I'll buzz you later. Over.'

'Roger, wilco, over and out,' I said.

I placed the walkie-talkie on the window ledge, and continued to stick the seeds to the window. It was extremely tedious, and, as I had been at it since breakfast time, I was beginning to find the whole task irksome. I should have been out painting and decorating and bringing in some cash. I even wondered whether this palaver was worth it. Some of the seeds were exceedingly small, and I kept dropping them into the flower bed. I had heard that a lot of the ones in bird food are actually hemp, and I worried that perhaps in the spring these would germinate. If the village bobby happened to pass by, I might get into serious trouble and cause a scandal in the village. So I was spending an undue amount of time on my knees on the damp lawn, looking for the seeds that I had dropped. No doubt many would be found by mice, but then the cat would probably jump on them and I would feel guilty about having lured them to their deaths.

That was the least of my worries. In fact, my whole life was turning into a series of irritating little problems, each of which required altogether too much time to deal with. In this instance it ultimately occurred to me that the sensible thing would be to cover the window with glue, and then just fling the seeds at it in the hope that most of them would stick. I tried this plan out, and it worked quite admirably. I stood back and contemplated my good work, whereupon the walkie-talkie crackled again.

'Mother to Archie-master. Are you back yet? Over,' demanded my mother. 'Only I just heard from the priest that you were late at Mass last Sunday, and caused a stir when you came in. Over.'

'I am back, Mother, obviously, and I would have been on time if I hadn't been late. I had to take Archie out before he did his business on the carpet. Over.'

'Well, that's all right then. Only it's a bad thing to get a reputation for lateness. It reflects badly. Over.'

'So it does,' I said. 'But let me point out that you didn't go to Mass at all. You were in bed with a magazine and your head full of curlers. Over.'

I went back indoors and into the living room. The smears on the glass looked horrible from the inside, and the seeds somehow didn't look right. I realised that I should have arranged them in some kind of artistic pattern. I could have made them into a portrait of a cockerel, or even a nice parsnip, but now it was too late. The walkie-talkie buzzed again. 'Mother to Archie-master. So why would you be sticking seeds on the windows? Over.'

'Mother,' I said, a little wearily, 'why can't you just come out of the kitchen and talk to me without using the walkie-talkie? I'm only in the living room. Have you lost the use of your legs? Over.'

'I'm making a cake and getting lunch. Bangers and mash and baked beans. It'll be ten minutes. I'll give you a buzz. Over and out.'

I sat in my armchair and waited to see what the response to the seeds would be. I realised that I could not expect results right away, but nonetheless I was extremely curious. While I waited for lunch I reflected upon the chain of events that had led me to adopt this desperate measure.

It had begun with the dog, a black retriever. The gypsy who sold it to us took advantage of our ignorance, saying that it was a golden retriever, and that it would turn gold later. All golden retriever puppies were black at first. He was obviously expecting us to fall in love with the dog, so that by the time we found out we'd been sold a pup, we wouldn't be wanting a refund. He was right, that was exactly what happened, only we got revenge by giving him a rotten rooster and telling him it was pheasant, well hung.

My mother wanted to call the dog Sooty, but the cat had already laid claim to that name, and we didn't fancy the confusion, so we called him Archibald Scott-Moncrieff instead, or Archie for short.

Archie was a lollopy friendly dog, and when he was very small he developed a predilection for shoelaces. You couldn't take a step without finding him fastened to your foot. We took to wearing slip-ons, and he just transferred his attentions to the kitchen trolley, biting at the wheels whenever my mother moved it about the house, and yipping at it incessantly when it wasn't being wheeled anywhere. We realised that we had acquired a dog with a terrible flair for obsession, and we decided to take his mind off the trolley. I brought him out in the fields with a walking stick and taught him to retrieve.

He was altogether the natural retrieving dog, and soon I was out there with a nine-iron and a golf ball, practising day and night for the pitch-and-putt competition, with Archie flying back and forth between the legs of the cows, my Penfold Commando in his jaws. I tried to train him to put the ball back on the tee, but his nose got in the way of his eyes, and he missed. He had a soft mouth and never put a single mark on the ball, and I had such good practice that soon enough I could hit the ball high and straight, and land it on any cow I chose. I could have given Christie O'Connor a match, and I would have won the competition but for a run of bad luck in the putting.

The trouble was that Archie wouldn't stop retrieving, and in his spare time he filled the house with junk. We'd be watching the goggle-box in the evening, as Archie rushed in and out with his tennis ball. We'd leave the front door open and throw the ball out of the living-room window, whereupon Archie would fly into the hallway, out of the front door and into the darkness. Through the window would come wafting the sound of Archie galumphing and crashing and snuffling in the shrubs, and soon enough he'd be back with his ball drenched in saliva, dropping it at our feet, looking up at us with liquid brown eyes full of pleading, and then one of us would go soft and throw the ball out again, saying 'Bloody dog' as we did so.

When we couldn't take any more, Archie just went out and fetched things that hadn't even been thrown. That's how my mother found her gardening gloves again, and that's how one evening we were presented with a frog, a log, a baby rabbit and a marrow that needed picking. One day Archie shattered the rake by trying to charge through the front door with the handle horizontal in his mouth. The only thing that Archie didn't retrieve was the cat, because Sooty wouldn't cooperate, and fluffed herself up into a chimney brush if ever he tried. Just as we were Catholics, in fact the only other Catholic family in Notwithstanding (everyone else being Anglican except for the brothers at the garage who didn't drink), retrieving was the nearest that Archie got to having a religion, and since we'd always practised toleration, we felt that we had to put up with his chosen way of life.

When Archie was about two years old he came in with a blackbird, but we paid no attention. The bird was dead, and we thought that he must have found it somewhere. But then the next day he came in with a song thrush and a starling, and we became suspicious.

In our village strange things happen from time to time. To this day we still talk about the time when Mrs Mac's sister went round telling us she'd heard on the radio that from now on the rain was going to fall upward, and sure enough it did. We sat watching it out of our windows, and it looked to us as if the drops in the puddles were actually little bursts of water heading skyward. We became anxious about the village pond emptying out, but it never did, and eventually Mrs Mac's sister confessed that she'd heard the radio item on 1 April. Even so, most of us were convinced by lengthy observation that in fact the rain had been falling upward, and we had some good arguments about it, for and against, until Sir Edward explained that it was a perceptual illusion caused by the well-known effects of intellectual confusion upon the eyesight under conditions of simple Galilean relativity, whatever that is. After that, the rain fell downward once more, and normality was restored.

Anyway, after Archie had brought in a pigeon, a linnet, a greenfinch, and a woodcock, we began to realise that his retrieving had gone too far, and it wasn't until I took to sitting in the living room after lunch that I discovered the cause of his success in retrieving dead birds that no one had shot. I was reading the *Sporting Times* one afternoon, when there was a fierce thump on the window. I looked up, startled, to see a robin sliding down it, leaving a thick trail of blood behind on the glass. A few minutes later Archie brought the little bird in, and, as usual, because it would be a shame to see it go to waste, I put it in Sooty's bowl. Two more birds committed suicide by crashing into the window that very same evening.

My mother and I discussed the possibility that the local birds were suffering from depression. We knew that sometimes in the human population a kind of self-destructive hysteria can sweep through – the last time it happened in Notwithstanding was in the eighteenth century when the calendar was adjusted and everyone thought they'd been deprived of several days of life. Somehow this didn't make sense with respect to birds, so we were forced to conclude that it must be a spontaneous collective amnesia about windows.

That's why I stuck birdseed to the glass, to teach them all about windows again, and, though I say it myself, it did work wonderfully. We had dozens of birds of all kinds flapping against the window, picking off the seeds, and the sparrows and tits learned to hover like hummingbirds while they pecked. My mother and I were quite chuffed to have contributed to bird evolution, especially when they also realised by experience to keep out of Sooty's reach. She only got two or three before they learned.

Nonetheless, it drove us barmy to see Sooty trying to get at the birds, leaping up and down with a mad expression on her face as though she were on an invisible and uncontrollable pogo stick. On top of that, the repeated sound of her claws dragging down the windows was worse than the scritch of a teacher's fingernail on the blackboard, so we moved the television into the other room, and Archie went back to fetching everything except birds.

# OBADIAH OAK,
# MRS GRIFFITHS AND
# THE CAROL SINGERS

Mrs Griffiths goes to the shop and stands next to Obadiah Oak, her nose wrinkled in distaste. Obadiah, known to all as Jack, lives with his daughter by the cricket green, in a cottage that has been handed down in his family for seven generations. Jack is the village's last peasant, and he and his house smell of two hundred years of peasant life; he exudes the aromas of wet leather and horse manure, costive dogs, turnips, rainwater and cabbage water, sausages, verdigris, woollen socks, Leicester cheese, fish guts, fraying curtains, mice under the stairs, mud on the carpet and woodlice behind the pipes, but most of all he reeks of six decades of neglected hygiene. Jack is considered a 'character', with his teeth like tombstones, his stubble like a filecard, his lips like kippers, his rolling Surrey accent and his eyes as round as plates, but newcomers avoid him if they can. They moved here in search of picture-postcard England, and are uncomfortable with a real countryman who knows how to wring the neck of a chicken and has no compunction about drowning kittens in a bucket. Jack is an anachronism, but he does not know it, and he is standing in the village shop because he has nothing to do, and not many to talk with. Every day he comes in and buys cigarette papers, so that by now he must have a roomful of them, and he engages the shop assistant in a dilatory conversation about the weather, punctuating his remarks with hawking. He used to spit it out, but nowadays he swallows it, having been roundly told off one afternoon by the squirrel-shooting Polly Wantage.

'Artnoon,' he says to Mrs Griffiths. 'Turned out nice again. Looks like rain though.'

'Getting chilly,' replies Mrs Griffiths crisply, hoping to avoid a prolonged conversation.

'Time o' year,' says Jack, 'what wi' Christmas on the doorstep. Going away?'

'Staying at home. I usually do.'

'Come and eat wi' us?' says Jack, knowing that she will refuse, because everyone always does. He does not in truth want to have Mrs Griffiths round for Christmas dinner, but he has always been the kind of man who tries to do his bit, the sort of fellow who will offer his sturdy back to a child who wants to climb a tree to fetch down conkers.

'Oh, I couldn't possibly,' says Mrs Griffiths shortly, without even thanking him. But Jack is not offended; he has a sense of his place in the world, and a sensible man expects snooty people to be snooty.

'Happy Christmas, then,' he says, and he touches the rim of his sagging hat. He leaves the shop and strolls home, directly across the middle of the cricket pitch. He has been asked not to, but cannot see the point of being tender in the winter about a pitch that is mangled every weekend of the summer.

Mrs Griffiths exchanges resigned glances with Mrs Davidson, whose turn it is to man the shop. It makes no profit any more; no one would buy it from the previous owner, and now it is run on a cooperative and voluntary basis by those ladies who have time on their hands.

'I don't know why someone doesn't tell that man to wash,' says Mrs Griffiths, crossly. 'It's a disgrace.'

'Oh, I know,' says Mrs Davidson. 'Polly Wantage told him once, you know, after she stopped him from spitting, and what he said to her was unrepeatable.'

Mrs Griffiths' eyes widen with a kind of horrified delight. Strong language is so far outside her world that when she overhears it, it is as exotic as Bengal tigers.

Mrs Griffiths buys a big box of Christmas cards because she wants Mrs Davidson to think that she has lots of friends and relations. She will send a card to the vicar and the doctor, and she will drop one through the letter boxes of the more respectable people in the village, so that they will send one back, and then, should anyone call round and glance at her cards, it will be clear that she is well connected and respected. She also buys mincemeat and ready-made frozen shortcrust pastry, because tonight she is going to make mince pies for the carol singers.

Mrs Griffiths has always hated the carol singers, even though they are the children of the better families. They arrive with their guitars and their recorders, and every year they sing the same two songs, 'Silent Night' and 'O Come All Ye Faithful'. They collect for the NSPCC, and Mrs Griffiths would really rather give money to the RSPCA; at least animals cannot be blamed for anything, and do not grow up to be thieves and yobs. Mrs Griffiths secretly resents the way in which the carol singers are so young and bright-eyed, so full of high laughter, so full of the future, and previously she has always turned out the lights when she heard them coming, so that she does not have to go out and listen to them, or give them money, or make mince pies and hot punch as everyone else does. The carol singers have always sung to her closed door and doused lights, and have then departed.

But things have changed. Mrs Griffiths lost her husband in the spring, and is slowly realising that at last the time has come when she has to make an effort to get on with people. She did not love her husband, he was boring and inconsequential, and she had not even loved him when they married. After he died, she felt merely a sense of relief, conjoined with the bitterness of a freedom that has come too late. Sometimes she wonders whether she has ever loved anyone at all, and certainly she has never loved anyone as they do on the television late at night, with all those heaving backsides. But, even though her husband was a cipher, nowadays Mrs Griffiths feels a certain emptiness, a certain need to reach out, a certain need to be reborn. Tonight she will make mince pies and punch, she will leave the lights on, she will come out and listen, and she will tell the children that their music is wonderful. She will ignore the fact that they know only one verse of 'Silent Night', their guitars are out of tune and their recorders too shrill, and she will wish them a happy Christmas even though they are beautiful and still have a chance in life.

Mrs Griffiths covers herself and her kitchen in dusting sugar, she deals with the frustration of pastry that sticks to the table and the rolling pin, she conquers the meanness that nearly prevents her from pouring a whole bottle of red wine into the punch, and then she waits, sitting on the wooden chair in the kitchen, warmed by the rich smells of baking pastry and hot wine, and lemon, and rum. 'After they've been,' she thinks, 'I will write all my cards, and then I'll draw a hot bath and read.' Since her husband died, Mrs Griffiths has taken to reading true-life romances that one can order six at a time from a special club. She has read so many that she thinks she could probably write one herself.

It grows very dark, and three hours pass. Mrs Griffiths goes often to her door, and opens it, to see if she can hear the carol singers coming. The night is very cold; there is a frosty wind, but she does not think that it is going to rain. They will be here before long.

Mrs Griffiths sits in her wooden chair and thinks about what she should say to the children; does 'Merry Christmas' sound better than 'Happy Christmas'? Does 'Thank you so much for coming' sound too formal? The young are not very formal these days. During the time when everyone was going on about the Beatles, the youngsters kept saying 'groovy', but that was probably not very 'with it' any more. She is not even sure if 'with it' is 'with it' these days. She experiments with 'Groovy Christmas', but decides against it.

Mrs Griffiths hears 'Silent Night' in the distance. The children are singing to the gypsies in their scrap-yard, causing the Alsatians to howl. Now they are singing to the Davidsons, and now they are singing to the baroque musicologist, and now they are singing to smelly Jack Oak. Mrs Griffiths listens very hard for the squeak of her garden gate and the experimental chords of the guitarists. She knows that, in between the houses, the children bray out songs from pop groups with silly names and working-class accents.

The children arrive at the garden gate, and the tall, lanky one says, 'What about this one?'

'Not worth it,' says the other guitarist, who is proud of the fact that he is going to get a shaving kit for Christmas. He strokes his invisible moustache with a nail-bitten forefinger.

'She's an old skinflint,' says the blonde girl who will be beautiful when she loses her puppy fat.

'Her husband died,' says the dark, sensitive girl with the brown eyes.

'It won't do any harm, will it?' asks the blonde girl.

'There's no point,' says the lanky boy, 'she just turns off the lights as soon as she hears us coming. Every year it's the same, don't you remember? She's an old ratbag.'

'Mum told us not to leave her out,' says the blonde.

'Who's going to tell Mum?' demands her brother. 'Let's go and do the Armstrongs.'

Mrs Griffiths sits on her wooden chair and hears 'Silent Night' coming from next door. At first she feels a livid pang of anger, and one or two of those vehement forbidden words spring to her mind, but not to her lips. She is indignant, and thinks, 'How dare they miss me out. They always come here. Why am I the one to miss out?' She looks at her inviting heap of mince pies and her steaming bowl of punch, and thinks, 'I did all this for them.' She wants to go outside and shout insults at them, but she cannot think of anything that would not sound ridiculous and undignified.

Alongside her anger and frustration, Mrs Griffiths abruptly feels more tired and forlorn than she has ever felt in her life, and she begins to cry for the first time since she was a child. She is surprised by large tears that well up in her eyes and slide down the sides of her nose, rolling down her hands and wrists, and into her sleeves. She had not remembered that tears could be so warm. She tastes one, in order to be reminded of their saltiness, and finds it comforting. She thinks, 'Perhaps I should get a cat,' and fetches some kitchen roll so that she can blow her nose.

Mrs Griffiths begins to write her cards. One for the vicar, one for the doctor, one for the people in the mansion, one for the Conservative councillor. She gets up from her chair and, without really thinking about it, eats a mince pie and takes a glass of punch. She had forgotten how good they can be, and she feels the punch igniting her insides. The sensuality of it shocks and seduces her, and she takes another glass.

Mrs Griffiths cries some more, but this time it is

partly for pleasure, for the pleasure of the hot briny water, and the sheer self-indulgence. A rebellious whim creeps up on her. She glances around as if to check that she is truly alone in the house, and then she stands up and shouts, 'Bloody bloody bloody bloody bloody.' She adds, 'Bloody children, bloody bloody.' She attempts 'bollocks' but merely embarrasses herself and tries 'bugger' instead. She drinks more punch and says, 'Bloody bugger.' She writes a card to the gypsies who own the scrapyard, and to the water-board man who had an illegitimate child by a Swedish barmaid, and to the people who own the pub and vote Labour. She eats two mince pies at once, cramming them into her mouth, one on top of the other, and the crumbs and the sugar settle on to the front of her cardigan. She fetches a biscuit tin, and puts into it six of the remaining pies. She presses down the lid and ventures out into the night.

When she returns she finishes off the punch, and then heaves herself upstairs with the aid of the banisters.

She is beginning to feel distinctly ill, and heads for her bed with the unconscious but unswerving instinct of a homing pigeon. She reminds herself to draw the curtains so that no one will be able to pry and spy, and then she undresses with difficulty, and throws her clothes on to the floor with all the perverse but justified devilment of one who has been brought up not to, and has never tried it before. She extinguishes the light and crawls into bed, but every time that she closes her eyes she begins to feel seasick. Her eyes glitter in the dark like those of a small girl, the years are briefly annulled, and she remembers how to feel frightened when an owl hoots outside.

At eleven thirty, fetid Jack Oak opens his front door to put the cat out and spots a biscuit tin by the door scraper. He picks it up, curious, and takes it back inside. 'Look what some'un left,' he says to his daughter, who is just as unkempt as he is, but smells more sweetly.

'Well, open it,' she says.

Jack prises off the lid with his thick yellow nails, and inside he finds six mince pies, and an envelope. Jack almost never gets Christmas cards. He feels a leap of excitement and pleasure in his belly, and hands the card to his daughter to read. It says: '*To dear Mr Obadiah Oak and daughter, a very Happy Christmas and New Year, from Marjorie Griffiths.*'

'Well, bugger me,' says Jack, and his daughter says, 'Now there's a turn-up for the books.' Jack puts the card on the mantelpiece, crams a whole mince pie into his mouth, and delves among the clutter for a pencil and the box of yellowing cards that he bought from the village shop fifteen years ago.

# ARCHIE AND THE WOMAN

'Mother to Archie-master, come in please. Over.'

'I'm digging potatoes,' I said to my mother, sighing as I held the walkie-talkie to my ear with my right hand, and gave up turning the heavy ochre clay. I thrust the spade into the ground. 'What do you want now? Can't it wait 'til lunchtime? Over.'

'I wanted to talk to you urgently,' she replied, 'while I remembered. Over.'

'Well, what is it? Over.'

There was a long pause, and then she said, 'Bless me, I've forgotten what it was. Over.'

'Tell me at lunchtime then, when you've remembered. What's for lunch? Over.'

'Steak and kidney pie with mashed neeps with a fried egg on top. It'll be half an hour. I'll be ringing you when it's ready. Over and out.'

I looked at the walkie-talkie. 'Bloody thing,' I said to myself, and hooked it on to the trellis. It had been a curse ever since my mother gave it to me for Christmas, because it meant that she could get hold of me wherever I was. Nowadays she did not even see fit to come the fifty yards to the vegetable patch, and I could clearly see her through the kitchen window, putting the walkie-talkie down and wiping the steam from her spectacles. If I left the gadget in the house, then she would roundly accuse me of ingratitude, and of a lack of respect for her poor old legs. Sometimes I just switched it off, and pretended that the batteries had run out.

'What was it then?' I asked her, as I pierced the yolk of my egg and watched the thick yellow goo trickle down the sides of a pyramid of mashed turnip.

She put down her knife and fork, and looked into her notebook, a small black one, with ruled lines and a red spine. In it she kept remarks and reminders that were to be addressed specifically to me. I used to call it 'Mother's Book of Complaints'.

'Oh yes,' she said, 'I've decided that it's about time you got married.'

I was aghast. I was so stricken by aghastness, or aghastitude, that my mind went quite blank, like a balloon that had suddenly popped on a briar. I paused with a forkful of mash in mid-delivery, and my mouth agape. 'What on earth for?' I demanded eventually. 'I'm only forty-two.'

'Even so,' she said.

'Oh, come off it. What would I want with being married?'

'It's not you I'm thinking of,' she replied, 'it's me. I need some company about the place. You're always out and about. When you're not painting and decorating or gardening, you're out playing golf. And I can't imagine you looking after me in my old age, so you'll have to get a wife.'

'You're only seventy-five,' I said, 'it'll be donkey's years before you'll be going gaga.'

Naturally I didn't take my mother seriously. When my dear father was dying in his bed, he had called me in to give me his final blessing, and, as I knelt beside him with the palm of his hand on the crown of my head, he had said, 'Now, son, you've got to promise me something.'

'Father, of course I will,' I had said. He closed his eyes, as if to marshal his final strength, and he said, 'Son, promise me faithfully that you'll never take your mother seriously. I never have. And try not to get married.'

'I swear it,' I spluttered (for the tears were making speech difficult), and with that his breathing stopped. There was a horrible rattling from his throat, and my mother, who had been standing there all the while, said fondly, 'The poor old sod.'

As the years have succeeded one another, I have increasingly appreciated my father's wisdom. The fact is that Mother gets curious fancies that fly into her brain one day, and fly out of it the next, such as the time when she started to make cabbage wine because she had conceived the notion that it was good for the pancreas. Of course, it was undrinkable, and so she gave it away at Christmas time as presents for folk in the village that she didn't think highly of. She sold some at the WI fete, and most people poured it straight on the compost after a single sip.

However, this idea that I should be getting married rankled in my mind like a bur in a woolly sock. It seemed a fine idea to have someone to share a bed with. I hadn't had a decent pillow fight for twenty years. And apart from that, a man needs a female, other than his mother, to rub along with.

The problem was, of course, that I had to find some women to meet with, so that I would have an idea of what there was in the offing.

I ruled out an advertisement in the lonely hearts; I hated to tell lies, and an honest description of myself would have put off all but the desperate. I wasn't so desperate that I would have taken someone else who was.

I thought about how one meets people in my village, and very soon realised that of course it was because of the dogs. Almost everyone had one, and most took their animals out every day, to stretch their legs and take a gander at what Mother Nature was doing to the common land or the Hurst. There was a regular ritual about all this, for if one met another dog, it was obligatory to pat it on the head, ruffle its ears, unclamp it from one's leg, and discuss its virtues with the owner while the latter performed the same ritual with one's own dog. First came the enquiry as to the dog's breed, which was usually a matter of some doubt, then followed anecdotes intended to illustrate its irresistible appeal, its great intelligence and its extraordinary powers of intuition. Then came news of its health problems, and the fact that garlic pearls in its food had been working miracles. Naturally, one could while away many hours in doggy conversations in the process of taking a long walk, and one could come back at dusk and say, 'I'm sorry I took so long, I got caught by Mrs John the Gardener, and she just wouldn't stop going on about that bloody mutt of hers. I'll dig the new potatoes and bring in the coal tomorrow,' and my mother would tut, and say something like, 'It was that woman's dog that put Sir Edward's Labrador bitch in the family way.'

I think I might have told you about our dog. He was a great big fool of a hound. We called him Archibald Scott-Moncrieff, which soon got shortened to Archie. He was a black retriever who took his vocation seriously. At one time Archie got delusions of grandeur, and came back from walks with fifteen-foot branches of oak in his maw. Then he would get stuck at the gate.

All this retrieving gave me a humorous notion, and so it was that one day at lunch I said to my mother, 'Mother, do you think it would be a fine idea to train Archie to retrieve eligible spinsters?'

My mother looked up from slurping her soup, and eyed me. 'Well,' she said, 'I have my doubts.'

'Why's that, then?'

'Because a dog's "eligible" might be a funny thing, and not to your satisfaction, I should think. He'd want her to smell of lady dogs.'

'Nonetheless,' I said.

'No harm in having a try, then,' she observed, 'but don't hang any washing on it.'

Of course, the difficulty wasn't with the idea, but with the execution. How does one train a dog to retrieve women who are specifically good-looking, intelligent, amenable, amusing, playful but faithful, fond of housework, and prepared to put up with my mother? The only way to do this would have been to identify such women myself, and work out a system of rewards for Archie whenever he got hold of one by the sleeve and dragged her in my direction. Clearly, if I had to find such women in order to train the dog, then I might as well just do the finding myself, and leave Archie out of it.

I decided to train him to find golf balls instead, and that's why I have five carrier bags of them in the cupboard under the stairs. I took him to the local nine-holer, which was a rough-hewn business designed by an aristocrat who used to own the big house. The course was like a First World War battlefield, in that it was sloppy with mud, and cratered with water-filled holes, there were rabbit scrapes all over the greens, and sheep browsing the rough. One par three was so constructed that you had to play your tee shot over the roof of the great house. The windows had to have steel shutters over them on playing days. If you muffed your shot, it might ricochet back over your head, and plop into the pond behind the tee, or you might have to go and chip your way round the house, avoiding the peacocks and the statues of naked girls with no arms. The best I ever did that hole was a birdie two, and the worst was forty-eight, if you don't count the ball that got stuck in the gob of the gargoyle on the west wing.

I soon found that no amount of training could get Archie to distinguish between a lost ball and one that was still in play. It was very embarrassing when he raced away on to another fairway, and came back with someone's perfectly placed drive, or their ball that was just about to roll into the hole for an eagle. Eventually I had to tie Archie to my golf bag, so that I could catch up with him when he tried to hare away after another illegitimate target. Sometimes he would fly off into the woods on the trail of a wild shot, and then get lost altogether, when his attention was distracted by a roe deer. Once he chased a deer all the way to Chiddingfold, and was spotted by one of the teetotalling brothers from the garage, who brought him back to Mother in the cab of his tow truck.

One day, as I was hacking up the first and someone else was coming down the third, Archie slipped his leash and scampered away with his ears flapping behind him. Off he lolloped, and before I knew it, he was back with a nice Dunlop 65, American size, all covered with slobber, which he deposited at my feet. 'Good boy,' I said, since he was so pleased with himself, and I didn't therefore have the heart to tell him off. I picked the ball up, wiped the dribble off on to my trousers, and began to walk towards its owner, who was striding towards me.

I was preparing my apologies, when I noticed that the golfer was a woman, and so I ran back and hid in a holly bush. Male golfers are usually quite jolly and placid, but female golfers can be terrifying in a variety of ways, and it is best to avoid them at all costs, just in case they turn out to be someone with a degree in Art and an amazing collection of conspiracy theories.

I didn't escape, though, and before I knew it she was poking at me through the prickly leaves with a four-iron. 'I know you're in there,' she said firmly, 'I can see your shoes.' Her voice sounded quite pleasant and mellifluous, with a happy burbling in it rather like a brook running over pebbles.

'I'm sorry,' I said, from the depths of the bush, 'but my dog can't help retrieving things. It's his hobby, and I can't stop him. I'll give your ball back.' And with that I tossed the ball through the branches, in the hope that she would be satisfied and go away.

'You're being very silly,' she said. 'It's your dog I want to talk to you about. I've got a bitch just the same, and I've been meaning to breed from her. Your dog looks just right. A very fine specimen. I'll pay you a stud fee and twenty pounds per pup. How about that?'

'Archie would enjoy that,' I said, disentangling myself from the bushes and coming face to face with a woman of about thirty years of age. She had blue eyes, and a mouth that curled up at the corners, as though she was always smiling and her mouth had to be ready on the blocks. For a lady golfer she seemed surprisingly on the level.

That's how it all started with Evie and me. All that hoo-ha and palaver about ovulation and being on heat, and making sure that there was penetration and fertilisation, gave us something in common, a good excuse to meet up and get to know each other. I think that talking frequently about mating must have got us all worked up subconsciously, and I can't imagine how many pots of tea we drank while we eyed each other up across the kitchen table, with Mother hovering outside in the corridor.

On the big day, Archie did his stuff pretty amateurishly, I'd say. He started at the wrong end, Evie's bitch got muddled, and we had to rearrange them. All the same, Evie was thrilled, and later that afternoon we went to the shop and bought a bottle of Spanish champagne. She made a shepherd's pie with caramel-flavoured Instant Whip to follow, and, well, you know how it is, how one thing leads to another.

# THE GIRT PIKE

The Girt Pike was caught in the days before the village pond had been sanitised. Once upon a time it was quite accepted that the village boys should spend their summers angling for rudd, squeezing pellets of dough on to size-twelve hooks, and casting out among the lilies. In the evenings the brassy rudd would skip for flies at the time of the hatch, and it seemed unbelievable that one small pond could hold so many fish. It was permissible in those days for people to throw sticks into the pond so that their dogs could fetch them, and the ragtaggle of semi-domesticated ducks would have to shift for themselves, paddling away in comical alarm. In later years the pond would be stocked with ornamental golden tench, little boys would be forbidden to fish, dogs would be forbidden to scare the ducks, and a fence would be erected around the banks to prevent erosion, and to prevent children from falling in. The pond became prettier, but in its prissified state it did not become better loved, and thenceforth it no longer played any part in cementing the friendships of the very young, or filling their holidays with sunshine and clean air.

Before it was sanitised, there was nearly always a party of little boys there in the summer months, usually on the bank nearest the road that led to the village green and the shop. There would be little girls there, too, making daisy chains or squinting against the sunlight as they cried 'Ugh, oh yuk!' every time a boy laid hands on a fish to unhook it. The girls never did understand why anyone could bear to get their hands slimy and smelly, and so they watched the boys with appropriate disdain and uncomprehending disgust. If any boy was using maggots or worms, there would of necessity arise a moment when one or more of the girls would be chased squealing round and round the pond by one or more of the boys, who would be threatening to put the worm or the maggot down their necks, or even down their knickers. These episodes would normally end with somebody falling over and hurting their knee or sliding down the muddy bank into the water.

On the morning that concerns us, however, one small boy was fishing on his own, his keepnet flashing at his feet with golden tiddlers. His name was Robert, and he lived in the small row of council houses on Cherryhurst, the road to the Institute of Oceanography, just past the house of Mr Hadgecock the spy, and the lane that led up to the house where Mrs Mac lived with her sister and the ghost of her husband. Many of the boys who fished were much posher than he was, but fortunately the brotherhood of the line counted for far more than deeply inculcated divisions of class and education, and he and they regarded each other with the kind of mutual awe tinged with fear which only a class-conscious Briton would appreciate. Robert used a small rod made of two sections of an ancient Avon rod that his grandfather had adapted for him. It had chrome-plated rings whipped carefully on to it in red button thread, and it had been craftsmanly rubbed down and varnished so that it gleamed. Many of the posher boys were envious of it, and once he had even refused an offer for it of as much as thirty shillings and a Goliath catapult, and a Milbro catapult that needed new rubber. Robert used a small brass centre-pin reel that his grandfather had also passed on, and which was the very same reel with which he had fished in the pond when he had been a little boy. Robert longed for a spinning reel, the kind where you could just open the bail arm and cast as far as you liked, but he was nonetheless adept at pulling out loops of line from the centre pin and placing his bait exactly where he wanted to. One day collectors would be paying implausible money for old brass centre pins such as his, but just now Robert wanted, more than anything, an Intrepid Prince Regent, which was even better than an Intrepid Black Prince, because it had a proper roller on the bail arm. Robert wanted an Intrepid Prince Regent just as much as other people wanted a Colston dishwasher or an E-Type Jaguar. The Prince Regent cost exactly thirty shillings, and so he was in the paradoxical and self-defeating position of being able to buy one only if he sold his rod to one of the rich boys.

Robert was reeling in another small rudd, hoping it would be bigger than it was, when a voice behind him said, 'Oh, you are clever. Do tell me what it is.'

'It's a rudd, missus,' said Robert, turning round and dangling the unfortunate creature in front of the lady's face.

The lady concerned was Mrs Rendall, blonde and pretty and vivacious, who, one day soon, would be carried away by cancer before she was forty. All the boys experienced a sensation of longing in the throat when they saw her or thought of her, and none of them could ever imagine growing up to be loved by someone as lovely as she. They thought of her husband as especially blessed, as if he were like God, his status much enhanced by the devotion of angels.

'How do you know it's a rudd?' she asked, with genuine interest.

'The mouth turns up, missus, 'cause it feeds on the top, and it's all golden. If it were a roach its mouth would turn down, and if it were a bream it'd be silver, and anyway, I just know it's a rudd.'

'You are clever,' repeated Mrs Rendall, genuinely impressed. She watched as the little boy unhooked it and put it into his keepnet. 'What do you do with them?' she asked.

'At the end of the day I count them up, and then I put them back.'

'Can't you eat them?'

'Don't know, missus. Haven't tried.'

'What's the most you've ever caught? In one day?'

'Twenty, missus,' Robert told her, exaggerating by five.

'Twenty! That's an awful lot!' She watched him as, very self-consciously, he cast his line back out. He was determined to do it beautifully, because Mrs Rendall was very nice and very pretty, and her niceness and prettiness made him want to do everything perfectly when she was near him.

'Have you ever caught a pike?'

'No, missus. I never even seen one.'

'Do you think that you could? Would you like to?'

Robert's eyes gleamed. There was nothing in the

whole world more marvellous than the prospect of catching a pike. It was probably more marvellous even than catching a shark. Robert knew someone who had been dangling his toes in the water when they had been savaged by a pike. He had heard of an Alsatian dog that had been bitten on the paw by one.

'I don't know if I could,' admitted Robert. 'I may not yet be old enough. If I was older, I reckon I could.'

'How old are you, then?'

'I'm eleven, missus.'

'I think that's old enough. In fact, I'm sure it is. Would you come and catch my pike?'

'What? The Girt Pike?' asked Robert incredulously.

Mrs Rendall lived in the Glebe House, opposite the cattle pound, and it had behind it a rectangular pond that must originally, perhaps a century before, have been a swimming pool. It was quite large, overhung with branches and it was absolutely full of starving tiddlers, as Robert had found out when poaching there from the shelter of a laurel. Robert had always kept an eye out for the Girt Pike, but he had never seen it. Everyone said it was there, and lots of people had claimed to have spotted it, or thought that maybe they might have done, but Robert never had, and he had become sceptical.

'The Girt Pike? Is that what you call it? Why "Girt"?'

'Don't know, missus. That's what it's called, dunno why. It's there, then, is it? I heard about it, but I wasn't so sure.'

'It's there all right. Every year the ducks and the moorhens and the coots hatch out all these gorgeous little fluffy chicks, and that pike just gobbles them up one after the other.'

Robert's eyes widened. 'You seen it, missus?'

'Yes. One after the other! It's awful! He just opens his mouth and his head comes out of the water, and that's one more chick, just gone! Every year! He eats all the chicks and there's never one left to grow up. I do wish you'd come and catch it.'

'You'd let me, then?' asked Robert, in disbelief.

'Let you? I'd be so grateful that you'd have to run away to stop me kissing you!'

'Gosh,' said Robert, thinking that he would probably have to run away as a matter of form, even if he did not actually want to. 'You'd let me, then?' he asked again.

'Please do come up and catch it. I'll bring you cups of tea and as many sandwiches as you can eat, I promise.'

'Peanut butter?' asked Robert, aware that posh people sometimes put truly revolting pastes made of rotten anchovies into their sandwiches.

'Peanut butter or jam, or anything,' said Mrs Rendall, much amused.

'I'll come up next week,' said Robert.

'Just knock at the door, and I'll make you tea and sandwiches, I promise.'

'Crunchy peanut butter,' Robert specified, with an intonation of warning in his voice.

'I'll go and get it now,' she said, and turned to go back to the Cricket Green Stores. When she drove past him a few minutes later, smiling at the wheel of her green-and-cream Austin Cambridge, she tooted the horn and waved a pot of crunchy peanut butter at him, with its red lid and label. Robert reeled in his line and began to pack up his tackle. His air had become deeply serious and determined. He was about to undertake the greatest task of his life hitherto, and he was gallantly doing it for a beautiful lady. This was what it might be like to be Sir Lancelot.

Robert had almost none of the equipment that one needs for pike, and he had very little money with which to acquire it. Nonetheless he went to Godalming on the bus, to C. F. Horne's tackle shop in Bridge Street. Mr C. F. Horne was a very kindly man with a bald top and a brown shop coat. He would mend any little boy's fishing rod very cheaply and beautifully, and nobody was ever aware, until he was one day found dead on the railway line, that his wife had been mentally ill for years, and that he had been suffering more stress and difficulty than most people could endure.

'I've got to catch a pike, mister,' Robert told him, adding, 'I've got to catch it for a lady.'

'How are you going to catch it, sir?' asked Mr Horne, playing up to the boy's earnestness.

'Live bait,' said Robert.

'Well, then, sir, you'll need a Jardine snap tackle and a trace.' He reached under the counter and brought them out, neatly coiled inside cellophane packages. 'Have you got a bung?'

'I found one in the Wey, mister.'

'How about the rod? Is yours up to it?'

'No, mister, but I can't buy another one. I ain't got the money.'

'That's a shame. Do you know what you're going to do?'

'Yes, mister. I got a plan. I need some line, though.'

'Is it a big pike, young sir?'

'It's the Girt Pike.'

'The Girt Pike,' repeated Mr Horne, unenlightened. 'Well, if it's the Girt Pike . . .' He handed over a fifty-yard reel of thirty-pound line, and said, 'This'll hold anything short of a shark.'

Robert felt the hefty monofilament with his fingers. It was thicker and more stiff than any line he had ever seen before. Mr Horne observed his apprehension and told him, 'Use the half-blood knot as usual, but wet the line first, or it'll be hard to draw tight.'

Robert counted out his money and realised that he was sixpence short. He stared at the coins in his palm, the threepenny bits and the halfpennies, and felt the leaden weight of disappointment in his heart. He looked and looked at his coins, as if looking might conjure up the extra coin that he had to have. Tears came to his eyes, but he mastered them, and slowly he offered back the brown paper bag containing his purchases. 'I ain't got enough,' he said.

Mr C. F. Horne looked down at him sympathetically, and then he had a brainwave. 'Let me look at those coins,' he said, and he took them, turning them over in his hand with a scholarly air. 'Ah!' he exclaimed theatrically. 'Just as I thought!'

He held out a blackened old penny that bore the all but deleted image of Queen Victoria. 'See this, young sir? This penny is very rare. In fact, it's so rare that it's not even worth a penny.'

'Isn't it?' said Robert, fearing that it was so worn out that its value might have been reduced to a halfpenny.

'As luck would have it,' said Mr Horne gravely, 'this penny is so rare that it's worth sixpence, and sixpence is exactly what you owe me.' He handed back the brown paper bag, saying, 'Thank you kindly, and good luck with the, er, Girt Pike. And don't go putting your fingers in its maw until you're sure that it's dead.' He watched Robert leaving the shop, and sighed and shook his head on account of his own foolishness. For months afterwards, Robert was to wonder somewhat ungraciously whether his penny might have been worth even more than sixpence, and half suspected Mr C. F. Horne of having diddled him.

The following day Robert took a small bowsaw from his father's shed, and went to the Hurst. It was dark, wet, criss-crossed with inexplicable ditches, and in some places it had been coppiced for centuries. One of the ditches was oozing with the old engine oil emptied into it routinely by the gypsies at the scrapyard, but in those days no one thought anything of it. It was a place of kingcups and bluebells, pheasants, and abandoned iron pans with the bottoms rusted out. Through it ran the old cart track that in former times had been the main road to Chiddingfold and Abbot's Notwithstanding. Nothing ever grew on it, and it remained a ghost road, or perhaps a road-in-waiting. He soon found a hazel that was in the ideal state, because he had often thought that one day such a wand might come in handy for something.

Not far off, Polly Wantage, apparelled in plus fours, was banging away at squirrels with her twelve-bore, and Robert worked quickly, with the fear in his breast that she might mistake him for a squirrel and give him a peppering. He whistled out of tune, very loudly, so that she would know he was a boy. His Uncle Dick frequently claimed to have been shot up the backside by irate gamekeepers, and liked to tell Robert that every evening he found lead shot in his underwear, where it had worked its way out of his bum during the day. He would put a hand down into the seat of his trousers, draw it out, and present the boy with pieces of warm swan shot, exclaiming, 'There you are, son, get a load a' that! Just think where that's been, eh! Makes yer wince, don' it?'

The holy grail and ultimate ambition of every little fisherman was a twelve-foot fishing rod. One day Robert hoped to own the very best, a Sealey Octofloat, which was made with real split cane, and was a proper twelve-footer. Twelve foot was long enough to reach out beyond the lily pads at the fringes of ponds, it was long enough to drop a float delicately next to the bubbles being sent to the surface by a tench, it was long enough to feel like a grown-up's weapon. Never mind if it was also long enough to get tangled in the branches overhead during lapses of concentration and periods of excitement. Robert cut a long hazel pole that looked as if it must be at least twelve foot, and pulled it out of the clump where he had found it. Rather self-consciously he walked back home with it, past the green and the village shop, and past Obadiah Oak, the village's last peasant, who made no acknowledgement beyond a friendly nod of the head, conscious that little boys often need long sticks for all sorts of purposes. Robert was worried that it might have been illegal to cut sticks in the Hurst, and his heart thumped with anxiety until he had arrived safely home, in case he was passed by the bobby on his bicycle, who would probably know straight away that the stick was a stolen one.

When he was home, Robert managed to get the pole through the house and out into the back garden with the assistance of his mother, who held on to the thin end to make sure that it didn't whip any ornaments off their shelves. When he had laid it out on the grass he fetched a tape measure, and, with mounting excitement, confirmed that his rod was indeed not just twelve foot long, but sixteen. What should he do? All the best rods were twelve foot, but why not innovate, why not go even further? He wedged the rod into a chink in the fence, and bent it at the tip. It was definitely too thin and weak, so he cut off two feet. He waved the rod about, feeling it flex, and it was just right. He knew instinctively that it had enough whip in it to resist and tire a big fish, bending without breaking. Robert realised that he was pioneering a new concept in extra-long rods, and he felt emboldened and excited.

The little boy whipped the end of the thirty-pound line on to the tip, carefully emulating the technique taught him by his grandfather. He tied a loop in his line and tightened it about an inch from the point of the rod, and then very neatly he bound it along the final inch with button thread, under which he had laid a short loop of fine line, so that he could pass the thread through the loop, and then pull it through under the binding, to fix it. This always worked better than knots. Robert waited impatiently until his mother went out to the village shop to get bread, and then he sneaked upstairs and raided her make-up table for clear nail varnish. He painted it heavily on to the whipped thread, enjoying the clinging, intoxicating odour of it, so that it would shrink the whipping tight and set it hard and solid.

Robert had enough experience to realise that the line couldn't be much longer than the rod, because otherwise he wouldn't be able to land the fish, and so he cut it off at fifteen feet, reasoning that this left some compensating margin for the line that in the future he was bound to lose while cutting knots away from hooks and traces. He rootled around in his treasure drawer and found the brightly painted pike bung that he had once rescued at great peril after spotting it abandoned, tangled up in reeds on the River Wey after the great flood. He pulled the stick out of the middle, laid his line in the slot, and replaced the stick. He resisted the temptation to tie on the trace and the treble hooks of the snap tackle. He had had a hook in his finger before, because of leaving his rod tackled up and ready to go. Uncle Dick had brought the hook through his flesh until it emerged, then he had cut off the barb and drawn it back out. The memory of the agony he had had to endure still made him clench his teeth.

Lastly Robert made a priest, because he knew that he was going to have to bash the pike over the head if he caught it. He found an old hickory broom handle, cut off a foot at one end, and drilled a hole in it. He decided to sacrifice some airgun pellets, and melted a handful in the lid of the tin, using Uncle Dick's blowtorch. With a pair of pliers he gingerly picked up the lid, swimming with molten silvery liquid, and poured the lead into the hole that he had drilled. He would need the extra weight to make a sufficiently convincing cosh. He left it to cool, and then found to his frustration and disappointment that the lead simply fell out of the hole, because it shrunk when it cooled off. After a half-hour's despair, Robert had a brainwave, and rummaged in his treasure drawer again. He had a big rusty bolt that he had found on the verge side, and this he glued into the hole vacated by the wilful lead. He smacked his palm with it a few times, and reckoned that it would be heavy enough.

So it was that two days later Robert called in on Mrs Rendall, ostensibly to let her know that he was there, but primarily to activate the flow of tea and peanut butter sandwiches. He had just had the most difficult bicycle ride of his life, because it wasn't easy cycling up hills with a bag of fishing tackle and a fourteen-foot pole, and all the mad drivers like Miss Agatha Feakes and the nuns from the convent made it that much more nerve-racking and hazardous. He had been glad to catch his breath by stopping and talking to the hedging and ditching man, who, in the attitude of Hamlet cradling Yorick's skull, had been examining the seized and rusted remains of an ancient gin trap that he had just found in the ditch. The hedging and ditching man had admired the hazel pole, and said that he would have been proud to have made something like that himself, and that if that didn't catch the Girt Pike then nothing would. When he finally arrived at the Glebe House, Robert was quite exhausted, his legs were aching, and he definitely needed tea and peanut butter before he could begin to catch a fish.

He set up his normal rod, because first of all he had to catch a tiddler to put on the snap tackle. It was a perfect day, balmy, with a light breeze that was propelling wisps of cloud across the face of the sun. The animals and birds seemed especially active and cheerful. With the tea and sandwiches lying pleasantly on his stomach like the weight of a cat in the lap, Robert settled on his tiny folding fishing stool, and hauled in one tiddler after another. There was such pleasure in catching so many sparkling silver roach with their bright scarlet fins that it put the

Girt Pike out of his mind. There was no sign of the great fish, and it receded into a distant possibility, a far potentiality, as if he suspected, or even knew, that he was not really old enough, or man enough, or ambitious enough, to catch it. He was also, in truth, reluctant to take one of those jewel-like fish, and impale it on treble hooks. Like all little boys, he had had his moments of gratuitous cruelty, but these beautiful little creatures were too perfect to violate.

He was in that hypnagogic state common in bank-side fishermen, when he became aware quite suddenly that something was happening at his feet. There was a stirring and a swirling in the water. He looked down and saw that the Girt Pike was tugging at his keepnet in an attempt to get at the tiddlers within. The great dark fish, casual, brutal and impudent, was actually within a hand's reach, and Robert felt his heart leap in his chest. He shouted and leapt backwards, knocking over his stool, and the pike flicked its tail and vanished. When Robert came back to the water, thankful that no one had been witness to his panic and foolishness, he could see the pike near the surface by the lily pad, fanning the water with its fins, and watching him. It must have been three feet long, and was the biggest fish that Robert had ever seen. It seemed impossible that such a creature could have lived in this small pond.

With his hands shaking, Robert took a roach from his keepnet and hooked it on to his snap tackle, just as it said in the books, with one hook through the dorsal fin and another through the lip. He did not enjoy doing this, but he had been taken over by a deep and ineluctable instinct. He knew that it was necessity, and that was all.

He swung the little victim out over the water, dropped it just past the lily pad, and drew it straight past the nose of the pike.

To his amazement and surprise, and so fast that he could not react, the pike lunged forward and took the bait. Robert knew that when a pike took, you had to wait a second before you struck, otherwise you could just wrench the bait out of its mouth, but in this case he was so astonished that he nearly didn't strike at all. When he did so, he felt the massive weight and strength of the fish at the other end, and began to experience an intoxicating terror that he would never in his life forget.

He would always remember the effort of trying to control his fright, and the temptation to do stupid or counter-productive things. He forced himself not to haul on the fish, not to risk breaking the rod, to let it tire itself out naturally against the spring of the hazel wood. He was amazed and bewondered by the energy and fury of the pike, as it surged one way and then another, bending the rod so that it bucked and leapt in his hands. Robert realised that he did not have his landing net ready, and understood too late that the net was far too small in any case. It was a little folding thing that he had found in the White Elephant in Godalming, and it had been originally intended for trout. He tucked the hazel pole under one arm, and managed to flick the net open with one hand.

He never knew how long it was that the mighty fish hurled itself about. Every time Robert thought that it had given up, the fish suddenly flamed back into furious resistance, rushing hither and thither, shaking its head, diving and leaping. Robert lost all sense of time and entered into another dimension that had something about it of eternity. He was holding on grimly, clutching his hazel pole more desperately than he really needed to, his knuckles white, his eyes popping in his head, and all the muscles of his arms and back aching with the strain. As the fish finally did begin to tire, as the intervals between its furies grew longer, he started to experience the terrible anxiety of not knowing how he was going to cope with such a monster once he had got it on to the bank.

Finally the Girt Pike was utterly spent, and Robert eased it towards him by raising the tip of the rod. Robert put his landing net into the water, and made the classic fisherman's mistake. No one had ever told him that big fish seem to know what a landing net is for. This is why you draw a fish over the net, and then lift it. You cannot risk pulling it straight into a net that is plainly visible.

The Girt Pike saw the net and with shocking suddenness it burst back into frenzied life and hurled itself out towards the centre of the pond. Before Robert even knew what was happening, it had wrenched the rod out of his hand and towed it away across the water towards the lily pad.

Robert wanted to cry, and he sat down on the grass gazing numbly out at his rod floating on the water, and the heaving of the lily pad as the pike thrashed about in it. Finally he stood up, shaking but determined, and took off his shoes, socks and trousers. He dipped a toe into the water. It seemed unnaturally cold for a summer's day. He worried that the water would be too deep, because he was not a good swimmer. He waded out, feeling the silty mud squelching between his toes, until he could grasp the butt of the rod. He raised it, and prepared to take up the strain of the fish. When he did so, it was the lily pad that responded, and he realised that the fish had wound the line round and round the massed stems. He pulled futilely on the line. The lilies moved but did not give, and his despair was renewed. The situation seemed irretrievable.

It was then that the speckled tail of the Girt

Pike rose up vertically from the water in the middle of the lily pad, rather like Excalibur, and just hung there, pointing straight up and not moving. Robert beheld it in wonderment, realising that the fish had wound itself so tightly around the lilies that it could no longer move. It was drowning ignominiously in the middle of its kingdom. This was an ignoble and humiliating end for a creature of such power and myth.

Robert waded back to the bank, took up his landing net and found his fishing knife. He re-entered the freezing water and approached the lily pad. He was already a wiser and more cautious fisherman. He got the net ready in advance, and slipped it under the fish, which did not respond. When he raised it, the fish flapped feebly, its huge body overspilling the sides of the net. Desperately Robert tried to saw at the line where it entered the water and tangled with the lilies. Finally he succeeded, and the fish was released into his possession. Robert brought it out of the pond, unable to believe just how heavy it was, and equally incredulous that he really had caught it and conquered it. He laid it on the lawn, where it continued to flap, and then Robert waded back into the water to cut the line again, so that he could retrieve his rod, which was still floating on the water.

Robert was bending over it, contemplating hitting

it on the head with his home-made priest, but actually too trepidatious to do so, when Mrs Rendall appeared bearing a fresh plate of peanut butter sandwiches in one hand and a fresh cup of tea in the other. 'Oh my goodness gracious,' she exclaimed when she saw the little boy, trouserless and his shirt tails dripping, crouched over the vast, gleaming fish. He stood up when she approached, and was deeply embarrassed about being bare-legged before her. 'It got tangled in the lilies, missus, an' I had to go in after it.'

'You're so brave,' exclaimed Mrs Rendall. 'You've caught it! I can hardly believe my eyes! How wonderful! How clever and brave you are!'

'It wasn't easy,' said Robert, in a manly tone of voice.

They stood side by side, gazing down at the gulping and dying fish that was now drowning in air. Robert had just learned that a swift and sudden death is not always the best. Sometimes a noble creature should be allowed to drift away with dignity, in a long and slowly fading dream that has no precise point of terminus. In the mouth of the great fish, the tiny silver roach, snared on the snap tackle, and much mangled, also flapped out the last of its meagre life.

'It's so beautiful,' said Mrs Rendall, looking wonderingly at the great olive stripes and the bright speckles of its flanks. 'And look at those teeth!

They're fearsome! I had no idea it was so beautiful! I almost feel sorry.'

'I feel sorry, missus,' said Robert, his voice a little choked, and when Mrs Rendall looked down at him she could see that indeed his eyes were brimming with tears.

Mrs Rendall took Robert home, with his hazel pole tied to the roof rack, and his bicycle hanging out of the open boot of the Austin Cambridge. At his feet, wrapped in newspaper and a plastic fertiliser sack, lay the body of the Girt Pike.

It would be hard to calculate the importance of these events in Robert's life. He was thereafter spoken of with awe by all the other boys in the village, and the little girls regarded him with something like fear mixed with desire. He became 'the boy who's got the pet rook, and caught the Girt Pike at the Glebe House pond', and when he grew up, he became 'you know, the man who caught the Girt Pike at the Glebe House when he was a boy, the one who had a rook'. In his house on Cherryhurst there would always be an overexposed photograph on the wall of the self-conscious and proud little fellow trying to hold up a pike that was too long and heavy for him. There would always be a photograph of the catch, laid out on the lawn beside a yardstick.

Robert's mother hung the fish up in the larder with its mouth full of salt, and next day it was eaten with great ceremony by the extended family and some of the neighbours. Robert did not think that it tasted very good because to him it savoured of guilt, but everyone else seemed to think it very fine. He received many a toast, many a pat on the head and many a congratulatory slap between the shoulder blades, none of which quite succeeded in drawing off his perturbing feelings of shame. He was haunted by how beautiful the pike had been when it was freshly out of the water, and how its beauty had already diminished when it had been out for only an hour. He knew instinctively that beauty should last for ever, and that this world would never be perfected until beauty was perpetual. Whenever he dreamed of his battle with the Girt Pike, what he remembered more than anything was the terror and panic of it, so that in retrospect his triumph took on more the aspect of a nightmare.

There was no doubt about the effect of the episode on Robert's self-confidence. He suddenly started to do unnaturally well at school, and passed the eleven-plus unexpectedly, so that his parents had to decide whether or not they could bear the expense and inconvenience of sending him to the grammar school in Guildford.

He had also been touched in another way. When the cancer took Mrs Rendall off a year later, he was heartbroken, and he wrote her a letter:

Dear Mrs Rendall,

I am so sorry that you have died,
because you were so pretty and so nice,
and you let me catch the Girt Pike, which
was the best thing ever, and you made me
tea and peanut butter sandwiches, and you
bought me the Intrepid Prince Regent reel
to thank me for catching the Girt Pike
and saving the ducklings, and it's the best
reel ever and just what I always wanted.

With love from Robert.


Robert folded up the letter very small and put it into one of his grandfather's discarded tobacco tins. He borrowed his mother's trowel and cycled up to the churchyard, where he buried his message in the upturned clay of the new grave, before crawling into the abandoned lime kiln nearby, where he could crouch in the wet darkness and bury his eyes in his forearm without being seen.

Robert used the Intrepid Prince Regent reel for the rest of his life, even though he never went pike fishing again. Content with perch and roach, he used the reel long after its manufacturer was bought out by a predator and asset-stripped, and he used it when he was middle-aged and everyone else was using superbly engineered reels made of lightweight graphite, which ran on roller bearings. Whenever he got it out of its bag and mounted it on his rod, he remembered the Girt Pike, the Glebe House pond, and pretty, vivacious Mrs Rendall. Every time he went to the churchyard he would pause in front of her grave, where the headstone was tilting and covered with yellow lichen, and, wondering if his tobacco tin and message had rotted away, would feel all over again his long-standing sorrow.

# THE AUSPICIOUS MEETING OF THE FIRST TWO MEMBERS OF THE FAMOUS NOTWITHSTANDING WIND QUARTET

It was a day in middle March, of the kind that for early risers begins sunny and uplifting, but which for late risers has already degenerated into the nondescript gloom that causes England to be deprecated by foreigners. The rooks were breaking off the ends of willow twigs and building their nests with raucous incompetence, most of the twigs ending up on the ground below, whence the birds could never be bothered to retrieve them. The box hedges were in blossom, causing some people to ring the gas board, and others to wonder what feline had pissed so copiously as to make the whole village smell of cat piss. Out on the roads, squashed baby rabbits were being dismantled by magpies, and frogs migrating to their breeding ponds were being flattened into very large and thin batrachian medallions that would, once dried out, have made excellent beer mats.

It was a Saturday, and the young man was driving along Notwithstanding Road, which leads twistingly and straitly from Notwithstanding to Godalming. Over time the lanes had sunk some fifteen feet below the surface of the ground, steep banks rose up on either side and trees so overarched the carriageway that the ensemble formed a kind of natural tunnel that gave people exhilarating intimations of being in fairyland. It was on this road that one was most in danger from the nuns who lived in the convent on the hill. Their bizarre disregard for safety on the roads was a source of constant wonderment to the locals.

The young man was taking a long cut into town in the spirit of exploration, since he was relatively new to the area, having recently taken up a post as assistant music teacher in a local public school. It was the kind of public school that one might have described as being in the top rank of the second-raters. He was not on duty this day, having been spared the embarrassment of refereeing any football games or supervising any detentions. Thus far he was not relishing his job particularly. The boys' attitude to music was more robust and jocular than musical, confining itself mainly to bawling out filthy rugby songs in the communal showers. Moreover, since he was accommodated in a spartan bachelor flat provided by the school, he had not experienced the customary welcome of newcomers to the village, which consisted in solidly constructed, inquisitive middle-aged women turning up with pots of home-made marmalade and general offers of assistance and advice. His flat was in a large house in a remote corner of the school grounds, and the other flats were occupied by the school chaplain, a sports teacher who thought that classical music was for 'queers' and a fey and unhappy young English teacher who almost certainly was one.

The music teacher was quite poor, and had no prospect of ever being otherwise. He drove a Morris Minor saloon which he had bought for fifty pounds at the age of seventeen. He and his father had dismantled and rebuilt it in the garden. The car was admittedly and visibly hand-painted, but it had already proved a faithful servant, and it worked well even when technically ill. He was fully reconciled to a long future with this car, even though his rowdier friends in better-paid jobs were roaring about in souped-up white Ford Escorts with red stripes down the sides and huge holes cut out of the bonnet in order to accommodate oversized Weber carburettors.

He had passed the hedging and ditching man, who was contemplating an old whisky bottle that he had just excavated from the mud. He was somewhere in the vicinity of the Glebe House when he came across a car that was stopped on the verge, unwisely near to a bend in the road. He felt reluctant to over-take it, in case a car should be coming round the bend the other way. Most of all, though, he stopped because the stationary car was also a Morris Minor.

Going round to the front, he met with a woman, standing and facing him with an expression that had something about it of embarrassment and shame. Her hands were behind her back, as if she were conceal-ing something. She was about thirty years old, a little plump, pleasant in the face without being pretty, dressed practically rather than for elegance or for effect.

'Ummm, hello,' said the music teacher diffidently. 'I'm so sorry to bother you, but I wondered if ... if you were in need of assistance. I mean, I thought you might have broken down, and, as it were, I drive a Morris Minor myself, and I always stop for Morris Minors if they're broken down. Usually I can get them going, you see. I've got a toolbox and some spares in the car. Solidarity and all that.' He looked at her, feeling foolish.

'Actually, I haven't broken down, so I'm not a damsel in distress, but thank you all the same. It was very kind of you to stop.' She smiled at him. It was the smile of someone who wishes that you would go away.

'The thing is, you're parked near a bend, so I thought ...'

'Yes,' she agreed, 'it's a silly place to stop, but ...'

'Yes?' It was then that he saw, behind her head, a pheasant. 'Gracious,' he said, 'poor little bugger.'

It had clearly been struck by a car while flying across the road and had hurtled into the side of the thorn hedge, near the top, where it had become stuck upside down, and died. The brown rump of the pheasant, as it protruded from the hedge, looked both comical and pathetic.

'Yes, poor little bugger,' she agreed. 'So many of them get splatted at this time of the year. God knows why.'

'It's the mating season perhaps? That's when all the animals get silly.' A thought occurred to the young man. 'You weren't . . . are you, er, if you don't mind me asking, planning to eat it? I mean, did you stop to get it out?'

She looked horrified, but also guilty. 'Gosh, no. They're so bruised when they're hit that the flesh goes all black and has a horrible texture. My dad ran one over once, and it wasn't at all nice when we tried to eat it. It's the kind of thing that everyone tries once. Not recommended.'

The young man scrutinised the bird. He was always fascinated by the intricate and beautiful patterns on pheasants' feathers. 'I wonder what happened to the tail,' he said. 'This pheasant doesn't seem to have one. The feathers can't have been knocked out by the car, surely?'

'Well, actually, I've got them,' she admitted, taking her hands from behind her back, and holding out the long, barred feathers. 'In fact, that's why I stopped.'

'What, for a hat or something?'

'Me? Can you see me in a hat with pheasant feathers in it? My granny, maybe.'

'Well, I suppose they're very pretty in their own right. I can understand why anyone would want one. Or even a handful.'

'It's not because they're pretty. It's because I play the oboe.'

'The oboe?' he said, trying to make the conceptual leap that might connect oboes with pheasant tails, and failing.

'An oboe,' she repeated. 'It's a wind instrument, and it has a conical bore that's very tight at the top. A pheasant feather is just ideal for cleaning it when you've finished playing. You could say it's traditional.'

'To get the spit out?'

She smiled wryly. 'I call it condensation.'

'So you play the oboe?'

'I just started again. You know, kids at school, husband at work, a bit of time on my hands. I got the itch again. It's not going very well, though. If you haven't got anyone to play with, you can't improve, and anyway my mouth seems to have lost the knack.'

'Trouble with the embouchure,' he said.

'You know about embouchure?' she asked eagerly, her enthusiasm triggered by the code word.

'Kindred spirit,' he replied. 'I play clarinet. I know what happens when you stop for a while. It always comes back eventually, if that's any comfort.' He said, 'I teach music actually, and I've been trying to find someone to play with.' They looked at each other for a long and portentous moment.

'Well . . .' She eyed him suspiciously. 'Perhaps you'd like to come round and meet my husband. We could try something out.' She placed a particular weight upon the word 'husband', a weight that was not lost on him.

'Delighted to. Perhaps you'd like to give me your number, and I can ring you later.'

'OK,' she said, and she took the old receipt from Timothy White's that he produced from his wallet. She wrote 'Jenny Farhoumand (oboe) 2380' on it, and handed it back to him.

'Farhoumand? What an intriguing name. Where does it come from?'

'I've no idea. I keep telling my husband that he ought to find out, but he's not very interested. He mainly likes mowing the lawn.'

'It looks French. Do you like Cimarosa's oboe concerto?' he asked.

'Love it. I played in it once.'

'I love it too,' he said.

As he was going back to his car, he turned and said, 'If you come across any dead cats on the side of the road, can you stop and cut off the tails? The clarinet has quite a big bore, and cats' tails are ideal. You could say it's traditional. You have to wait till rigor mortis sets in, though, or they're too floppy.'

She was only fooled for a moment, but she never forgot the thrill of horror that ran through her for the split second when he was driving away, and she thought he was being serious.

# MRS MAC

Mrs Mac's cottage found itself down an unmetalled rutty lane that had been so frequently resurfaced over the centuries that, merely by remaining where they were, the ditch on one side and the cottage on the other seemed to have sunk far into the earth. The ditch became seven feet deep, and in summer it grew rank with briars, nettles and docks. Dogs that plunged into it re-emerged caked in stinking black slime, much to their own delight and their owners' horror. Local children tortured their friends and enemies alike by pitching them into the mire, where wellington boots would be sucked away to an ignominious end. Many a child howled with panic having answered a dare to go in, only to find that there was no way out.

Every autumn the hedging and ditching man would clear the banks with the aid of a billhook mounted on a two-yard pole, and then, protected by waders, he would descend into the abyss and heave the black mud up on to the banks so that the waters could flow unhindered in the winter. For some reason he never removed the mud altogether, so that it lay glistening and reeking on the edge of the track, gradually being washed back into the ditch by the rains.

The hedging and ditching man was an unexplained person. He was at that time in his sixties, very slim and fit. He wore braces and a flat cap, and worked in shirtsleeves even in the winter. He had laid hedges and cleared ditches since he was a youth, but nobody knew who employed him or paid him, or where he lived. Parents told their gullible children that he was a supernatural being appointed by nature, who turned into a birch tree at night, and ate leaf mould in his sandwiches. The generally credited rumour was that he was the wealthy scion of an aristocratic family, who hedged and ditched in order to escape the fathomless tedium of an idle life filled with scones and trivial conversation. Housewives took him mugs of tea when he was at work outside their houses, in order to hear him speak, and were convinced that his rich Surrey accent was indeed a thin disguise. They differed as to whether or not he might be Lord Dunsfold, or Lord Munstead, or Lord Chiddingfold, but all agreed that, without him, the village of Notwithstanding would long ago have disappeared beneath a canopy of hawthorn and a viscous sea of clay.

At the bottom end of Mrs Mac's lane lived a man who owned a large and gracious house surrounded by a high laurel hedge, and who was widely known to have been a spy. There was confusion as to whether Mr Hadgecock had worked for MI5 or MI6, as indeed there is still confusion as to which is which, but nobody liked to ask him, since his being a spy was supposed to be a secret. This was a very conservative area, and it would have seemed unpatriotic to ask him directly. It was also a very considerate area, and no one wanted to hurt his pride by revealing to him that his years of absolute discretion had been a failure. Mr Hadgecock lived his secret life, innocently unaware that the secret of his secret was secret only to himself, and he wasted his weekends dutifully, making damp bonfires in the hope of seeming to be like every other paterfamilias in the village of Notwithstanding.

Mrs Mac's cottage was at the other end of the track. When Mac and Mrs Mac were younger, the house had been smart, albeit very small, and the tiny garden had yielded eglantine, wallflowers and neat rows of diminutive cabbages. Now the conservatory glass was dirty and mossy, the paving had cracked and heaved, and in the wooden garage Mac's beloved black A35 rusted on deflated and perished tyres, unused for ten years. Mrs Mac kept the beds weeded, but nothing was grown in them any more, so that even in the spring and summer the place had the air of waiting for the resurrection.

Mac and Mrs Mac had three elderly cats who had done their duty in this life, and now they meditated all day in their appointed places, one on the roof of the shed, one by the scraper at the back door and one upon the gatepost. They seemed simultaneously to be a kind of garden statuary, and a variety of bearskin, as though three foot soldiers of some Ruritanian regiment of palace guards had capriciously disposed of their headgear in this greenest and most English part of southern England. The cat on the gatepost hissed at those who tried to caress it, but it did not budge or lash out, as if it were anticipating worthier opponents, and was merely keeping its bad temper up to scratch.

Inside, Mac, Mrs Mac and Mrs Mac's sister existed in two small rooms downstairs and two small rooms upstairs.

Mac was grey, watery and insubstantial, sitting silent and still at the bare wooden table, but Mrs Mac was lively even though she had been bent double by the thinning and warping of her bones. Her sister was fatter and more upright than she, but her brain was not as sharp, and her function in the house was more to flesh it out than to contribute to its life. Mrs Mac's sister would seem to have had no name, since she was known by everyone simply as 'Mrs Mac's sister', and Mrs Mac herself simply addressed her as 'dear'. She would nod happily, unoffended, when introduced to others as 'Mrs Mac's sister', as if anonymity were a natural and ultimately preferable state.

Mac and Mrs Mac had been known as such for so long that it occurred to almost nobody that their real name must have been something other than that. Occasionally somebody was struck by the idea that they must really have been 'MacDonald', or 'MacGuire' or 'MacCrae' or 'MacEwan', and this somebody would resolve to ask Mrs Mac about it one of these days, but would then forget to do so; this was in any case a village where almost everyone had a nickname such as 'Buzz' or 'Totty', or was known simply as 'So-and-so's Owner'.

Mac had always lived in Notwithstanding, but Mrs Mac was an interloper from Abbot's Notwith-standing, a mile to the south. They had married after the Great War, when she was a bonny laughing girl of eighteen, and he had already been reduced to semi-silence by the infernal din and carnage of Ypres and Passchendaele. They were of a generation, more than any other that has ever lived, that had been cauterised by history, and come through it all with the conviction that there is no higher aim in life than to live with common decency. Children felt safe with them, because they had been so intimately touched by death.

In those early years of their marriage when sleep evaded Mac at night, and fits of trembling seized him, Mrs Mac had been the Ariadne who had spun back together the threads of his sanity, binding up the wounds of his experience with equability and tranquillity. He found hard and cathartic work on the de Mandevilles' farm, where he was to remain for the rest of his working life, and, although he and Mrs Mac were never to have offspring, they built a world between them that was all the more particular for being impenetrable to others.

Mac, Mrs Mac and Mrs Mac's sister were spiritualists, and had been ever since Mrs Mac discovered her abilities in 1922. She awoke one morning in the summer, on the same day that Field Marshal Sir Henry Wilson was assassinated by Irish terrorists, and asked Mac, 'Who's Robert?'

'Robert?' repeated Mac.

'Robert,' said Mrs Mac, 'with sandy hair, blue eyes and one of those sheepskin flying jackets. He says he wants you to know that he's all right. Then he said "Toodle-oo" and disappeared.'

Mac sat up in bed and looked at her, his mouth hanging open, and a cold shiver travelling the length of his spine. 'I knew a Robert,' he said, 'and he always used to say "Toodle-oo". Got burned in a Bristol Fighter.'

'He's dead, then, is he?' asked Mrs Mac, realising

all at once the significance of her dream, and Mac nodded. He was recalling the best friend of his youth, who had managed to become an officer, and campaigned so vigorously to be seconded from his regiment into the Royal Flying Corps, only to be killed accidentally, three weeks after winning his wings, on the second-to-last day of the war.

In the aftermath of that war these islands were in tears, and never before had there come about such a rending of the veil between this world and the next. Mediums sprung up like cuckoo pint in the spring, among them the fraudulent, the genuinely gifted, the innocent but deluded, the disingenuous, and those who could be both spectacularly right and wrong within the space of a single sentence.

Mrs Mac sought neither money nor notoriety, but gathered around her a small group of people from all walks of life, who crammed themselves into the tiny room, sat holding hands around the wooden table, and received messages from those they had loved, as well as some from complete strangers, as if the dead were as promiscuous as the living in their need to speak across the abyss, and as desperate for reassurance.

Mrs Mac began her meetings with a short prayer, calling upon the Lord to bless their undertaking, and to protect those gathered together from the mischief of the uncouth spirits that inhabited the lower ether, and then the lights were quenched, with the exception of a single candle in the middle of the table, upon whose flame Mrs Mac would focus until her vision blurred and the dead would appear before her inner eyes, queuing up behind each other as it well behoved the British dead.

As the decades passed, Mrs Mac's circle of spiritualists passed on, one by one, until those who had once sat expectantly in the chairs became the very visitors who stepped out of the candle's yellow flame to bring their cryptic messages and declarations from the other side. Increasingly, Mrs Mac dwelt not in this corporeal sphere, but in the next, until the two elided and coincided, and any distinction between them became redundant. It was as if Mrs Mac had died while remaining alive, or as if she had taken to living among the dead. She subsisted without terror, fearing only the pain and inconvenience of transferring from one condition to another when her own moment of death arrived, and looking forward to the better state of health whose enjoyment she envisaged on the far shore. Many in the village considered her mad, or at least half-baked, but she was sweet-natured, kindly and fascinating, and therefore those who did not believe in her phantoms simply humoured her. 'She's harmless,' people would say, shrugging their shoulders, 'and, you never know, there might be something in it.'

One day Joan called in on Mrs Mac, saying, 'I'm

just going up to the church to do the flowers, and I wondered if you'd like to come.' Joan took village responsibilities seriously and ran a kind of localised social services organisation that was entirely of her own devising. She was a devout conservative, perceiving that if all the world were made up of communities such as this one, and if every such community had people like herself and her friends to help anyone at any time, then there would be no conceivable need for socialism. The trouble with socialism, thought Joan, was either that it told you to do what you were going to do anyway, and therefore made you not want to do it, or else it took things out of your hands and did them worse than you would have done, but at far greater expense.

Joan was an implacable Utopian, envisaging a world where individuals were responsible, rather than the state, and it was she and her husband, the Major, who would one day start a revolution whose aim was independence from Waverley Borough Council.

Mrs Mac and Mrs Mac's sister considered Joan's offer; they had many old friends and relations to visit in the graveyard. 'I'll just go in and ask Mac,' said Mrs Mac, and in she went, to see what her husband thought. 'Mac, dear,' she asked him, 'Joan's offered to take us up to the churchyard. Would you like to come?'

It was often hard for Mrs Mac to get Mac to pay attention; he seemed to exist for much of the time in a state of profound contemplation, his head bowed, and his hands folded in his lap; extreme age had reduced him to the semblance of a philosopher. Mrs Mac repeated her question more loudly, and Mac raised his hoary head slowly. Their eyes met, and Mac's mouth twitched at the corners into the slightest of smiles. He nodded. Mrs Mac went back outside and told Joan, 'Mac says that he'd like to come. I do hope that that's all right. Of course, if it's any trouble ...'

Joan had been prepared for this; Mrs Mac was notorious for consulting Mac about every single thing, always running back and forth from the garden gate to the house, and more often than not she took him with her, talking to him continuously and very loudly in public, so that people who did not know her looked at her askance, and giggled to each other. Mrs Mac was growing deaf, and did not realise just how public her monologue was.

Mrs Mac went back indoors to fetch Mac and re-emerged with one arm akimbo, so that Mac could thread his own arm through, for support. 'Good morning, Mac,' said Joan, who was used to their ways, and Mrs Mac said, 'Mac says "Good morning", don't you, Mac?' She turned to her sister and said, 'Let's put Mac in the middle. Then we can share him. Doesn't know his luck, does he?'

Mrs Mac had to cope with Mac's usual dis-orientation, and spent some time coaxing him into the back of Joan's Rover. Joan patted the gatepost cat on the head, being rewarded with the usual impartial hiss, and then she picked holly from the hedge by the bank, so that she could give it to Mrs Mac and her sister, for their loved ones' graves. She already had variegated holly and ivy from her own garden in the boot of the car, but was determined that they should go in a vase beneath the window to St Peter, whose church it was. She had the reputation of a flower arranger *sans pareil*, and her husband, the Major, had often remarked that if she had chosen an art form less ephemeral, she might easily have become quite as famous as Picasso, but with considerably more justice. Joan was immodestly proud of her facility with sprigs and flowers, and rightly so.

Joan drove carefully past the convent at the apex of the hill, because the nuns had a habit of emerging from their driveway at full tilt, without looking to right or left, and then she drove just as carefully through the central cluster of the village. Here the road was only a few feet wide, very sinuous, and just as likely to be carrying upon it a carload of jeopardous brides of Christ. Equally one might be run upon by Miss Agatha Feakes in her antique car, often with a piebald goat on the back seat, her white hair flying as she pumped the horn in lieu of using her brakes. They passed the hedging and ditching man, who, amid the steam of his own breath, was contemplating the skull of a fox that he had just found in the ditch. 'Alas, poor Foxick,' jested Joan, aware that her pleasantry would probably be lost on the Macs. She drove through the arches of oak trees that spanned the lane. In summer they gave drivers the sensation of entering a tunnel in Arcadia, but now only a few tenacious brown leaves rustled on those great boughs that seemed to be upheld in beseechment to a white, implacable sky. Finally Joan turned right, up the very steep hill to St Peter's Church. Since the church was Anglican, this road customarily had no nuns upon it, and so Joan speeded up a little in order to gain some momentum for the ascent, sounding her horn at the two most dangerous corners. 'Nearly there,' said Mrs Mac to her husband, and Mrs Mac's sister echoed, 'Yes, nearly there.'

St Peter's Church was truly very small, having been founded in Saxon times, and rebuilt several times without ever having been expanded. A rough path in Bargate sandstone led to its door, and two enormous yew trees overshadowed much of its graveyard, whose level had risen greatly over the thousand years in which its soil had been turned up for the new dead. The oldest headstones dated only to the seventeenth century, but the oldest bones were already browned and crumbled when Geoffrey de Mandeville took these lands in fief from the Conqueror, and divided them up in turn among his captains.

Joan stopped the car outside, and pushed the gear lever into first, just in case the handbrake was as unreliable as she suspected. She clambered out, opened the rear doors for the Macs, and then went to open the boot in order to fetch out her cuttings and her secateurs. Mrs Mac's sister emerged first, and then Mrs Mac, who turned to assist her husband, holding out an arm for him, even though she herself was so bent that she could scarcely see a dog's length in front of her.

'I'm going into the church,' said Mrs Mac's sister, who was a woman of simple pleasures, and liked nothing more than to sit in a pew, gazing around at the stained glass and the tablets on the walls, soaking up the atmosphere of the timelessness and perversity of God. She also thought, as always, but falsely, that it might be warmer inside than out.

Joan fetched the substantial old key from its usual hiding place in a crevice in the brickwork of Piers de Mandeville's tomb, and unlocked the black oak door of the church. Until recently it had never been locked at all, but lately there had been a rash of theft from rural churches as the larcenous classes had finally lost their sense of sacrilege. 'I'm going to do the arrangements,' she told the others, somewhat superfluously. 'Shouldn't be more than half an hour.'

'Mac and I will do the graves, then,' said Mrs Mac, and the old couple moved slowly away, bearing each other's weight, to visit the graves of those they had loved, as well as those for whom they had felt particular sorrow. Mac's mother and father were in there, and two of his sisters; there were three members of their defunct group of spiritualists; there was poor Mrs Rendall, who had been so blonde and pretty and vivacious, carried away by cancer before she was forty; there was Pamela Diss, who had committed suicide inexplicably at the age of twenty-three, when she had a family that adored her, and her whole life to look forward to. Mac and Mrs Mac paused before each headstone, reading the inscriptions and epitaphs that they already knew so well, and Mrs Mac, as always, could not help the tears of sentiment that inevitably welled up in the corners of her eyes. 'All gone before, all gone before,' she said to Mac, wiping her eyes with a tiny crumpled handkerchief, and then blowing her nose. 'Last one,' she said, and they moved slowly towards the grave under the western wall that was habitually the final one on their rounds.

Mrs Mac was always mildly dismayed by the state of it, frustrated by the manner in which time confounded her efforts. Sometimes she brought a scrubbing brush with her to remove the yellow lichen, and sometimes she brought a small bottle of systemic weedkiller which she had prepared at home, to defeat the brambles, the ground elder and the dog's mercury. Today she tutted to herself, and peeled away a long tendril of darkest-green ivy that had begun to obscure the writing on the stone. 'That's better,' she said, and straightened herself painfully. For the thousandth time she read:

Joseph MacMahon
Dearly beloved husband of Agnes
5 December 1896 – 15 July 1968

Underneath was inscribed 'Behold, I am with you always', a quotation that Mrs Mac particularly loved and understood, and underneath was carved, in bold capital letters, the single word 'MAC'.

# COLONEL BARKWELL, TROODOS AND THE FISH

The villagers of Notwithstanding considered that of all the retired officers in the parish, Colonel Pericles 'Perry' Barkwell was the most peremptory. He spoke with virtuosic economy, mercilessly pruning unnecessary words from his sentences, and his voice was a rich and resounding baritone that might have excited envy in an actor. When he sang in church on Sunday his voice was so much the most powerful that, over a period of years, the idiosyncratic embellishments to the standard hymn tunes that had been one of the quirkier customs of his former public school had perforce become the generally accepted ones in Notwithstanding. Even Sir Edward Rawcutt, a stickler for the ways of singing hymns and psalms learned at his own public school, had become used to Colonel Barkwell's versions. On one occasion the Rector had attempted to introduce a new melody to an old hymn, and the Colonel, perennially disgusted by new-fangledness in general, had resolutely sung the old tune over the top of the congregation until the organist had given up and reverted to it. In the responses, when the Colonel replied to the Rector's 'God be with you', his stentorian 'and with thy spirit' perturbed the bats in the bell tower, and caused the bronze of the bells to vibrate in sympathy. The congregation felt assured that their communal prayers would be answered, because not even God would have dared to decline a demand from the Colonel. Therefore his presence in the community was conducive to the maintenance of its spiritual calm, despite the disconcerting volume of his crisp sentences, and the abject terror aroused in the breast of anyone who crossed him.

The Colonel, an old Coldstream Guardsman of heroic height and bearing, had served in several campaigns, some of which had apparently taken place without the knowledge of the British public, and had received both the DSO and the Military Cross. In the village itself his lionheartedness had been a legend ever since he had brained a burglar with a number seven iron, and the jury in Guildford had, despite the clear direction of the judge, resolutely declined to convict him for the use of unnecessary force. Without the knowledge of the judge they had instead had a whip-round for the sum of ten pounds towards the purchase of a new golf club.

Mrs Barkwell, on the other hand, was an elegant and slender lady with a penchant for blue cocktail dresses, who played bridge regularly with a circle of friends, with whom she liked to sip cold German wine and talk about the latest comedy at the Yvonne Arnaud theatre, and the latest modern drama at the Redgrave in Farnham. She contributed thoughtful verse to women's magazines, and was an indefatigable collector of money for charitable causes. Some people thought her excessively distant, but those who knew her well found her warm and humorous, seldom calling her by her real name, which was Helen. Instead they referred to her as 'Leafy'. Almost no one, it has to be said, was known by their real name, and, more often than not, no one knew wherefore any given person possessed the nickname that they did. Leafy Barkwell was, without even understanding it herself, utterly devoted to the Colonel – he had only to enter the room and she would glow with visible warmth – and sometimes she counted up the years of their marriage on her fingers, as if such perdurable happiness were something intrinsically incredible.

Their sons and daughters had left home, and there remained only a maid and a cat. The maid had originally come to them as a nanny, provided gratis by the army when they were stationed in Germany, but now, even so many years after the children had grown and flown, Anna stayed on. As soon as their youngest child had reached the age of five, Perry and Leafy Barkwell had tried to encourage her to find more suitable and remunerative employment, but she had tearfully refused, accusing them in German of wishing to be rid of her, and demanding to know what she had done wrong. 'Damned awkward,' the Colonel had said to his wife. 'What on earth can we do?' she had asked. 'Nobody has a servant these days.'

The Colonel, fearless in the face of terrorists, bullets, burglars and high-explosive shells, was readily defeated by a woman's tears, and so Anna stayed on, romantically and absent-mindedly caressing the ornaments with a duster, her gestures curtailed and curiously melodramatic. She was a relentless furnisher of cups of tea, made in the British Army style with condensed milk and heaps of white sugar, and she seldom spoke except to exclaim '*Gott im Himmel*' or '*Ach, du meine Güte*'.

Naturally she understood English perfectly, but what few words emerged were cloaked in an accent thick with years of linguistic apathy. She lived in the attic, which had been converted into an upper room, and there she played with her hair in front of a mirror and hugged her breasts to herself while singing snatches of nursery songs whose words she had muddled up over the passage of the years. The Colonel had a theory that she had been interfered with by the advancing Mongolian hordes in Berlin in 1945, and that this explained her tenuous grip on reality and the skewed angles of her psyche.

Anna never went out, and never spent her exiguous wages. Under her bed she kept rows of jam jars full of the obsolete pre-decimal coinage of her first years with the family and in others she kept all the notes that she had ever earned, with the intention that when she died all the money they had ever paid her would revert to them. Anna, because she had been a nanny, was, of course, known to the entire family as 'Nanna', and she had never once expressed a wish to return to Germany, even out of curiosity.

The cat, the final member of the household, was named Troodos because Mrs Leafy Barkwell had so much enjoyed being stationed in Cyprus, until Makarios and Grivas between them had turned their pleasant existence into a nightmare. Troodos was a genial tabby of about six years, with green eyes and an unappeasable appetite for voles. Most cats disdain them for their bitter taste, but Troodos would sit for hours in the long grass, waiting for a blade to stir. He could leap twelve feet or more, and land on the rustling object with perfect precision. He would swallow them head first, much as a snake does, bolting them down in great gulps. If he caught too many to eat he would bring them in and lay them down in rows on the carpet, much as the moleman's cat, Sergeant Corker, did with his moles.

It happened that one day Colonel and Mrs Barkwell were preparing a dinner party for a few friends, while Nanna polished the banister ball. She liked it to be shiny because it reminded her of the round head and glistening brown hair of the Barkwells' youngest daughter.

Mrs Barkwell had bought a large salmon which she was intending to poach in a steel fish kettle, and was looking over the Colonel's shoulder as he gutted and cleaned it. 'Whopper,' he commented. 'Tough one to land.'

'Oh dear,' worried Mrs Barkwell. 'Do you think it's all right?'

'Tickety-boo,' said the Colonel.

'You know, I do think it might be a bit off. Oh Lord. What do you think, Perry?'

The Colonel lowered a reconnoitring proboscis, and sniffed. 'Smells of fish,' he declared. 'What d'you expect?'

Mrs Barkwell was still worried. 'You don't think it's a bit ripe? I mean, wouldn't it be awful if we made everyone ill?'

'Folderol,' said the Colonel. 'Perfectly good fish.'

'Nanna,' called Mrs Barkwell, 'do come and smell this fish; I think it might be off.'

Nanna came into the kitchen and poked the flank

of the salmon. Then she sniffed her finger, first with one nostril, and then the other. She wiped it on her apron, and said, with a connoisseur's air of finality, '*Weiss nicht. Entschuldigung.*'

'I've eaten pheasant so high, maggots in it,' declared the Colonel. 'No harm done.'

'Pheasant's different, Perry dear, fish has to be fresh,' said his wife.

'Portugal,' said the Colonel, '*bacalao*. Months old. India, Bombay duck, years old. Prehistoric.'

'Years old, and dried and salted,' rejoined Mrs Barkwell. 'This is supposed to be fresh from the lochs.'

'Cat,' suggested the Colonel.

Mrs Barkwell raised a finger and touched him on the tip of his nose. 'Clever boy,' she said.

Troodos was accordingly summoned from the orchard by the vigorous rattling of his biscuit box. There had not been much action on the vole front, and he was certainly ready to try the fish. He was so fussy about his food that in the evening he would not even eat from a tin that had been opened that morning, and Perry and Leafy Barkwell placed great faith in his gastronomic expertise.

Nanna, the Colonel and Mrs Barkwell bent over and watched Troodos contentedly polishing off a lump that Leafy had cut out of the side that was to be downward on the serving dish. '*Er schnurrt,*' observed Nanna, and the other two listened with satisfaction as Troodos accomplished the daily miracle of purring and eating at the same time.

'Well, pussy likes it,' said Mrs Barkwell, and the Colonel patted Troodos somewhat brusquely on the head, saying, 'Good soldier, what? First class, first class.'

The salmon was duly poached. All the same Mrs Barkwell could not help but wonder whether or not the fish really was all right. She had sown a doubt in her own mind that was very hard to uproot, and this doubt also began to infect the Colonel, despite his implicit trust in the cat's considered judgement. 'Crossed fingers, what?' he said to his wife.

Sir Edward and Lady Rawcutt had cried off, but the Rector, Polly Wantage and her artist friend, and Joan and the Major turned up at eight as planned. 'Slight worry about the fish,' the Colonel informed them as they sat down. 'Hope it's all right. Should be. In fact, damned sure it is. Tried it on the cat. Can't fool the cat.'

'Please leave it if you have any doubts,' said Mrs Barkwell. 'There's plenty of everything else. I won't be at all offended.'

'All the more for puss, eh?' said the Colonel.

'One has to be so careful of salmonella, these days,' said Polly Wantage's artistic friend, oblivious to the pun. 'And wisteria.'

The Colonel regarded her incredulously; he had

always thought her a little ill-connected in the brain department, a typical airy-fairy artist type, in fact. 'Wisteria is a card game,' he told her, 'listeria's the one.'

'Whist is the card game, I think you'll find,' offered the Reverend Godfrey Freemantle, diffidently. 'Wisteria is a climbing plant, *floribunda*, *formosa*, *sinensis*, *venusta* ...' Here he caught the Colonel's hostile eye, and added, 'But, of course, as Perry says, it is indeed listeria that causes gippy tummy.' Once more he smiled at the Colonel, who was notoriously irked by being corrected, and who, on account of just this very flaw, had once narrowly missed the opportunity of being made equerry to the Queen.

The guests tucked into their fish, and declared it perfect, wonderful, superb, just right, and the best they had ever had. But the sorry fact was that Colonel and Mrs Barkwell had managed all the same to insinuate doubt into their guests' minds as well. 'It would have been better not to have said anything at all,' reflected Leafy Barkwell, as she surveyed the mildly worried expressions upon their faces.

The Rector had a second helping, motivated by Christian supportiveness, explicitly putting his trust in God by means of a fleeting supplication, and the Major had seconds because, as he put it, 'In my time I've drunk water from a petrol can, and I've cooked fried eggs on the bare metal of an armoured car in the middle of the desert, and I'm damned if anything will ever make me ill again.' He ate his second helping as a direct personal challenge to the fish, and to any and all bacilli that it might contain. Joan, his wife, who had heard this speech about petrol cans and fried eggs a hundred times, loyally corroborated the Major's assertions. 'Oh yes,' she said, 'the Major's never ill. It's positively alarming what his stomach can put up with.'

The Colonel glanced at the Major somewhat balefully. There had been a strong undercurrent of rivalry between them ever since the Major had disclosed that he had been in the only Foot Guard regiment senior to the Coldstreams. It was indeed an unfortunate coincidence that a former Grenadier had turned up in the same village as a former Coldstreamer, especially as both of them were of titanic build and forceful temperament. In this instance it irked Perry Barkwell that a Grenadier should lay claim to a cast-iron constitution, and so he countered with: 'Ate a boa constrictor in Belize. Damned tasty actually. Not bad at all. Ate a dog in Malaya. Emergency. Not quite so good.'

'Oh Perry, don't, how could you?' demanded Leafy Barkwell. 'How perfectly horrid.' She had not heard this story before, and suspected that her husband was elaborating falsehoods from somewhat base motives.

The carcass of the salmon was cleared away, and in the kitchen Mrs Leafy Barkwell heaped its remains

into Troodos's bowl, having decided that it was probably not a good idea to keep it over for the following
day. Nanna went out to rattle the biscuit box, and
Troodos appeared shortly through the catflap, an
anticipatory purr rattling in his throat. It was his right
to eat leftovers, and he was never far away from the
catflap at about eight o'clock in the evening, after
which his night's adventures could begin. The left-
overs would be followed by flirtation, a little hunting,
a little chromatic yeowling, and, with any luck, an
exhilaratingly good battle with a farm cat. Troodos
would often appear in the morning with the outer
sheath of a claw embedded in the middle of his forehead like a piece of Ruritanian military regalia, and
Perry Barkwell would extract it, saying, 'Damn good
soldier. Chip off the old block, what?'

Dessert was served and eaten, and then the
Colonel and the Major announced their intention to
waive their right to stay on at table and pass the port
while the ladies withdrew.

They both felt uneasy because, naturally, the
Reverend Freemantle would be remaining with them,
and they would feel inhibited about coming out with
the odd 'bugger it', or worse, and risqué anecdotes
or even talk about old campaigns would be out of
the question. The Rector, they suspected, was a
milksop, a nice chap, but with no balls at all. Accordingly they all removed to the drawing room, and

Nanna served coffee, returning to the kitchen to begin the washing-up, which she did with her customary fanaticism, polishing the plates until they glowed.

Polly Wantage lit her pipe, and began a long discourse about a squirrel that she had recently shot. The Colonel and the Major listened with admiration, for Polly, with her plus fours, her pipe, her legendary past in the England women's cricket team and her monocle, was the kind of woman a chap could really rub along with; none of that damned female nonsense about headaches and manicures and hairdos.

'And so,' said Polly, puffing on her pipe and creating the atmosphere of a damp bonfire in autumn, 'there he was, the little bugger,' (here everyone glanced at the Rector, who merely smiled theologically) 'and I gave him the right barrel. Boom.' (Here Polly wielded an imaginary twelve-bore.) 'And bugger me, I missed. And then the little bugger takes a leap, and, like a flash, boom, I'm after him with the other barrel, and blow me down, I got him in mid-air, and he spins over and drops, and there he is, stone dead on the pine needles. One bad shot, and one blinder. Just like life, what?'

Polly looked around with satisfaction, and the Rector observed, 'Such a rich metaphor,' while the Major and the Colonel responded almost in unison with 'Jolly good, old girl. Splendid.'

Joan and Leafy exchanged glances, and the former

summoned up her courage. 'Polly dear, I can't help wondering why you have this thing about squirrels.'

Polly puffed vehemently on her pipe, and then pointed the stem at Joan, stabbing the air with it for emphasis. 'Rats,' she said. 'Rats with fluffy tails. Tree rats. Vermin. Full of fleas. Disgusting.'

'Oh, I think they're rather sweet,' said Joan, unthinkingly.

'It's the songbirds,' explained Polly. 'You can have squirrels or songbirds, but not both. These grey squirrels eat the eggs, and they eat the heads off the chicks. Nice and crunchy, you see. I'm voting for songbirds. Bugger the squirrels. Got to get rid of them. Do you remember Eric? Before your time, I should think. Eric Parker? He was the last man to see a red squirrel in the village.'

Just then Nanna flung open the door, hurled herself into the centre of the room and exclaimed, '*Oh mein Gott, mein Gott, du lieber Gott, der Kater ist tot. Der arme Kater, oh oh oh.*'

The Colonel stood up abruptly, exclaiming, 'What? What? What?' and Nanna clutched the sides of her face with both hands, her eyes full of horror, tears running down her cheeks. She swayed like an opera singer imitating the effects of a storm, and Joan and the other women exchanged a 'What do we do now?' kind of glance.

'Pull yourself together, woman,' cried the Colonel,

grasping Nanna's shoulders, and for one horrible moment everyone thought that he was going to slap her, as if she were the stock hysterical woman in an old-fashioned film. Nanna looked up at him and managed to say, her voice choking with distress, '*Tot, tot, tot ist der Kater.*'

The guests went pale in unison, and in unison their stomachs began to feel unwell. 'Pussy's dead,' said Mrs Barkwell, horrified both by the news and by what it meant. A wave of social shame swept over her, for the time being postponing the jagged grief that she would feel for her beloved pet. 'The salmon,' she blurted out, looking to her husband for strength. 'Oh my God, the salmon.'

The Colonel had not spent all those years in the Coldstreams without learning the art of dealing with an emergency. 'On the double,' he roared, 'quick march,' and everybody, galvanised by this vocal explosion, jumped up out of their armchairs. 'Into the hall,' commanded the Colonel. He turned to his wife. 'Start the car. Round the front!' She seemed a little confused, but was electrified into action by his 'Jump to it, woman, jump to it'.

The Colonel addressed his troops. 'Stay calm. Calmness essential. No hurrying. Cool head at all times. Women first.'

'Where are we going, old boy?' asked the Major.

'Hospital. Stomach pump. Bloody obvious, man.'

The Major was nettled by this last phrase, implying that he was short on understanding, and he stiffened. 'Not for me, old boy. Cast-iron stomach. Waste of time.'

The Colonel was nettled in turn. 'Do as you're bloody well told,' he said coldly. 'My responsibility.'

The Major, deeply riled, replied coolly but with clear hostility, 'We are not in the army here, old boy, and, even if we were, a major of the Grenadiers does not accept orders from a mere colonel of the Coldstreams.'

'Mere?' repeated the Colonel. 'Mere?' He stabbed at his chest with a forefinger, indicating his natural superiority. '*Nulli secundus*,' he exclaimed, 'second to none, second to none!' repeating the motto of his regiment.

The Major stiffened and drew himself up to his full height. 'Second to one, second to one.' He struck his own chest. 'Senior regiment. Grenadiers. Damned Coldstreams, bloody sheepshaggers.'

Colonel Perry Barkwell became livid beyond all reckoning. 'Sheepshaggers?' he spluttered, outraged by this ancient but ever-hurtful slur. 'Sheepshaggers? You'll answer for this, sir, you'll answer for this.'

The two elderly giants were by now eyeball to eyeball, their faces puce, their white clipped moustaches quivering, and it took their respective wives to intervene. 'Get off me, woman,' they both cried, but allowed themselves to be prised apart. The Major and his wife were hurried through the front door by the Rector, followed by the Colonel's bellows of 'You shall be answerable, sir, you shall be answerable'. At the gate the Major turned round and intoned 'Baaaa, baaaa' and thus he continued his derisive bleating until well out of earshot while the Colonel trembled with implacable ire.

In the car, on the way to hospital, Mrs Barkwell reflected that there would not have been room for all of them anyway, and she hoped that the Major and Joan would be all right. 'Damn them both,' exclaimed the Colonel fiercely, and no more was said on the subject as he drove, in the grip of an ecstatic rage, pell-mell through the sinuous country lanes towards the little casualty unit at Haslemere hospital. The other four did not know whether they felt sick from the salmon, or from the terrifying and vertiginous speed of their journey, or from being crammed together like dates in a box, or from retrospective horror at the viciousness of the quarrel that they had just witnessed. They were flung against each other unmercifully as the old Rover skidded and screeched around the corners, and the Rector prayed aloud, his left upper arm forced against the copious but unmaternal bosom of the resolute Polly Wantage, whose overpowering aroma of wet tweed, dogs and bitter pipe dottle contributed generously to the general feeling of sickness and nausea experienced by all the passengers in the bucketing car. Polly's companion whimpered softly to herself, and Leafy Barkwell, white-faced in the front seat, closed her eyes and tried not to think. She realised suddenly that they had forgotten poor Nanna altogether, and that Nanna had also eaten the salmon, but somehow she lacked the will to tell the Colonel to turn back for her. A wave of unhappy fatalism overcame her, and she decided to try not to think about what it would be like to die by overleaping a ditch and crashing into an oak tree.

When the car left the twisting lane and reached the main road from Brook to Haslemere, everyone felt relief tempered by the knowledge that the Colonel's wrathful driving could still easily leave them dead. Polly Wantage realised she was longing to know about the origins of the 'sheepshagger' jibe, but even that formidable lady baulked at the idea of raising the subject when the Colonel was still in an incendiary state of vexation. She would keep a straight bat on this exceedingly sticky wicket, and hope that it would see her through. Certainly she had not felt such trepidation since she had faced the fast bowling of Tricky Trent-Donovan in that memorable match in which she had almost been caught in the slips for a duck before going on to get fifty-six not out.

At last the Rover slewed to a halt in the hospital car park, and its occupants staggered out, bewildered, sick, but relieved to be alive. The Colonel corralled them together and shushed them towards casualty like particularly troublesome sheep. 'Get a move on, that man,' he said curtly to his wife, and 'Jump to it' to the Rector.

It was not a busy night in Haslemere hospital, and in the waiting room there was only a doleful man with a fish hook embedded in his forefinger and a diminutive nun from the hilltop convent in Notwithstanding, who was suffering from superficial abrasions because she had been dragged a short way along the lane when her habit had caught in the door of Sister Concepta's minivan. The Colonel's party was met by a small, plump Asian doctor, who came from behind the partitions and wished them 'Jolly good evening'.

'Bloody awful evening,' riposted the Colonel, who then pointed his finger at his unfortunate knot of dinner guests. 'Food poisoning. Stomach pump,' he declared. 'Chop-chop.'

The doctor bridled; he had always resented the way in which a certain kind of person tried to push him around as if he were a mere orderly. Knowing that the stomach pump was invariably unpleasant and humiliating and could even be painful if passed down the gullet with sufficient lack of sympathy, he squared his shoulders, looked the Colonel in the eye, and said firmly, 'Very good, sir. You first.'

\*     \*     \*

It was an hour and a half before Colonel Perry Barkwell and Leafy returned to their house, pale and weakened after their ordeal, crushed and tired beyond all reckoning, almost too overwhelmed by the awfulness to be able to speak to each other. Leafy Barkwell was sure that never again would they be able to give another dinner party, and the Colonel could still feel the pain of the prolonged and energetic sluicing that his guts had had to endure. He felt unsteady on his feet, and all his imperial bravado had vanished. He leaned on his wife's shoulder for support and wiped his white moustache repeatedly with a monogrammed handkerchief, repeating, 'Oh God, oh God.'

The pallid couple were met in the hallway by Nanna, who was clearly perfectly well, albeit still tearful about the untimely demise of the misadventurous Troodos. 'Oh Nanna,' exclaimed Mrs Barkwell, her voice trembling with horror, 'it was simply dreadful.'

Nanna held out her hand, in which she was holding a small piece of paper. '*Der Kater,*' she said. '*Eine Nachricht.*'

Mrs Barkwell took the note and eased herself wearily down on to the chair beside the hall chest. She began to read it, and then said, 'Oh God, oh my God, oh God . . .' She looked up at her much-diminished husband, who was holding himself upright by clutching on to the banister ball that

Nanna loved so much to polish. 'It's about the cat,' she said. 'It's from Totty Banks.'

The Colonel took the message and read the first lines. '"Dear Leafy and Perry, I am so dreadfully sorry about poor Troodos. I do believe that I was almost as fond of him as you were ..."' The Colonel raised his eyebrows. 'Damned curious,' he said. 'Letter of condolence already. Rum do.'

'Read the rest of it,' said Mrs Barkwell softly, and the Colonel continued, reading aloud, '"He was a very great character, a real personality in the village, and, if it wasn't an insult to such a fine cat, I would have said that he was almost human."'

'Quite. Quite,' agreed the Colonel, and then he continued once more. '"I dearly wish that I could turn the clock back, believe me, and I am so desperately sorry that I could do nothing about it. I suppose that Troodos was crossing over into the field to look for voles. I do hope that you will be able to forgive me, but I just didn't see him at all until the last minute, when it was too late to swerve ..."'

# ALL MY
# EVERLASTING LOVE

He spent the morning shooting at daffodils with his
air rifle. To be more exact, he was trying to shoot
through the stalks so that they keeled over. He would
not have tried shooting through the flower heads,
since he was not insensitive to their beauty, and, in
any case, that would have wrecked his mission. His
mother Joan had sent him out to pick daffodils for a
dinner party that she was having in the evening.

When she had asked him, he had grimaced and
his heart had sunk. This was a girl's job. His jobs were
to empty the waste-paper baskets and burn the
rubbish, chop wood, prune the fruit trees, rescue birds
and mice from the cats, walk the dog, scoop up pet
vomit, dig trenches, cut the hedge, go up ladders to
clean out the gutters and roam around the countryside with his catapult and air rifle. The only girl's task

he ever did was to make the coffee after supper. His sisters had to clean and tidy inside the house, activities from which he was exempt, apart from emergencies that required the use of the Hoover. His father washed up after supper and also hoovered in emergencies. It was an enlightened household, in which it seemed as though the women did all the work, but in which anything very unpleasant or strenuous always fell to the men.

Peter would not have had it any other way. He had just turned thirteen and had only recently left behind his shorts and become eligible for jeans. He loved his jeans, as the whole country loved jeans. They were the epitome of comfort and modernity, without being either modern or comfortable. It was the late sixties; disreputable people had taken to wearing them. They were raffish and daring and they proclaimed the beginning of a more casual age, when the platoons of commuters walking to the station suddenly gave up wearing bowler hats. Even his father, the Major, had taken to wearing jeans at weekends, and even the Major's hair had become fractionally longer owing to the subversive influence of the Beatles and the Rolling Stones. The Major and Joan disapproved strongly of the Beatles and the Stones, even though they had once had a soft spot for Elvis, and so it had been Granny who had taken all the children to see *Help!* and *A Hard Day's Night*. Granny thought that George and Paul were sweet. The Major used to say that those bloody pop stars (who couldn't even sing, with or without a fake American accent) should serve some time in the forces; that would straighten their ideas out. It was discipline they were short of. What he really wanted was to tie them down, gag them, cut their hair off and then shoot the lot of them, along with George Brown and Harold Wilson. But his hair became longer nonetheless. One day, perhaps five years hence, he would even sport sideburns in the wake of his wife's crush on Engelbert Humperdinck, and he would wear, briefly, a kipper tie with paisley swirls. But he would never sink so low as to wear brown shoes with a black suit.

Just now, however, young Peter had been told to go and pick daffodils, at the very time when hormones were bursting to life in his body and there was nothing more important in life than not being a girl.

Adolescence had already damaged him. Nowadays his psyche had degenerated into a whirlpool of resentments, longings and animal impulse, but a couple of years before he had been so bright and intelligent that he had been able to memorise a poem in three readings. At Guildford Grammar he had regularly achieved 100 per cent in several subjects during end-of-term exams. He had won double-plus marks for his French composition. Joan used to boast that he had got his brains from her side of the family, from her father, a mathematician who even understood relativity and could calculate the dimensions of circles in his head, using pi to three decimal places.

Above all, the twelve-year-old Peter had been happy. His mind had buzzed with energy, his religious faith had been instinctive, and he had lived unquestioningly in his little universe of Latin verbs, punch-ups at school, edifying parables, catapults, yo-yos and marbles.

Like everyone else he had eagerly awaited the arrival of his first pubic hairs, without realising how much they would hurt him. He had thought that the first one was a stray hair floating on the surface of the bathwater, and had not realised that it was his until he had plucked at it in order to drop it over the side of the bath. That sharp and astonishing twinge, however, was as nothing compared to all the psychological agonies that followed.

Peter started to wonder why life was meaningless. Given his Anglican inoculation, it was perhaps strange that this should have happened. But it wasn't that he knew life was meaningless; it was that, deep in his bowels, he began to experience it. His bones and blood began to tell him that one day they would be nothing but earth or ash.

What was it that would make the world seem like the fresh, uncomplicated place it had always been before? What was it that would restore the purpose in life that puberty had removed? He began to feel unhappy. Fits of horrible violence came over him and he wanted to go out and kill. He felt that he wanted to fight, and not stop until he was dead or victorious. He began to play furious games of football with his friends that would go on for three hours or more, because afterwards he felt purged enough to be equable for a while, to sleep peacefully. Recently he had been unable to turn his mind off at night, sweating in his sheets, tormented by everything in general and nothing in particular, a detainee and plaything of his own whirling brain and dissatisfied heart.

Nothing would have sorted Peter out except for the arrival of a large platoon of indulgent nymphomaniacs, an eventuality of little likelihood in Notwithstanding. It might at least have quietened the canker of physical longing that gnawed in his throat and guts. Even that would not have been enough, for Pandora's box had opened more completely than that. Not only did he crave incessantly a satisfaction he could barely imagine and could not have, but he had fallen in love.

He had been in love as a child, it is true: with his hamster, with a little blonde girl at primary school, with the picture of his father as a young man, with Diana Dors and Valerie Singleton on the television, with the family dog; but these kinds of in-love did not hurt and grieve.

Now he was in love with a friend's sister, and he

was in a state of spiritual pain. She was chestnut-haired and freckled, skinny and bouncy. In the summer her freckles joined up. She was slightly croaky in the voice, and she was a Methodist, which didn't seem to matter now, because love had made him broad-minded. He knew nothing about Methodists apart from the fact that they didn't burn people at the stake, were opposed to enjoyment and might not be proper Christians. Because of her voice, everyone called her Froggy. She was twelve, she lived half a mile away up the hill, and she and Peter's little sister spent much of their time together, giggling a great deal and conspiring in hushed voices. One of their favourite topics was discussing what it might be like to have periods, how big their breasts were likely to grow once they got started, and how relatively 'developed' were the various friends they knew. They were fascinated by sex, but knew that it was immoral and that any girl who had it was a tart. Peter knew, contrariwise, that any boy who had it was inconceivably lucky.

Froggy was also in love with Peter, but they hardly ever spoke. They could think of nothing to say, too tongue-tied and awkward to speak to each other at all. They never managed more than 'hello', and Peter spent most of his time with his friend Robert, and Froggy's brothers. They liked to collect conkers or small dead animals, and put them on the railway line, just to see what the trains did to them.

Instead of speaking, Froggy and Peter exchanged a whirlwind of letters. Hers he would always keep. *'My Darling One . . . I miss you,'* she would begin. When they arrived his heart would leap at the sight of the rounded handwriting. The letters were breathless with longing, incandescent with passion. *'My darling darling darling,'* they read, followed by pages of news about her friend Andrea, and about the savage teachers who attacked and oppressed them at school. Froggy wrote, *'I love you, my darling, I love you,'* and she concluded her letters with *'All my everlasting love'*, or *'All my tons and tons of all my special love ever faithful'*.

Their epistolary passion had endured for a year and yet they had never held hands, kissed, or said anything other than 'hello'. On the day before his mother's request to go and pick daffodils, however, a day of the spring holidays, he had contrived to break the impasse, by slipping a note into Froggy's plastic adolescent handbag. He did it on two false assumptions, the first being that girls go through their handbags every day, and the second, that upon finding the note she would come to the assignation. He did not know that women are not what you think; they have limitations and peculiar fears, a sense of right-timing and self-preservation that is obscure to men. Neither did he know that a handbag, even that of a twelve-year-old, contains more than a woman's essential supplies. His note vanished into a congeries of brush, purse, broken biscuits, tissues, coagulated make-up, old bus tickets and chocolate wrappers, much of it being of extraordinary antiquity. The note read: '*Come and meet me at the Maclachlan bench at two thirty tomorrow. Today is Tuesday.*' It had not been easy to find a moment when he could put the note in her bag, but somehow he had done so when she had left it momentarily abandoned in the hall while she was upstairs, giggling with his sister.

Peter did not know precisely what he and she would do up on the common at the Maclachlan bench. Perhaps they would kiss, hold hands, declare their love outright. Perhaps she would take him in her arms and he would feel the length of her sweet and burgeoning body against his. Peter did not imagine that they would have sex. If he had known that it was imaginable, he certainly would have imagined it. He was in love, and he thought he knew the cod wisdom, frequently passed on from his mother while his father sat in resentful silence, that sex and love were different and not really connected.

Peter did not sleep at all that night, and was forced to sit up and read a book. He read *Lady Chatterley's Lover*, which his parents had hidden on the shelf in a brown wrapper, making it the most obviously tempting book in the house. His parents might just as well have written on its spine 'Attention all children! Read this book! It's got sex!' All the children did read it, and none of them understood it much. In any case, the book wasn't as explicit as they might have hoped. Peter read it that night without taking it in. He was too much consumed with anxiety and speculation.

Spending the morning lying in the orchard, shooting down daffodils and thereby picking them in the manliest possible fashion, seemed the only way to pass the time without going mad. He was quite a good shot, but his Webley Junior was only a small-bore 177, and sometimes when he hit a stalk, the flower still didn't topple. He decided that any hit counted as a plucked flower, otherwise he would never get enough of them in time for lunch. Sometimes he would aim at one flower, and another immediately behind it would topple over instead. The dog kept sabotaging his efforts by pouncing on him, snuffling in his face and wandering about in the line of fire. One of the cats, who enjoyed every spring sitting motionless and upright among the flowers, watched them both as if they were mad. 'He thinks he's a daffodil,' Joan used to say. Next door, Miss Agatha Feakes, wearing her brown peaked cap and one of her vast home-knitted cardigans, threw seed to her chickens and milked the goats. A white-headed black-bird came down nearby. She'd known it for nearly ten years. She listened to the repeated pneumatic cough of the air rifle, and reflected that boys will be boys.

Joan made corned-beef fritters and baked beans for lunch, and afterwards Peter sought hopelessly for something to take up the slack until it was two o'clock and time to go out with the dog. There was only half an hour to wait, but it was, in emotional terms, a year. He emptied the waste-paper baskets, even though it wasn't Thursday, and separated out the things that were not inflammable, small bottles and aerosols for female potions and lotions. They were often lilac-coloured. He had to watch out for his father's discarded razor blades. The residue, which included the women-folk's balls of cotton wool with suspect deposits, and rough drafts of his own apostrophic poems to Froggy, Peter burned in the incinerator.

At a quarter past two Peter called the dog, who had been sighing pointedly ever since early morning. The dog sighed and waggled his eyebrows every day until he was walked, affecting an air of suffering, but as soon as anyone went to the walking-stick stand or fetched wellington boots, he would lift off vertically into the air, bouncing straight up and down so rapidly that it was impossible to attach his lead. You had to throw one arm around his neck and restrain him while his back half continued to cantilever up and down. In order to avoid unmanageable explosions of excitement, the family had had to learn to avoid mentioning the word 'walk' anywhere near the dog. Thus they progressed through 'W-A-L-K' to 'promenade', to

'Spaziergang' to 'paseo' to 'peripateion', with the dog always only one linguistic step behind.

Peter set off up the road past the big house where the famous actress lived with her charming but alcoholically outrageous bisexual husband, and past the council houses. In one of these houses lived John, gardener to the Shah of Iran, who had kept a motorcycle combination secretly from his wife all the years of their married life. He passed the hedging and ditching man, who was up to his waist in mud, brambles and nettles. He was cradling in his hand a cantankerous tortoise that he had found at the end of its hibernation in the bank side. Peter passed what was to become the Institute of Oceanography, unaccountably sited in the middle of the countryside rather than by the sea. Once a large workhouse, it was at this time Notwithstanding Homes. It housed a tribe of noisy and emotionally damaged children, who felt a natural and reciprocated disdain for the fortunate children of the village. Once Peter and Robert and Froggy's brothers had got into a stone-throwing fight with some of them, which had ended with one of the Homes' children receiving a large and ragged gash in the forehead. Peter, who had thrown the stone, had been aghast and guilt-stricken, and from then on all hostilities had ceased, both sides understanding at last the appalling consequences of war. The disadvantaged children retreated behind their twenty-foot wall.

Peter entered the woods and strode along a track that, after centuries of use, had sunk fifteen feet below the level of the forest floor. The banks on either side were thick with blueberries that, the moment they were ripe, fell victim to old ladies and squirrels. To the left was a stand of enormously tall Scots pine, where Polly Wantage, to the detriment of squirrels, ventured forth daily in brogues and plus fours, armed with her twelve-bore, and to the right lay the sandy hillside, brackened and bridle-pathed, which was known as Busses Common even though no one knew who Buss had been.

At the end of this track was a low white house whose owners had two Mercedes, were rumoured to possess an aeroplane, and were said to drive all the way to Harrods in order to buy butter. Peter turned right and followed the fence that separated the nuns of the convent from the outer world. Peter could not conceive why anyone would want to be a nun and renounce sex for ever. He had never had any himself, but he knew a priori that it would be as mad, self-defeating and bizarre as renouncing respiration or water.

There was a gentle slope to these tracks and paths, but at the summit of it, at Maclachlan's bench, people realised that they had unwittingly gained a very great height. There was a sapling oak next to the bench, just right for a child's first climb, and steep paths descended from it, down which it was customary to have vertiginous races, and where, in winter, the children, the dog and their mother careered together on toboggans, whooping with exhilaration, numb in face and finger, breathless with the exhaustion of dragging the sledges.

From the bench one could see across the ocean of trees to sombre Blackdown, where Tennyson and his friends had fled in order to avoid literary tourists on the Isle of Wight. In these parts Helen Allingham had painted her pictures of rose-draped cottages and the rural life thereabouts, to be condemned for ever by urban art snobs as a sentimentalist, even though those places were exactly as she depicted them, and often still are. The England that Peter saw, and Allingham before him, was the England that the English used to love, when England was still loved by the English.

Even though he had always lived there, this countryside that he surveyed from the crown of the hill still seemed to Peter an enchanted place, not because it was home, but because it had the archaic atmosphere of Arthurian romance. Because of the density of the trees one could see no dwellings in any direction for tens of miles, and when there was a mist in the low places, rising up off the fields and following the lines of the brooks, it took very little imagination to conceive of squired and mounted knights wending their way through the Hurst on quests. Down among the trees there was even a pink tower, of curiously suggestive appearance, where, had it not been a structure for the pumping of water, a fair demoiselle might have been imprisoned.

To the south among the breasted downs in the far distance rose Chanctonbury Hill, with its unmistakable ring of trees, tall and majestic, unreduced as yet by the great hurricane, where everyone said that the Sussex witches danced naked at Sabbaths. Folk would say that they wouldn't go there, it was frightening, frightening and weird. North of the down, nothing could be seen at all because of the trees, but amid them lay the sagging cottages of agricultural workers, and the unpretentious houses of the rural middle classes, red-tiled in the Surrey farmhouse style from first floor to gutter. Disappearing beneath a forest of rhododendrons lay Sweetwater, a deserted dark tarn that had all but died of oblivion, where Peter had fished for years without ever seeing anything but moorhens and minnows. Once he had been caught poaching there, with Robert from Cherryhurst who was famous for catching the Girt Pike at the Glebe House.

This was the scenery that framed Peter on the occasion of his first tryst. He saw little of the beauty around him, because his consciousness was fixed upon the booming and buzzing of his inner life. The dog, holding no brief for this, lay at Peter's feet, huffing and whining for the entire two hours that they waited for Froggy to come.

Growing more and more despondent, frequently looking at his watch (the first he had ever owned), his heart aglow with ever diminishing hope, anticipation and excitement, Peter sat on the Maclachlan bench, scrying through the trees for any sign of movement from the direction of Froggy's house. He often thought he saw the glimmer of chestnut hair, the luminescence of pale skin, the white furry ruff of her purple coat. The last half-hour he spent with his elbows on his knees, his face buried in his hands.

During the following months he spoke to no one about what had happened, since nothing had. He resolutely replied 'Nothing' when Joan repeatedly asked him what the matter was. He sat in his room, night after night, sometimes all night, at the desk that the Major had made for him, and tried to write things down. For the first time in his schoolboy's literary life, he found no adequate words.

He was caught up in the inexpressible turbulence of a grand love's first emphatic disappointment. It was like a window through which he perceived for the first time the unsatisfactoriness, the faultiness, the mess and futility of the world. He saw that life would not after all be as he had dreamed. Everything falls away, everything escapes. He became infuriated, almost to the point of hysteria, about slippery, errant destinies and unembraceable loves. He knew now about optimism's loss, which no philosophy can console.

Froggy was the focus of this rage. When she wrote to him (*'My darling darling, I'm so so sory I found your note but it was too late I didnt look in my bag til last night please forgive me I wold have come if Id known really I would Im so so sory how will you ever forgive me?'*) he cursorily sent her note back, with all the spelling and punctuation mistakes corrected.

Thus pompously, capriciously, inexplicably did Peter end the affair and fall out of love. For a short time, and only occasionally, he even felt some pleasure at his new freedom. When he and Froggy saw each other they said hello, and then nothing, just as they always had, so that her heartbreak and his rancour never knew the light. She even took his dog to a competition, winning the event for the dog most like its owner, but no word passed between them about the abortive tryst.

Peter would always think that he had infected the bench with disillusionment, resentment and injured pride. It rotted soon, and had to be replaced. Even when he sat there, decades later, he could feel the ache that came up through the sodden oak of its legs and planks. There was still the taste of dust on his tongue. The beginners' oak tree had become too tall and difficult to climb. The rollicking dog and its amiable successors were buried beneath the roses.

It was true that the common gave him other pleasures. He loved the memory of his tiny daughter planting acorns at the path sides in the confident expectation that they would be trees by the weekend – but he was always sad on the bench. It was there he learned that nothing works out as it should.

Since Froggy's day he had walked that hill and lain in the bracken with other lovers, and had come to see that places are only precious because of the ways in which one has loved there. There was a sandpit near Sweetwater where he used to sit and write love poems to Froggy and those who came after, always, it seemed, accompanied by a patient collie. Near the Hurst there was a small woody glade of bluebells and kingcups between two ditches, which became at first the site of future solitary romantic misery and, later on, an enchanted place to take a rug and make love on the moss in dappled light.

Certain locations have the ability to retain the emotions of generation upon generation, until they begin to exude them like the resin that forces itself out of the veins of a pine. On Maclachlan's bench at the top of Busses Common, in sight of Blackdown and Chanctonbury Ring, Peter would always think that others must have been able to feel what had happened to him. It was the natural place for rendezvous, and since Peter and Froggy's youth there had been any number of lovelorn village teenagers who had ineptly failed to meet there.

# THE DEVIL
# AND BESSIE
# MAUNDERFIELD

At sixteen, Bessie Maunderfield was petite, vivacious, ingenious and undeferential. Despite these disqualifications, she obtained employment at the manor house, not least because she was related to both the cook and the groom, and her mother had been a childhood friend of the housekeeper. Naturally, it was envisaged that she would leave the job as soon as she married, but for the time being she arose at six, and, whatever the weather, put on her pattens, and clumped a muddy two miles along the Chiddingfold Road that ran through the Hurot. If she was lucky, there might be a lift to be had on a cart, but it was no quicker than walking. If it rained, she held a tray over her head to protect her black curls, and, if the worst came to the worst, she had a canvas cape that was well smeared with pork lard. The cape was the invention of an uncle who had served with the West Surreys, and seen something like it being used by fishermen in a foreign land where he had been on campaign. It was very effective, but it smelled dreadful, so the housekeeper would make her hang it up on a nail in the stable.

It was of course traditional for the sons of squires to fall in love with serving maids. The sons of squires frequently found themselves unattracted to the women of their own class, since there is a limit to the amount of time one can listen to halting renditions on the piano in between discussion of one's mutual acquaintance. The sons of squires usually did eventually fall for one of them, or become resigned to one, but they married with very little expectation of pleasure, and indeed, very little pleasure did they receive. They took to staying out as much as possible, or, if the house was a very large one, contriving to find themselves always at the opposite end of it. For the son of a squire a serving maid seemed like a cheerful and affectionate creature who might have been prim and virtuous in her own way, but seldom became a prig before the age of thirty.

For the maid, the squire's son was a thrilling creature, quite unlike the young men of her own class, who were given to slumping in front of the fire with pipes and jugs of ale that gave them halitosis, hawking gobbets of phlegm into the cinders for the pleasure of seeing them sizzle, and whose conversation was mainly about the weather. The squire's son rode a beautiful shiny big horse that gave him well-muscled thighs. He had elegantly cut clothes with more buttons than were useful, his top hat was tall and well brushed, and when he spoke he never grunted, but employed long sentences containing many unusual and lovely words. Best of all, until he married, he had high spirits and joyful eyes.

Piers de Mandeville, however, was not the kind of squire's son who assumed that a serving maid was his by right. He was a more democratic sort. He was naturally able to find more or less anyone interesting in some way or other, and understood that hearts should be protected. He particularly appreciated liveliness and intelligence wherever he found them.

He found both on a day in early midsummer when he entered the withdrawing room one morning, with the intention of playing some airs on his violin. His fingers were neither fast nor dexterous, but he had a feel for the soul of a melody, and he was looking forward to playing through a collection of airs by James Hook, which had arrived the previous day by the hand of a cousin who had presently come down from Merton. It had occurred to him that at that time of day there should be no one to discommode in that particular room.

Bessie Maunderfield was there, however, cleaning

out the hearth on her second day of employment, and already regretting her sore knees. 'Ah,' said Piers de Mandeville when he saw her.

She got to her feet and executed a little curtsy, saying, 'Sir.'

'You must be new,' he said.

'Started yesterday, sir,' she said.

'And what might be your name?'

'Bessie Maunderfield, sir,' she replied, 'an' it may please you, sir.'

'Maunderfield? Of the Chiddingfold Maunderfields?'

'Yes, sir.'

'Well, Bessie, I am Piers de Mandeville, and I regret to inform you that I am not the son and heir of this house. That honour belongs to my older brother, who is, as we speak, planting tea in a much hotter place where skins are darker, diseases even more foul and languages incomprehensible.'

'I am pleased to make your acquaintance, sir, and I hope you will find my service satisfactory, sir,' said Bessie, glancing up at his face and finding herself looking into a pair of humorous grey eyes.

'I am sure I will,' he replied. He paused, and added, 'Did you know that the Maunderfields and the de Mandevilles are supposed to have been related, distantly, once upon a time? The origins of the name are the same, it seems.'

'I did hear that, sir. People do commonly say it; they say that our side fell on hard times and your side never did, sir. They say it was because of our being greatly in the wrong cause in the Civil War, sir, and our house got terrible burned by fire setters.'

'Well, Bessie, one day perhaps all will be reversed. The wheel of Fortune might spin and there you'll have it – lo and behold! – a de Mandeville girl cleaning out the hearth of a Maunderfield as he scrapes on a fiddle in the withdrawing room of a great house in Chiddingfold.'

'Well, I do hope not, sir.'

'Really, Bessie? Why not? The thought should give you some satisfaction, should it not?'

'No, sir,' said Bessie, 'I wouldn't wish cleaning hearths on anyone, sir. Hearths would clean themsen, sir, if it had anything to do with me. Now you must excuse me, sir, I have the parlour to do, and I wouldn't be wanting the housekeeper to scold me.'

'Not on your second day, certainly. Indeed, I do excuse you. I am sorry to have detained you with my chatter.'

Bessie bobbed, glanced at him and hurried out with her copper bucket of ash. She set it down on the parlour floor, and clapped her hands together softly in a gentle gesture of delight. She smiled and kneeled to clean out the grating. In the withdrawing room Piers de Mandeville began to play through his James Hook with a light heart.

Love being what it is, Piers de Mandeville contrived to run into Bessie quite often. The best pretext, he found, was to be looking for something that he had mislaid. It gave him a reason to be moving about the house somewhat randomly. He would greet her with 'How now, my pretty distant cousin?' or 'How now, my distant pretty cousin?' Bessie very quickly realised why he kept losing his possessions and was both flattered and frightened by turns. She could not deny that her heart seemed to flutter to her mouth every time that she saw him. He found himself in a similar condition, merely at the thought of her, and at night, the two of them, she on her palliasse in Chiddingfold, and he in his goose-down bed in Notwithstanding, would exhaust themselves as they slept, on account of the febrile longings and repetitive pretty dreams. It was not long before both of them saw quite clearly that an inevitable intimacy was developing.

One day Piers de Mandeville turned up below stairs, upon a somewhat feeble excuse. Bessie teased him. 'Now why would my master be looking for his timepiece in the scullery, when he never has any business there?' to which he replied, 'Sir Isaac Newton, of late philosophical memory and immortal renown, established it as a universal law of nature that lost objects gravitate inexorably towards places where they would least expect to be found. Objects, my pretty distant cousin, have a natural and innate perversity. In fact, it seems likely that for this reason objects must be feminine, even though, in the French language, merely half of them are.'

'Could it be that the lost object is indeed of the female kind and that you were looking for a particular maid, sir, and a very likely place to find her might be in the scullery?'

'I confess it. That is indeed the reason, and I am very glad to have chanced upon you.' They stood looking at one another for a long moment, and then he found himself stroking her cheek gently with his hand. 'How very sweet and lovely you are,' he said quietly, adding, 'my pretty distant cousin.'

'You're not so bad yourself,' she said, removing his hand, 'but you must be cautious, sir. Think of all the other servants coming in and out. It wouldn't do to get caught now, would it?'

'You're quite right, Bessie, of course you are, but I think we need to talk about certain things, don't you?'

'I would say we do, sir.'

'Where shall I see you?'

Bessie Maunderfield thought quickly, and said, 'This evening, sir, have your groom saddle your horse, and tell the family that you are riding to Chiddingfold.'

'On what pretext, Bessie? What can I tell them?'

'That's for you to decide, sir. I shall be walking home, and you will pass me on your horse and turn into the Hurst, and if there is no one about, then I shall follow you in. The Hurst is full of hidden places, sir.'

Somewhat in advance of the hunting season, Piers de Mandeville set off one evening to scout the Hurst for fox earths. He encountered his particular little vixen at a place near one of the ponds where, within living memory, Prince George of Denmark had got bogged down in his carriage on the way to Petworth, and the men of the village had gathered to disembog him. Checking that no one else was about, he dismounted, and together they walked into the wood, he leading his horse by the bridle. The latter was tied to a sapling of ash, and the couple spread his cape on the ground by a little stream, barely a pace wide, which in those days was populated by diminutive brown trout.

They sat shoulder to shoulder, with their arms around their knees. 'Do you love me, Bessie?' he asked at length.

'The question is, sir, do you love me?'

'I asked first.'

'My question is more urgent, sir.'

'How so?'

'A maid has more to lose. A maid might lose her

very self, a maid might be sore hobbled, but a gentleman might lose very little.'

'Very well, then, I do love you. You know that I do. I can think of very little else but my pretty distant cousin. Does she love me, though? Is she tormented, as I am?'

'But how is it possible? What can we do? I know you would never marry me, and I would never be a mistress.'

'Are you saying that you love me, then?'

'Oh sir, I am miserable with love.'

'We shall be married then, Bessie. There is no other way.'

'Don't be goosey, sir. Your family would never accept it. I can just imagine your father roaring and your mother weeping. What a furore there would be. You know it.'

'Yes, I know it. Even so, love makes all things possible.'

'Only in fairy tales, sir. Here in this place everything depends upon who you are.'

He fell silent, and finally said, 'I will marry you. I have resolved upon it.'

'You have yet to ask me, sir.'

He got to one knee, and spread his arms wide. 'Bessie Maunderfield, my pretty distant cousin, will you marry me?'

'I will marry you on one condition.'

'Oh Bessie, what is that?'

'When we are married and in a public place, or at dinner before the servants, you must call me madam, just as your father does your mother.'

'This is a very small condition, Bessie.'

She shrugged and smiled. 'I have always wanted to be addressed as madam.'

'Then madam you shall be. Of course, under similar circumstances I shall expect you to call me sir.'

She suddenly became deeply grave, and looked at him directly, as if searching his eyes for honesty. 'Do you swear that we shall be married?'

He tried to field the question lightly. 'I swear by these trees, and the yellow kingcups, and the blue-bells, and by my right hand, and even by His Majesty the King's best gilded chamber pot.'

'Don't make me laugh, now. I am serious. Do you swear that we shall be married? Do you swear it on the Holy Bible?'

'I do. I swear it on the Holy Bible, and may the Devil have my soul if I don't.'

'You swear that the Devil may have your soul if you don't?'

'I do, Bessie, I do.'

'Put your hand on your heart and say, "I Piers de Mandeville do solemnly swear that if I do not marry Bessie Maunderfield, then the Devil may have my soul."'

The squire's son sighed, and lifted his eyebrows in humorous resignation. Nonetheless he put his right hand over his heart and swore the oath. 'There,' he added, 'the deed is done. I am yours, or Beelzebub's.'

'Now you may kiss me, sir, if you please,' said Bessie. Piers de Mandeville discovered that she kissed very sweetly indeed, and soon they were lying side by side on the cape, kissing with ever greater degrees of oblivion. De Mandeville's mare watched them indifferently as she waited to go home to her stable.

Their recklessness and ardour increased by the day, especially after a small room on the top floor of the house fell vacant owing to the departure of another servant. The housekeeper, wishing to spare Bessie her long trudges back and forth through the Hurst, allowed her the room, which was at the back of the house next to the top of a narrow flight of stairs. It was perfectly placed for a furtive liaison. They made love with his hand over her mouth as she bucked beneath him. Sometimes there was a full moon hanging in the window, filling the room with delirious silver light, and Piers de Mandeville and Bessie Maunderfield would lie crammed together on the narrow bed, confounded to find themselves in paradise, incredulous with happiness.

Their liaison had been established for about six months, when four things happened in quick succession. Firstly the Rector died of an apoplexy brought on by becoming infuriated about politics when drunk on claret, leaving behind him no son to inherit the living. Secondly the new Rector arrived with three accomplished and charming daughters who were looking for husbands to match their station. Thirdly the Rector's wife quickly discovered that there was an unmarried son in the manor house, and the fourth thing was that Bessie Maunderfield came to the inescapable conclusion that she was pregnant.

Bessie said nothing for a month, frightened to tell her love, and believing that he would be angry with her. At St Mary's Church on Sunday, beneath the stern gaze of Earl Winterton and his family in their own private gallery, she even begged God for a miscarriage. During that time she became ever more alarmed at the frequency of the visits from the Rector's wife and her three marriageable daughters. They seemed to have an inexhaustible appetite for cakes, scones, tea and lively chatter, and it was quite plain to all that the eldest daughter was making specific efforts to be charming to Piers de Mandeville. She tossed her golden ringlets very fetchingly, praised his playing inordinately and listened wide-eyed to his opinions. When she passed by him, she brushed just a little closer than one ordinarily would, and he often caught the scent of lavender from her clothes. Emily Sutton went to the lengths of learning the fortepiano accompaniments to certain violin pieces that he had always wanted to play. Everyone who observed them also observed that they seemed a very well-matched pair. This thought was not lost on Piers de Mandeville, who now began to waver in his determination to marry Bessie Maunderfield.

Not least among his worries had been that he had proved himself too cowardly to confess his intentions to his parents. Terrified of their rage, and equally terrified as to what would become of him, once disowned, he procrastinated daily, despite many bold resolutions to grasp the nettle.

Bessie Maunderfield, entering and leaving the withdrawing room invisibly and discreetly as a servant must, could not help but notice what was happening, and she quickly became desperate. She foresaw fatal chasms opening up beneath her feet, a storm of recrimination and disgrace about her head. She was forced to tell her lover about the child.

'Are you sure?' he asked her repeatedly, as if there might be the slightest possibility that the swelling was an attack of colic.

'You will marry me, won't you?' she asked him repeatedly, sick with anxiety and dread. 'You will marry me before the little one comes?'

'I will, I will,' he promised, and she reminded him solemnly that he had vouched his soul to the Devil if he did not.

He fell into such a state of agitation that he

thought his heart would give way. It seemed to flutter in his chest like a panicked bird, and his concentration left him. He would pick up his violin, and then immediately lay it back in its case. He went out and walked at furious speed, taking the sandy paths on Busses Common as far as Sweetwater Lake, or tramping along Vann Lane all the way to Pockford Road, or down Malthouse Lane all the way to Brook, where he could take to his cups in the Dog and Pheasant, believing that no one there would know who he was. Ultimately, because of the difficulty of walking home inebriated in the dark, Piers de Mandeville began to ride there on his mare, knowing that she would find the way home without any instruction or intervention from him.

Naturally, everyone knew within days that the squire's second son was drinking and falling into bad company at the Dog and Pheasant. Bessie heard it from her cousin, the groom, and then she heard it again from her own sister who had heard it from the blacksmith's wife in Sittinghurst.

It became impossible for Bessie to dissemble her pregnancy any longer. Her mother noticed first. She had in fact suspected for some considerable time, because she had not seen Bessie washing her clouts. Fury was followed by hand-wringing, followed by accusations of bringing disgrace upon the family, followed by the decision that Father would have to be

told. Then the same sequence of rage and recrimination had to be endured all over again. Lastly came
the sensible consideration of practicalities.

Bessie endured these terrible scenes with tearful
resignation, at first refusing to name the father, but
assuring her family over and over again that the culprit
had promised to marry her before the child was due.
'He said that if he didn't then the Devil may have his
soul. He swore it on the Holy Book,' she told them.

'Now that's a fearful oath,' said her father, 'a fearful
oath indeed.'

Another month went by, and Bessie lost her situation at the manor. At a stroke it became almost
impossible to meet up with her beloved, and it even
seemed to him that perhaps this was for the best. 'Out
of sight, out of mind,' she thought bitterly, when she
had not seen him for a full week.

Finally, so desperate that she could hardly think,
she confided who the father was, and her mother
and father immediately felt better about the entire
situation. How very advantageous it might be if only
Bessie were to marry the son of a manor house. 'I've
got a plan, Da,' said Bessie, and when she had
explained it, her father leaned back in his chair, his
eyes twinkling. 'Well, Bessie my dear, I think that
might be well worth a try. I'd enjoy doing that.'

There ensued many days of energetic and creative
activity on the part of the entire household. Her

brother John was dispatched to the slaughterhouse to fetch back the head of a cow. It was boiled to remove the flesh, which was soon eaten at dinner, and then he set about sawing off the crown. He bound the tips of the horns thickly with sackcloth, and soaked them in pitch. Setting off early one morning, mother and sister went all the way to Godalming on a cart to find bolts of red cloth. Mr Maunderfield rode down to Malthouse Lane on his cob to select a good site, and was fortunate to find an oak stump at the side of the road that was four feet high. At the back of it he cut toeholds with an axe. Bessie herself shredded paper and cloth into a pail, and mixed it all up with glue. She made a former out of clay, allowed it to dry, smeared it with butter, and then carefully coated it to the depth of her little fingernail with the mess from the pail. When it was dry she painted it red and lifted it off the mould. Mr Maunderfield stood in the kitchen and practised his speech, in the deepest voice he could muster. He sang bass in the church choir, and therefore began with a considerable advantage.

On the designated night, Piers de Mandeville, half asleep, his tongue stinging and bitter from cheap tobacco, stupid with alcohol, and as much drunk with despair as spirits, hacked slowly home on his mare. There was a half-moon, but it was dark beneath the overhanging trees, and the night was cold but quite still. Wisps of black cloud passed slowly across the face of the moon, casting gossamer shadows. Foxes coughed in the woods, and owls screeched or hooted according to their kind. When Piers de Mandeville passed the crossroad at Lane End, where once they used to bury the suicides, Bessie's brother John, hidden behind the hedge, put his hands together and blew into the cavity they formed. Three long identical hoots were the signal. Quietly he slipped through the hedge, and followed Piers de Mandeville at a small distance. At the spot where in the distant future would stand the half-tiled house inhabited by the naked general and his rhododendrons, Mr Maunderfield opened his tinderbox and repeatedly struck the flint. Once the tinder was smouldering, he handed the box to his wife, and carefully mounted the stump, feeling for the axe notches with his feet. He then released the cord binding up his robes and let the drapes of cloth fall down around the stump. When Piers de Mandeville was barely twenty yards from him he bent down and whispered, 'Now!'

With a lit spill caught in the cleft of a long stick, Bessie's mother ignited the pitch-soaked rags, and Mr Maunderfield stood erect and roared.

So startled was de Mandeville's horse, that she leapt sideways and then reared. De Mandeville, too drunk even to have managed to get his feet into the stirrups, slipped backwards off her hindquarters and landed in the muddy road on his rump. The mare bolted ahead, whinnying, and de Mandeville scrambled to his feet.

He beheld a most terrible apparition. Ten feet tall, robed in red, stood a vast creature. It had a huge and hideous red face, with large blank eyes, and above its head rose curved horns that flared at the tips, the flames casting violent shadows as the figure waved its arms and nodded its head.

'Piers de Mandeville, of Notwithstanding Manor in the county of Surrey, Esquire,' announced the creature, which had a strong local accent that Piers was too drunk to find peculiar.

He gazed at it, wordless with horror, clutching his hat in his hand.

'How pleased we are, how very pleased we all are, that you have generously yielded up your soul. How very pleased we are that within such a short time we shall be relishing your company in Outer Darkness, where there is weeping and wailing, and gnashing of teeth.'

De Mandeville fell to his knees. 'I beg you,' he began, but was unable to continue. He started to whimper with terror, but could not take his eyes off the figure of the Devil.

'You shall be ours on the night the child is born, you shall be ours, you shall be ours on that fatal night. Is that not so, my brothers and sisters?'

From behind, in the trees, came laughter and

shrieking, and whooping, and the dinning of wooden spoons on copper pans.

The Devil held up his arms for silence, and asked in his booming voice, 'What do you plead to that, Piers de Mandeville?'

'Spare me,' said the young man, simply, 'spare me.'

'That was the bargain. Do you deny it?'

'Only if I do not marry,' said de Mandeville weakly.

The Devil hissed, 'No, no, you must not marry. No, no, marry not.'

From the trees behind came howls of rage and disappointment. First one flame on the horn extinguished itself, and then the other. To be alone in the dark with a Satan that he could not see was too much for Piers de Mandeville. He crawled a short way, then struggled to his feet and ran, bent double as if to avoid blows, scarcely able to run in a straight line, scarcely able to run at all. Laughter followed him up Malthouse Hill, and a deer ran out across the road in front of him, adding startlement to his fear.

Three days later in the evening Piers de Mandeville arrived on horseback before the Maunderfields' cottage. He dismounted and began to tie his horse to the ring set in the wall. Bessie, by now heavily pregnant, saw him from the window and came out.

'Oh sir, you do look terrible awful,' she said. He did indeed look very bad. He was pale and wild-eyed, and seemed to have become wasted and thin almost overnight. He did, however, have a mature air of purpose about him.

'Bessie,' he said, 'I have come to tell you that we shall do what we should have done a very long time ago. I have been a most shameful coward. We shall be married in St Mary's as soon as the banns are read. My father is resigned to it, and my mother is saying nothing further against it. They ask only that I marry in your parish rather than theirs, and that they should not be expected at the wedding. We are fortunate indeed that I am not the first son. If I had been my brother, God knows what would have happened.'

'Come in and meet my father, sir,' said Bessie mischievously. 'I believe you first have to ask him if he is willing to give me up. I fear you might have to overcome his reluctance.'

'Ah, Bessie, there is plenty of time for that. All I want for now is to take a walk with you on my arm, and confer about what we shall do. I imagine you are sufficiently well to walk?'

'Well, sir, it's only fine ladies who take to their beds when a tiddler's on the way. The rest of us just carry on as needs must.'

They walked slowly through the Hurst, with her arm through his for support. Piers raised his hat to those they passed, ignoring their astonished expressions. As they drew near the pond, Bessie said,

'Shall we go into the woods? We can find our special place.'

Piers de Mandeville laid his cape on the ground and they sat side by side by the stream, just as they had so many months before. For a little while they were silent, and then Bessie asked slyly, 'What was it that made up your mind, sir?'

'Well, Bessie, have you heard the story of Saul on the road to Damascus?'

'Yes, sir, I have heard it.'

'It was something very like to that.'

'Indeed, sir? And is Emily Sutton very down-cast?'

'I presume to hope that she might be, but not for too long, I trust.'

'And what about your other promise, sir? The other promise you made in this same place?'

Piers de Mandeville laughed quietly, and looked at her askance. 'I believe, madam, that you wanted me to call you madam, did you not, madam?'

'I did indeed, sir, but don't go overdoing it, sir.'

# THE AUSPICIOUS MEETING
# OF THE THIRD MEMBER
# OF THE FAMOUS
# NOTWITHSTANDING WIND
# QUARTET WITH THE
# FIRST TWO

There were two Morris Minor saloons, both grey, parked in the small driveway of Jenny Farhoumand's house as well as a large Hillman Hunter. The latter belonged to Jenny's husband, who was an auctioneer with Messenger May Baverstock in Godalming, and the Morris Minors belonged to Jenny herself and to the music teacher at the public school. He had come round on a Saturday afternoon in spring, to rehearse a few duets by Devienne for a little concert in the church, in order to raise money for a new set of steps up from the church to the road. Neither of them were believers, but the churchgoers were always prepared to consider outsiders to be honorary members of the congregation when it came to fundraising. There was not much of a repertoire for clarinet and oboe, and so they were playing flute duets. Brian, the clarinettist, was manfully transposing on sight, and Jenny was playing her flute parts on the oboe. Sometimes it sounded quite good and sometimes very strange.

'It's lucky that Devienne is dead,' said Brian. 'I can't imagine what he'd think of us doing this.'

'I think it's wonderful, how you transpose like that,' said Jenny. 'I don't know how you do it. You must have to split your brain in half.'

'It does your head in after a while,' he admitted, 'but you get used to it, and the exercise is probably very good for you. I'm hoping it'll make me more intelligent.'

'Why don't you use a C clarinet? Wouldn't that be the really intelligent option?'

'I haven't got one. They don't sound quite as nice as a B flat.'

'Why don't you get one, though?'

'Maybe I should start saving up my pocket money. That's not a bad idea, actually.'

'Then you can save up for a basset horn. I'm sure they pay you masses at that posh school.'

'Yes, and pigs fly. I'd love a basset horn, though.'

'By the way,' said Jenny, 'can you see the kids anywhere?'

'They're all in a heap, fighting on the lawn,' said Brian, looking through the window. 'Suzie has just bitten Annie, and Andrew is crying, and the dog is digging in the flower bed, and your husband is doing something to the lawnmower. By the way that his lips are moving, I would guess that he's swearing. I can't see the cat, but I think the rabbit's got out. There's a black one in the vegetable patch.'

'All's right with the world, then,' said Jenny. 'Shall we try something else?'

They were halfway through a fairly vigorous allegro when Suzie, aged six, blonde, tousled and filthy, came running in. 'Mummy, Mummy, there's a strange man outside, and he was listening under the window. I saw him, I saw him!'

'Have you told Daddy?'

'Yes, I did tell Daddy, and Daddy's got him and he's going to kill him.'

'Oh dear, really?'

'He's got a big spanner, Mummy.'

'I suppose we'd better go out,' said Brian, putting his clarinet carefully on to its stand, and replacing the cap.

Outside they found a small, bespectacled middle-aged man in a brown jacket and waistcoat cowering between a wall and a rhododendron, while Jenny's husband, already enraged by the intransigence of the mower, loomed over him with a large wrench and demanded explanations.

'Peter, darling, please, be careful with that thing,' said Jenny. 'You might do some damage, and then they'll take you away in a Black Maria, and tomorrow you'll miss Sunday lunch, and we'll have to give your share to the dog.'

Peter lowered the spanner, and said, 'All right, but who the hell are you, and what are you doing underneath my window? And don't you know any better than to walk on other people's flower beds? It compacts the soil. Don't you know that?'

'No. I'm not a gardener, I'm afraid. I really am most terribly sorry. It was the music.'

'The music?' repeated Jenny.

'Yes, the music. I just love that kind of music. I love Devienne. It's a bit light, I suppose, but I don't mind. I've never heard it done like that before, on oboe and clarinet. I couldn't resist listening. I really am so sorry . . . for the damage to the flower bed . . . and for intruding.'

'You knew it was Devienne?' said Brian, much impressed. 'Are you a musician yourself?'

The little man nodded, and said, 'Bassoon.'

'Bassoon!' exclaimed Jenny and Brian together, both struck by the same thought.

'Prove it,' said Peter, who was still enraged by his mower, and desired a little more confrontation and aggression.

'Prove it? Why, do you have one?'

'Tell us the K number of Mozart's bassoon concerto in B-flat major,' said Jenny, mischievously.

'And the opus number of Weber's bassoon concerto,' added Brian.

'Oh, for God's sake,' exclaimed Peter, 'bloody musicians!'

'It's 191 and 75, respectively,' said the man. 'I've played both of them in my time.'

Jenny and Brian were astounded. 'You've played them both? Entire concertos?'

'I used to be a pro, but then I got married. You can't support children and a wife, especially not my wife anyway, if you're just a bassoonist. Now I play with whoever wants me. I keep my hand in. One of these days I'll be back on the road, God willing. Well, wife willing.'

'Would you like a cup of tea?' asked Jenny.

'Oh no,' said Peter, waving his spanner, 'I can just see what's coming. God save us all.' He strode away to renew battle with his mower. The children, who all this time had been standing dumbly by with their thumbs in their mouths, returned to their scrum on the lawn.

'So what were you doing round here?' asked Brian.

'I'm a de Mandeville,' said the man, as if that amounted to an explanation. 'Or man-devil, as my wife likes to say.'

'I don't see . . .' began Jenny.

'I'm Piers de Mandeville. Piers is a family name. There've been lots of us. You've probably noticed the big tomb just outside the door of the church. It's the one where they hide the key. That's the Piers de Mandeville I'm descended from. We used to be the lords of the manor, you know, in that house where the musicologist lives. Unfortunately we went down in the world. It was the South Sea Bubble, apparently. The family lost a fortune.'

'How do you know all this?' asked Brian. 'I don't even know the names of my great-grandparents.'

'I'm a genealogist. When I'm not a bassoonist, I spend my time finding the ancestors of Americans, mainly. It pays surprisingly well. They're all convinced that they're related to the royal family. Or Irish chieftains.'

'It's like people who believe in reincarnation,' said Jenny. 'They all think they were Cleopatra.'

'Do they?' said Brian. 'They say I've got an ancestor who was hanged for being a highwayman.'

'Well, anyway, I like to come here and see where Piers and Bessie are. It's a sad story.'

'Go on,' said Jenny, 'depress us. Do come in and have a cup of tea.'

Once in the drawing room de Mandeville continued. 'Well, Bessie was from the poor side of the family, who lived in Chiddingfold. The Maunderfields. They were farmers. Apparently she and Piers fell in love, and they got married rather late in the day, after a lot of opposition from his family. Three months after they married, poor Bessie died. It says "dyed in childbed" on the tomb.'

'Oh, I saw that,' said Jenny. 'It always makes me feel sad. And there are three little children in there by a second wife. They are all called John and they died one after the other in the space of three years. It's awful.'

'After Bessie, he married one of the Rector's daughters. Emily Sutton. They had eight children, so losing three wasn't so bad, I suppose, by the standards of the time. I'm descended from Bessie, the first wife. The little baby survived and they sent it to Chiddingfold for the grandmother to look after, and then when Piers remarried the boy was sent back to the manor. They called him Perditus.'

'Perditus?' said Brian.

'Little Lost One. Since then, some of us have had it as a second name.'

Jenny suddenly felt tearful. She was a sentimental person, and her feelings came easily to the surface. She dabbed at her eyes with her sleeve.

'He did well, though. When he grew up he started quarrying Bargate stone. All the old buildings around here are made of it. You know the old lime kiln next to the church? I think they probably used it for making mortar, as well as lime for the fields. Anyway, that's the story. I was visiting Piers and Bessie and Emily and the three little boys, and when I came back down the hill, I heard you two playing. By the way, there were two old ladies in the graveyard, and one of them introduced me to someone who wasn't there.'

'Wasn't there?' repeated Brian.

'She had someone on her arm, as if she was supporting him, and she kept talking to him, but he wasn't there. When she noticed me looking, she said, "This is my husband." Well, I didn't know what to do. I wondered if I ought to pretend to shake his hand. Then the old lady said, "We've just been visiting his grave." It was quite bizarre.'

'That's Mrs Mac,' said Jenny. 'She's a spiritualist. She lives with her sister and the ghost of her husband. He's called Mac. She even goes on the bus with him and tries to pay two fares.'

'How very entertaining,' said Piers, and then he frowned. The tone of his voice changed, and he looked at Jenny. 'I'd like to know if you know the K number of Mozart's oboe concerto in C major.'

'No,' she said.

'Then why did you expect me to know the K number of the bassoon concerto?'

'We didn't know it, anyway,' said Brian cheerfully. 'You could have said anything you liked.'

'Do you drive a Morris Minor, by any chance?' asked Jenny.

'No, I've got an old Minx. Why?'

'We have eligibility criteria.'

'I'm sorry?'

'Oh, never mind,' said Jenny.

'You have to bring offerings of tail feathers from pheasants,' said Brian.

After the bassoonist had gone home in his Minx to his difficult wife, Jenny and Brian went out into the garden. The children clambered up Brian and draped themselves from him like human flags. 'Oh God,' he said, as he toppled over.

Peter relaxed the throttle lever on the mower and stopped making his stripes. 'I just thought I'd tell you, darling,' said Jenny, 'the bassoonist is coming to Sunday lunch tomorrow. I'm sure there'll be enough for all of us. There just won't be any leftovers for warm-up. And he's bringing his wife. And his bassoon.'

Peter sighed and pursed his lips. He put on a funereal Scottish accent and said, 'We are doomed, Captain Mainwaring, doomed.' Then he throttled up the mower and resumed his work.

As Jenny said goodbye to Brian, she remarked, 'Talking of pheasant feathers, I wonder how you clean out a bassoon.'

'Alsatians' tails,' said Brian.

'Not very practical. I don't think you'd get one round the bends.'

'You hardly ever find a dead one,' said Brian, 'and it's a bit cruel cutting them off when they're still alive.

149

When they come round from the anaesthetic, they're all off balance for a while.'

'We just need a flautist, now,' said Jenny. 'One that plays in tune, and breathes at the right times, and isn't mad.'

Brian shook his head. 'There's probably more chance of finding an Alsatian's tail sticking out of a hedge.'

# FOOTPRINT IN
# THE SNOW

Back then every parish of the Anglican Church still had its own vicar or rector, and many of them still lived with modest gentility in substantial houses inherited from more prosperous and faithful days, when God was indisputably in His heaven, and all was right with the world. These were the times when one was not respectable unless seen in church, at least at Christmas and Easter. For teenagers it was a chance to eye up the prospects, and for middle-aged and elderly women it was a chance to remark upon who wasn't there, and to deplore each other's hats.

The Reverend Godfrey Freemantle, together with his wife, three pretty daughters, a yellow Labrador and two tabby cats, occupied a substantial rectory at the foot of the hill below St Peter's Church. It had fifteen rooms and was supposed to be haunted by the ghost of a pregnant serving maid who had been found dead under suspicious circumstances in 1879, shortly after the Tay Bridge Disaster. It was said that her wraith wafted about the attic rooms of the former servants' quarters, wringing its hands and looking for Epsom salts in the cupboards. No one had ever seen it, but the Reverend Godfrey Freemantle often liked to suppose that from time to time he detected a chilling of the air when he was up there at the skylight, observing the moon through his telescope. Occasionally he had thought of performing an exorcism, but he felt a little embarrassed about the idea of approaching the Bishop for permission, and he was too trepidatious to go ahead and do it without.

It was mid-morning, shortly before that Christmas that would always be remembered as the last in the village when it actually snowed on Christmas Day, and the Reverend Freemantle was in his study with a Handel flute sonata crackling and clicking on the record player, as he flicked somewhat despairingly through his collections of sermons for one that he might plagiarise for the family service. The composition of sermons was a weekly torment to him, as he was conscious of never having in all his life as a minister come up with something fresh or original. He was tired of repeating himself, but lacked the nerve to go to the pulpit unprepared. The Church of England was not an extemporising institution. What made it worse was that he often found God a difficult customer to deal with, and at this time was fresh from wondering what God could possibly have been up to when He let poor pretty Mrs Rendall die horribly of cancer while she was still so young. He wondered if God realised how difficult it was for him to keep making excuses on His behalf.

As he browsed a sermon on the True Meaning of Christmas, it suddenly occurred to him that he had not for some weeks seen Sir Edward at Holy Communion. The thought alarmed him.

Sir Edward Rawcutt (pronounced Rawt), fifth baronet, was not the squire of the village, although he performed that function to some extent, simply by being the only resident who was a baronet. The manor itself was occupied by an eminent musicologist, who was rumoured to drink tea and write about baroque music all day, emerging only in the evening, with his chamber pot perilously brimming. Few people had ever seen him, but his only daughter caused some comment by being dark-haired, passionate, black-eyed, beautiful, and always dressed in romantic white dresses, even for her forays to the village shop to buy mentholated Du Maurier cigarettes. The musicologist was to come into his own quite suddenly at the time of the great hurricane, when it transpired that it was the duty of the manor house to keep the pathways of the common land clear. He and his son took on the monumental task with amazing alacrity and efficiency, and thereafter the son never lost his interest in it.

Sir Edward Rawcutt occupied a late-Victorian Surrey farmhouse. It was substantial and imposing, with numerous low sag-roofed annexes attached to it at the back in a somewhat arbitrary fashion. Its croquet lawns were kept in immaculate condition by young Robert from the council houses, who often mowed with his pet rook resolutely perched upon his shoulder. He was paid five pounds a time, plus unlimited peanut butter sandwiches. The marvellous rose beds were tended by Lady Gemma Rawcutt herself, who was never without a pair of secateurs secreted somewhere about her person. She was a notoriously nimble-fingered and furtive snipper of cuttings from all the great gardens of southern England, from Great Dixter and Bateman's to the Royal Horticultural Gardens at Wisley. There were many in the gardening club who dreaded her yearly visits to their own homes when it was their turn to act the host. So adept was her pilfering that she had never actually been caught, even though everyone knew that it was she who was responsible for their mutilated shrubs and bushes. She was, despite this almost unforgivable personality defect, well loved on account of her graceful figure, her crisp accent and her charmingly spontaneous peals of laughter. She was a regular member of the team of ladies who arranged flowers in the church by rota, and this also was taken into consideration as an extenuating circumstance.

Sir Edward himself was an affable and energetic gentleman approaching his middle sixties. His energetic and reckless youth had been followed by a raffish and adulterous middle age, and this in turn had recently been succeeded by the unexpected return of the simple piety that had been his most remarkable trait before the onset of adolescence. Conscious, no doubt, of the beat of death's drum, he had taken to attending every possible communion in the village church, and was fond of comparing the relative merits of various sung Eucharists which he had attended in cathedrals as far apart as Wells and Peterborough. There were those who considered this preoccupation a harmless eccentricity, and others who felt a warm glow in their hearts at the thought of such a prodigal's wholehearted return.

The Reverend Freemantle himself was unconcerned as to why Sir Edward had returned to the fold; if God moved in mysterious ways, it was clear that many others did also. What concerned the Rector was that he had not seen Sir Edward for some time, and the latter had not yet responded to his note asking him if he would read one of the lessons in a forthcoming service. He had a feeling that something must be wrong.

He was on the point of picking up the telephone

when he was startled by an urgent knocking at the door. One of his predecessors had installed an enormous brass knocker in the shape of a lion's head, and he had never ceased to be shocked when its percussions suddenly reverberated through the house.

He heard someone go to the door, and shortly afterwards his oldest daughter appeared, and said, 'Daddy, there's an old lady here to see you.'

'Who is it?'

'I don't know, Daddy, she didn't say.'

'Oh well, you'd better send her in, then.'

'She doesn't want to come in, she says she's in a hurry. She's waiting at the door.'

'Oh hell's bells.'

'Not a very godly attitude, Daddy.'

'Oh drat, I suppose I'd better come out. Tell her I'm coming straight away.'

'She's a bit strange.'

'Is she? Oh lor'; as if I didn't have enough to worry about.'

The Rector put down his address book, stood up and stretched. He came out into the hallway and went to the front door, where he beheld an elderly woman dressed in black, who was anxiously rubbing her hands together and biting her lip. The Rector thought that she looked very familiar, but he was quite unable to put a name to her. His forgetfulness was one of the problems that he still had with this parish even though he had been there for nearly twenty years, and it caused him little pangs of shame from time to time. He always dreaded having to make introductions, and even had some difficulty with recollecting the names of some of the more mousy ladies of his Bible Study Group on Tuesdays, who were grimly but steadfastly reading their way right through the entire New English Bible, from the first word of Genesis to the last word of Revelation. They were at present reading with some horror of the numerous divinely inspired atrocities in the Book of Judges.

'Do come in,' he said, 'it's really quite cold out there. I think we might be in for some snow.'

'I prefer to stay where I am,' said the old lady, 'if you don't mind. I have something of great urgency to tell you, and I will require only a moment of your time.' She spoke with precision, and some hauteur.

'Oh dear,' said the Rector, 'has something dreadful happened?'

'Not yet, sir, but I have to tell you that Sir Edward is very seriously ill and is in need of communion. You know how much comfort he derives from it. I must ask you to come as soon as you possibly can. He's not long for this world, I am sorry to say.'

The Rector felt a pang in his heart; he was really very fond of Sir Edward, and the thought of him being at death's door, or even very ill, was particularly painful. 'Tell him I'll come right away,' he said.

'Thank you, sir,' said the old lady, 'it will be very much appreciated by all of us, I do assure you.'

After she had gone, the Reverend Freemantle set about rummaging for all the things he would need for a private Eucharist. He would have to pick up some of it from the church vestry. He found his little leather case with its chalice, paten and cruet of wine, and then sat down at his desk and scrawled a list – *Abbreviated order, Bible, prayer book, oil? Two small candles, matches, small crucifix, little table? White linen cloth? Purificator, chalice, host, water jug, stole.*

He underlined the things that they would surely have at Sir Edward's house, and decided that he would take his cassock and surplice, as the dying man was quite High Church by inclination. His daughter came in, and said, 'Strange, wasn't she?'

'Strange? Who?'

'That woman. She looked as if she dressed in stuff from a play. That lacy white collar thing, it was almost a ruff. And her hair all tied up like that, it must take hours. And that funny little hat with the silver-mounted claw. She actually had hatpins.'

'She was all in black, wasn't she? I thought she was just an old widow.'

'Widows don't wear black any more, Daddy. Honestly, where have you been all these years?'

'Don't they?'

'No, Daddy, they don't.'

'Oh dear. Well, as you often like to point out, I am just an old fossil, aren't I? I don't really notice what people are wearing these days anyway. You get Polly Wantage in plus fours, and sometimes when you call in on the General, he's not wearing anything at all, and you wear skirts hardly wider than a belt. Anyway, tell your mother I've had to go out. Sir Edward's ill, and apparently it's very bad.'

'Oh how awful,' she said, putting her hand to her mouth.

After an anxious search for his car keys that eventually involved the entire population of the house, he finally got into his maroon Singer Gazelle and drove up the hill to the church. He parked next to the disused lime kiln, retrieved the great key from the tomb of Piers de Mandeville, let himself into the church and raided the vestry. He realised that he was panting from the exertion of all this hurrying and worrying, and he started to sweat about the head. He crammed all he needed into a carpet bag, and strode back out to his car, harmlessly forgetting that he had left the key in the door of the church, where he would find it upon his return.

He drove back down the hill, tooting his horn as was customary at the bend, and turned right along Notwithstanding Road, past the pound and the Glebe

House where the legendary Girt Pike had been caught by young Robert. He drove by the hedging and ditching man, who was contemplating a small blue-and-white enamelled saucepan that he had just unearthed from the ditch, and headed towards the golf course. Miss Agatha Feakes hurtled by in a pink cloche hat, waving cheerily, with a piebald billy goat gazing out lugubriously from the back seat of her 1927 Swift convertible. Many of the houses had Christmas-tree lights twinkling in their windows, and the Rector felt a twinge of sadness at the idea that anyone should be about to die at Christmas.

He turned into the driveway of the Rawcutts' house, parked on the gravel sweep before the front door, gathered up his paraphernalia and knocked anxiously. There was a frantic barking and then the door was opened by Sir Edward himself.

'Edward!' exclaimed the priest.

'Godfrey, what a pleasant surprise! Are you coming in? Is it too early for the holy ones to drink sherry? I've just poured one for Gemma.'

The Reverend Freemantle was thunderstruck and embarrassed.

'What's the matter, Godfrey? Anyone'd think you'd seen a ghost.'

'You're all right then?'

'All right? Of course I'm all right. As you see. In the pink.'

'I was told you were dying!'

'Dying, Godfrey? I just played two sets of squash with my eldest. Damn near beat him too.'

'Well, I'm so pleased. I was informed that you were dying and asking for communion!'

'Really? A prankster? You should have telephoned and saved yourself the trouble of coming up.'

'It was an old lady. She came and asked me to get here as quickly as possible.'

'An old lady? Really? Which one?'

'Well, to be honest, Edward, I can't remember her name. I know I've seen her before.'

'Not in the congregation?'

'Well, I don't think so. Edward, I'm so pleased you're all right. I was going to phone you anyway because I hadn't seen you at communion for a couple of weeks. I was beginning to get worried.'

'Nice of you to be concerned, but I thought it would be fun to go to one in Chiddingfold, and the week after I tried out Peasmarsh.'

'Fun? Really, Edward, the Eucharist is supposed to be a very solemn thing. You can't go round doing it for fun.'

'Isn't it supposed to be fun?' asked Sir Edward. 'I've always enjoyed it tremendously. It's such an improbable joy to have a God who actually enjoins the drinking of wine. It's so wonderfully reasonable. Such a pity that communion wine seems to be made of treacle. Still, one can always go home and have the profane stuff for lunch.'

The two men looked at each other, and then Sir Edward said, 'Well, as you've come all this way to give me communion, why don't you give it to me anyway?'

'Really?'

'Well, why not? I'll try not to enjoy it. I will be most solemn, Godfrey, quite fantastically solemn, I promise.'

'I've done Communion for the Sick in someone's house before, but not an ordinary one.'

'First time for everything! Go on, Godfrey, be a sport. We can do it in the study, and then Gemma will give you crumpets dripping with butter.'

'Anything for Gemma's crumpets,' said the Rector.

'Let's not do the whole caboodle, though,' said Sir Edward. 'I know the Ten Commandments already. We'll do the prayer for the Queen, and the creed, of course, and you can do one or two sentences, if that's in order, and then the exhortation, and then you can do the business.'

The Rector was amused. 'What, no general confession?'

'No point, old boy. Haven't done anything worth confessing for ages. Awfully dull. Don't want to waste the Lord's time listening to anything pointless, do we?'

'Sorry, Edward, I think you'll have to confess. We're not allowed to miss that out, I'm afraid.'

The two men went into Sir Edward's study. He cleared his desk, and the Rector unpacked his carpet bag and laid everything out on it, covering it first with the clean white linen cloth. He looked around at all the leather-bound books in their glass-fronted cabinets, and wondered whether Sir Edward had read many of them. He suspected that they had all belonged to Sir Edward's father. Sir Edward dropped a cushion on to the floor by the desk, and knelt upon it. He clasped his hands together, closed his eyes and bowed his head. The priest watched him praying, his lips moving silently, and not for the last time was a little ashamed at the fact that so many of his flock really did seem to have a stronger, simpler and purer faith than he did himself. Sir Edward opened his eyes, blinked and said, 'Righto, Godfrey, let's do the prayer for the Queen.'

It all went very well, though it was mildly disconcerting for the Rector to be giving communion to someone who knew the service even better than he did himself; Sir Edward was quite obviously reciting the sonorous words of the Book of Common Prayer to himself as they were being read. He grew positively excited when being delivered the bread and wine, and afterwards recited the Lord's Prayer with gusto. He accepted the blessing with sighs of satisfaction and pleasure, so much so that the priest thought it almost indecent.

Afterwards, over tea and crumpets, Lady Gemma, the Reverend Freemantle and Sir Edward discussed the weather, the state of the church roof, the best way to get rid of moles, the daunting prospect of having hundreds of relatives to stay over Christmas, why it was that the little crowd of teenage carol singers who came round every year only knew two carols, and the possible identity of the mysterious old lady. Sir Edward proposed that she must be some old biddy with bats in the belfry, and this proposition received the general assent of the company. 'Never mind,' exclaimed Sir Edward, 'it was terrific fun to have communion in the study. Godfrey, I am so grateful.'

The Reverend Freemantle then gathered his para-phernalia together, collected a Christmas peck on the cheek from Lady Gemma, and had his hand shaken vigorously by Sir Edward, who repeated, 'Tremendous fun, marvellous!' a great many times. They waved from the porch as the Rector departed in his Singer, to call in first at the church, where he returned some of his things to the vestry. Thence he went back home, and resumed his desperate perusal of old sermons, even-tually finding an appropriate one in a volume compiled by a certain Reverend Colin Sykes, late of St Andrew's College, Berkshire.

On Christmas Day it began to snow just as

everyone was leaving church, and by the afternoon three inches of glistening blanket had settled on the lawns and meadows of the village. With the brilliant whiteness, there arrived a wondrous hush.

Just when all was utterly quiet, the steady tolling of a single muffled bell in the church tower began. It rang three times, paused, rang three times more, paused, and then three times again. After a few moments it began a steady, slow mournful tolling, as if thereby something were being counted. Some people in their warm houses wondered what it might possibly mean, but most, illiterate in the reading of bells, thought nothing of it at all. Down in the rectory, in his armchair, the Reverend Freemantle awoke from his nap after lunch and listened. 'Now, what's that?' he asked his wife, who had challenged herself to a solitary game of pelmanism and had spread cards all over the coffee table.

'It's the bell, dear,' she said unhelpfully. He listened, and for some reason he felt a heavy sensation in the pit of his stomach. 'It's a passing bell,' he said, 'I'm sure it's a passing bell.'

'A what, dear?'

'A passing bell. The Strilling Out for the Dead. I've heard it before somewhere. I'm sure that's what it is. It's what they always used to do.'

'I'm sure you're right,' said his wife, who of course had no idea what he was talking about.

'I'd better go.'

'Oh why? Do you have to? It's awfully cold, and the road'll be frightfully skiddy.'

'I'm going, I really think I ought to be going.' He went into the hall, and swathed himself in scarf, hat and gloves. He went to the back door and fetched his wellington boots, just in case the car couldn't manage and he was obliged to walk back.

It was frightening in the extreme trying to get the Singer up the hill, but fortunately there had been no other cars using the road since this morning's service, and so the snow had not yet been packed into ice. In first gear, and with one or two alarming reverses, he made it up the slope, frequently wiping the condensation from the windscreen with the back of his driving glove. It was freezing up again the moment he got it clear. Leaving the engine running so that the demister could get to work on the glass, he crunched his way through the virgin snow to the door of the church, and pushed it open. It seemed far colder inside than it had been out in the fresh air. The tolling of the bell ceased, and a second later someone emerged from behind the curtain that separated the bell tower from the nave.

The old woman in the long black dress with the white lacy collar approached him, and brushed lightly past. He caught a scent of mothball and lavender. She turned at the door, and looked at him imperiously for a few moments, as if appraising him steadily. She nodded, and said simply, 'Sir Edward.' He watched her go, looking in wonder and stupefaction at the ground beneath her elegant laced-up ankle boots. She opened the gate, waved and smiled courteously, and set off down the hill without the slightest regard to the snow.

After another frightening and erratic journey, the Reverend Freemantle found the Rawcutt house in turmoil. Lady Gemma answered the door, her face pale and her lips trembling, exclaiming, 'Oh Godfrey, thank God you're here. How did you know?'

'Where is he?' he asked.

Sir Edward, dressed in a dinner jacket, bow tie, red cummerbund and wing collar, was laid out on his back on the drawing-room floor, with his lips blue, his florid complexion vanished away, his eyes staring and his mouth wide open. He had a sprig of holly in the lapel of his dinner jacket, and a gold paper hat lay beside him on the floor. He was plainly dead. 'Oh God,' said the priest, dropping to his knees beside the body. He bent down to listen for a breath, and then sat back on his heels. Without knowing precisely what to do, he made the sign of the cross on the dead man's forehead, and said, 'The Lord gave and the Lord hath taken away. Blessed be the name of the Lord.' Then he sighed, and said, 'Goodbye, old fellow. Bon voyage.'

'We're waiting for the ambulance,' said Lady

Gemma. 'We tried the kiss of life, and everything, and the ambulance'll never get here with all this snow. Oh Godfrey, it's just too awful.'

'It's too late for an ambulance,' said the priest. 'We should all just take this chance to say goodbye.'

Reverently they formed a kind of ring around the dead man. Two sons and a daughter, their spouses, Lady Gemma, the Rector and the family dogs. Those who were not sobbing were waiting numbly for the tears to come. From the doorway peered in the confused white faces of four small grandchildren, all of them dressed in their best party clothes.

'What happened?' asked the priest.

'We were playing "Are You There, Moriarty?"' said Lady Gemma. 'It was his favourite game, he loved it. It's so silly, it was right up his street.'

'"Are You There, Moriarty?" I know that one. He made me play it once. Well, it's good to know that he died having fun. Good old Edward.'

It was a highly energetic and hilarious game in which blindfolds were placed on the two contestants, who were then laid down on the floor, facing each other and holding the other by the left hand. In their right hand, each one held a rolled-up newspaper. They took it in turns to ask 'Are you there, Moriarty?' in the strongest and most bogus Irish accent possible, whereupon the other would have to reply 'Here I am, to be sure!' and then move out of the way to avoid being struck by the rolled-up newspaper. The first to achieve ten successful strikes was the winner.

'Did he win?' asked the priest.

'He always won,' said Lady Gemma, smiling through her tears, 'he was a grand master.'

'He died laughing,' said his daughter, 'he was doing his victory dance, and then he just went straight down.'

The Reverend Freemantle remembered Sir Edward's victory dance very well. He had been known to perform it on the cricket green, and beside the eighteenth green of the golf course, right in front of the clubhouse. He did it even if he had merely won a prize in a tombola. It was a flamboyant business, involving much whooping, cavorting, prancing and stamping which he swore he had learned from a Cherokee, whose acquaintance he had once made in Dorking during his rugby-playing days.

It turned out to be the saddest Christmas in the parish since the year that almost an entire family had perished on the night of St Stephen's Day, in a fire brought about by candles on a tree. It was a melancholy time, doubly remembered still for its beautiful mantle of snow and for the entire village turning up to the funeral, during which the Reverend Freemantle had wept throughout his entire oration, but without any break in his voice.

At the drinks and canapés party after Sir Edward's

burial, the Reverend Godfrey Freemantle found himself, glass in hand, standing before a large portrait facing the staircase. He gazed at it for some minutes, and then called to Lady Gemma, who was passing by with a small silver tray loaded with cocktail sausages. She was pale, but very becoming in her black dress and hat. She had been making conversation and smiling bravely, even though she felt that really now there wasn't much to live for. It was doubly difficult to lose a man who had been well loved by so many, because the nice things they were saying made her want to cry.

'Who's this?' asked the Rector, indicating the portrait with his glass.

'Oh that,' said Lady Gemma. 'It's Edward's grand-mother, Jenny. She absolutely adored him apparently. She called him Tedda and told the most marvellous stories. He's got a drawer somewhere full of all the toys she gave him when he was tiny, and every year on her birthday we went to her grave and put flowers on it. I think he loved her more than he loved his mother, to be honest. She's in the churchyard in Chiddingfold.'

'Do you know much about her?'

'Only what Edward used to tell me. I never knew her; she was before my time. Why?'

'I wondered where I'd seen her before,' said the priest. 'Of course, it was this picture. I must have seen it every time I came here, and never really noticed.' He smiled at Lady Gemma, raised his glass and said, 'Here's to the old lady.' He took a draught of the champagne, and said, 'I know something about Grandmother Jenny that you don't.'

'Really?' she said.

'Oh yes, I certainly do.' He fell silent, took another sip from his glass, paused, and said, 'She leaves no footprint in the snow.'

# THE HAPPY DEATH
# OF THE GENERAL

The General, MC, DSO, veteran of Burma and the
Malayan Emergency, late of Sam Browne's Cavalry
and the 9th/12th Lancers, goes out into his garden
at half past seven in the morning and inhales the air
deeply. Across the de Vico fields comes the cuckoo
call of Miss Agatha Feakes as she summons her
menagerie, and from behind the row of council houses
comes the splutter of John the gardener's secret
motorcycle as he sets off to work on the stud farm
of the ever-absent Shah of Iran.

The General flexes and stretches the muscles of
his arms, and then squats down and bounces against
the elastic sinew of his thighs. It would be clear to
any observer, should there be one, that here is a man
who has been strong and healthy all his life. He is
barrel-chested, solid and hairy. There is something

faintly simian about both his body and his face. His eyes are small, round and black, and the skin of his back is dark brown from years under the sun both in the tropics and in his Surrey garden, where he cultivates azaleas and hydrangeas in the acidic soil. The General believes in cold showers, the Englishness of God and the civilising effect of the Empire. He loves his country, his wife, his walking stick, his pipe collection, his old black Labrador and his Rover P4. He has had them respectively for eighty-five years, fifty years, forty-five years, forty years, twelve years and ten years. His wife has recently died, taken off by cancer's cruellest devising, but it doesn't seem to have sunk in yet, and he still makes two cups of tea in the morning, uncomplainingly removing hers from her side of the bed as soon as it goes cold. He improvises strange crude suppers for both of them, and eats her portion cold for lunch on following days. He has attempted to use the washing machine and has now, on maximum temperature, shrunk all of her old jerseys and cardigans, folding the felted, miniaturised versions back into the woollens compartment of her chest of drawers. Now that she isn't wearing them, it seems a good opportunity to get them all clean and ready.

Anyone observing the General's robustness as he deep-breathes in his garden in early summer, amid the blooms of his azaleas, would find it easier to do so on account of his nudity. He has emerged in a state of nakedness out of sheer innocence, and now he goes back indoors with the fixed intention of driving to Haslemere to buy something, although quite what he does not yet know. He scrutinises himself in the hall mirror, and beetles his brows in puzzlement. 'Dear me, old boy,' he says to himself at last, 'you've forgotten your tie. Letting yourself go. Can't have that. Have to give yourself a good dressing-down.'

He strides upstairs, reaches a regimental tie from the wardrobe, realises that he needs a collar around which to tie it and fetches a shirt from its hanger. He then understands that the ensemble is incomplete owing to the lack of a waistcoat and blazer. He calls his ancient dog. 'Bella, Bella, old girl!'

Bella is deaf, but she is already waiting by the front door, her tail wagging on her portly rump. Her dugs are blotchy, dark and pendulous after three litters (one of them accidental), and her muzzle is silver. The wrists above her front paws are swollen with painful arthritis, and she waddles breathlessly when she walks. She is the last and the best of the General's gun dogs, but, like him, she has given up shooting. Now, like him, she just likes to go out in the car.

The General opens the door of the Rover, and Bella puts her front paws up on the back seat. The General bends down, grasps her rear legs, and propels her into the interior. This is how they have managed it for the last two years, ever since Bella seized up.

The General starts up the car and guns the accelerator. It feels peculiar, and he realises that he has forgotten to put his shoes on. He goes back inside and wanders about until he looks down at his feet and remembers what he was after.

Bella and the General go the back way to Godalming, a town once famous for being the first to have street lighting, and for being the home of Mary Tofts, who was frightened by rabbits in the spring of 1726, and consequently gave birth to a litter of eighteen of them in November. Nearby, and less explicably, the ghost of Bonnie Prince Charlie strolls beneath the trees of Westbrook.

The General motors up Malthouse Lane, past the convent. He passes the hedging and ditching man, who, in the attitude of Hamlet cradling Yorick's skull, is waist-deep in the verge-side ditch, inspecting the freshly excavated hubcap of a Riley 1.5. The General drives past the Glebe House, through Hascombe, and finally parks his car behind the new Waitrose. He sets out past the public conveniences, past the Christian cafe, and out into the high street, where he pauses in puzzlement. It all looks wrong. He scratches the top of his head in bemusement. He stops a middle-aged woman and asks, 'I say, please do excuse me, but is this Haslemere?'

She looks at him in horror and alarm, says 'Godalming' and hurries away. 'Damn and blast!'

exclaims the General. Now he can't buy whatever it was that he intended to get in Haslemere. Never mind, he will go to Lasseter's instead, because a man can never have too many nails and screwdrivers and clothes pegs and whatnot. He might go and look in the window of William Douglas, too, because he has never lost his love for the things of boyhood, such as cricket balls, catapults and airguns.

He is but halfway there when he is accosted by a police officer. 'Excuse me, sir,' says the latter, in that portentous tone much favoured by the British police, 'may I have a word?'

The General trusts and approves of anyone in uniform, and he smiles delightedly. He thinks that no doubt the policeman has some weighty issue to deal with, and feels the need to take advantage of his wider and deeper experience. The policeman ushers him gently into the alleyway beside the pub where Peter the Great once stayed, when Godalming was on the main wool route to London. 'Do you realise, sir,' asks the officer, 'that you have gone shopping without your trousers on?' Sensitively he refrains from mentioning the lack of underwear. Fortunately the tails of the shirt are long, and any indecency is sufficiently concealed in shadow.

The General looks down, but sees only the polished toes of his shoes. He raises a knee and beholds the nakedness of his leg. 'Ah,' he says. 'Damned embarrassing. Can't imagine … so sorry. Have to keep an eye on that, eh? Can't be having that, can we? Definitely not cavalry. Damned embarrassing. No socks either. Whatever next! Have to give myself a rocket!'

'May I ask your name, sir?' enquires the policeman. 'Then we might be able to help you.'

The General puts his hand to his eyes, and thinks hard. 'Remember my number,' he says at last. 'Always remember my number. In case of capture, you know. Second Lieutenant, um … 734 …' he begins, but then stops. 'Damn it! Damned if I haven't forgotten. Won't do at all.'

'I think you'd better go home and put some trousers on,' says the policeman. 'Do you think you can find your way? Perhaps you can tell me your address?'

The General reflects futilely, and offers, 'Used to have a place in Simla. Little bungalow. Hot season, you know. Unbearable anywhere else. Wives and children always sent to Simla.'

The policeman sighs, and then asks, 'And where did you leave your car, sir?'

'Is this Haslemere?' asks the old soldier.

'Godalming, sir,' says the policeman.

'Blast it,' says the General.

The policeman takes the General by the arm and they walk around the car park looking for his car. The policeman has radioed into the station and they have advised him of the probable identity of the old warrior and his vehicle. This has happened several times recently, but the General usually recovers in between. Social services have been informed, the children are making arrangements and wheels are in motion.

Eventually they find the green-and-grey Rover, and the policeman strokes the wing appreciatively. 'Lovely cars, these,' he says. 'I learned to drive in one. Built like a tank, never go wrong. Bit heavy on the old petrol, though.' He notices that the keys have been left in the ignition.

Bella wakes up and greets her master with all the joy that old age and stiffness might allow. She eyes the policeman suspiciously, but allows him to fondle her ears.

The General loves it in his new home. Bellevue is simply vast, the biggest house he has ever had. It is even bigger than his childhood home in Gloucestershire, the great house that was demolished because of inheritance tax. He has an enormous staff of servants who are more conscientious than all the wallahs, orderlies and batmen he has ever known put together. He wonders why the regiment never thought of having women help out in the mess, but of course in his day it simply wasn't done.

Best and happiest, his wife has unaccountably returned, radiant with all the adorable golden prettiness that first besotted him, in the form of a twenty-two-year-old nurse who has become very fond of him and pays him special attention. She makes sure that he remembers his trousers and his tie, and speaks to him in the soft and musical voice that he has so acutely but unwittingly missed these last few months. He tells her frequently that he has washed all her jerseys, ready for when she comes back, and she strokes his cheek, thanks him and plants a chaste kiss on his forehead. He is as much in love with her as he ever was, and calls her 'my darling' as he reaches out to take her hand.

In the daytime the General sits on a bench by the front door, with his walking stick at the ready and with Bella at his feet. She is brought in every day by the old lady who now cares for her, and is fed left-overs by the staff. The General walks her slowly round the grounds, which are full of magnificent rhodo-dendrons, and gives advice and instruction to the two tolerant gardeners.

Whenever anyone comes through the door, the General, when he is at his post, rises courteously to his feet and greets them. 'Do come in! Delighted to see you. Let me call someone to take your coat. What can I get you? Scotch? Don't touch the stuff myself. Sherry? Medium or dry?'

The visitors and staff get used to the distinguished, sweet old man, they humour him affectionately and politely, and some of them listen with diminishingly reluctant interest as he regales them with highlights from his adventurous past. They can hardly believe that once upon a time in the Khyber Pass this ancient man, mounted on a bay horse, charged into battle with a sabre, and they will miss him for weeks when one day Bella is not at her place by his feet, and he is neither in the garden, nor at his bench by the door.

# RABBIT

Joan walks with the Major, and with Leafy, wife of the redoubtable Colonel Pericles Barkwell. It is an evening late in March, but the day has seemed more like one from the end of June. They have gone out warmly dressed, because it is only March, after all, and now they are huffing and sweltering as they circle the bounds of the fields behind Joan's home. Joan doesn't like to sweat so much because she doesn't want people to know that she has been struck by the menopause, and it is beside the point that this particular sweat is brought about by a very English refusal to concede that any March day might be other than cold and blustery.

The Major is clad in green wellingtons, corduroys, a grey woolly jumper and a khaki-coloured quilted body warmer that enhances his military mien. In his pocket is a supersonic whistle for the dog, which he never uses because he has trained the dog to respond to parade-ground orders. 'Dogs will retire. Ab-o-u-t turn!' he roars, and the black Labrador obediently comes to heel. The supersonic whistle is a present from his son in the City, who believes in high-tech solutions to problems which no one had previously recognised as problematical.

Leafy Barkwell is dressed in wellies, and a tweed skirt that has seen smarter days. Its wool has been teased by bramble and thorn for a decade, and some people have taken to commenting unkindly that it looks like a sisal doormat. It is the only scruffy garment she has, because indoors she is elegant, and indoors is where she most likes to be. Today, however, she has succumbed to the warmth of the day and has come out at the same time as the primroses, with which she shares some of her delicate beauty, even though she is no longer young.

In the clump of elms at the end of the field noisy squadrons of rooks croak and squabble. It is nesting time, and the birds are raiding all the surrounding trees for twigs, which they bring back to the elms, where other birds try to snatch them away. There are quarrels and tugs of war, and the booty almost inevitably gets dropped, whereupon the birds fly off back to the willows and oaks in order to break off more twigs with elaborate exertion that involves much acrobatic risk. The fallen twigs they stupidly do not bother to collect, so that under the rookery the ground begins to look as though a small hurricane has just passed by. In the old days when the peasants had been poor, when, in fact, there actually had been peasants, they used to come and collect the fallen twigs, and bind them into faggots. Now there is only one peasant left, malodorous old Obadiah Oak, with his teeth like tombstones. Jack Oak is probably the only person left who can remember what it was like to collect rook faggots and to know that young rooks aren't scared of guns. The adults flew away, but you just took your rook gun and shot the youngsters off the branches where they sidled about in confusion. Then you cut out their breasts and made rook pie.

Leafy begins to compose verses in her head that one day she might send to *The Lady*, or *Country Life* magazine. She writes mainly about the beauties of nature, which normally she experiences from the other side of her drawing-room window. Her poetry is very like the stuff that used to be anthologised in the 1920s by people like J. C. Squire, and she represents an England that urban intellectuals and university lecturers assert to be dead, merely because they wish that it were so, and do not realise that it is not. Millions of country people are quite unaware that this version of pastoral England is supposed to have gone, and so they continue to live in it with perfect calm and acceptance. Leafy writes poetry that rhymes inexactly, and struggles to scan, about blackbirds singing on fence posts, and woodlarks up in the blue, and about clouds, and about hearts beating in unison. She is as unaware of being quaint as she is of the gnomic poetry of T. S. Eliot or the angry verse of Adrian Mitchell.

On the village green the man with the ridiculous dog called Archie is throwing golf balls in the hope of training it to retrieve them. On the other side of the copse the crack of Polly Wantage's twelve-bore announces that she is once more persecuting squirrels. Up the hill Miss Agatha Feakes sounds the horn of her vintage Swift as she careers past the convent with a goat on the back seat as usual. On the common the Rector, armed with a plastic sack and a yellow plastic beach spade, is patrolling the bridleways and collecting horse droppings for his roses. In the graveyard of St Peter's Church, Mrs Mac converses with the ghost of her husband. She asks him if he remembers the time when they were little children and all thirty-two of the pupils in the village school managed to pile into the hollow centre of the gigantic yew. In her house on the green, Mrs Griffiths opens a gin bottle and pours herself a tiny tipple which she dilutes with Ribena. She has thought of a new plot for her latest bodice-ripper, in which a beautiful young orphan called Venetia discovers that she is really an heiress, and has to choose between a handsome lord who probably wants her for her money, and the boy who was her teenage sweetheart, but has no prospects. In the middle of the field, a small posse of Friesian cows stands motionless beneath the huge oak that has been there since the English revolution. In the wood the bluebells are up, but have not yet blossomed, and the snowdrops and winter aconites have flowered awhile and gone.

Joan exclaims, 'Ooh look, what's Wellington up to?'

The other two follow the line of her pointing finger and see Wellington the black Labrador bounding up and down on the spot, his ears flopping forward. He appears to be nudging something. He goes down on his forepaws, his backside in the air, and barks senselessly.

'He must have found something,' says Leafy.

With one accord they change course, and fifty yards later they see that Wellington has indeed found something. Joan makes Wellington sit, and slips on the lead. Side by side they look down, without a word.

'Poor little bugger,' says the Major at last.

'It's so awful,' says Leafy, her voice trembling with shock and sorrow.

'It makes you sick,' says Joan.

'To think this was introduced on purpose ... by man,' says the Major. 'It's vile, it's damned vile. What a bloody thing to do. Whoever invented this ought to be strung up and flogged.'

At their feet, in the last extremity of its suffering, is a myxomatosis rabbit. Its flanks have caved in from thirst and starvation, its lustreless coat is loose, hanging in folds. Deaf and blind, it cowers in the long grass, dimly aware that something is happening, but too weak to move. It is attempting to eat the grass, but its mouth is too swollen. It chews on nothing, or perhaps on the ulcers of its own tongue. It chews mechanically and thoughtlessly, as if, by this token eating, it can assuage some of the hollow agony of its unassuageable hunger.

The little creature is so abject, so miserable, so pitiful, that it is heartbreaking just to stand and look. The worst thing, the most horrifying, is that its eyelids are stuck together, and what were its eyes behind them have inflated to the size of table-tennis balls. The effect of this swelling is entirely grotesque, the horrifying globes transforming the rabbit into something that seems other than a rabbit. It has become a monster imagined by the cartoonist of a horror comic.

'I can't bear it,' says Leafy Barkwell.

'The poor little mite,' says Joan.

The rabbit does not try to get away. It remains still and quiet, trying to eat, hoping that if it remains still for long enough, everything might begin to get better. It is so harrowed by misery that it has lost all sense of self-preservation. For days now it has stayed out in the same place in the grass, unable to find its burrow, freezing and shivering by night in the March frosts, drenched by the March rain, buffeted by the March gales, enduring the slow cruciation of this casually inflicted death, its own insignificant, tiny, world-destroying Calvary. It stays perfectly quiet, and never loses hope, but it is a most unfortunate miracle that it has not yet been found by a fox.

The Major is an old soldier, and he knows his duty. He takes no pleasure in saying, 'I am going to have to kill it.'

Leafy puts her hands to her face and exclaims, 'Oh please, not with me here.'

'Wait till we've gone,' pleads Joan.

The Major is relieved not to have to do it immediately. He says, 'I'll come back with the airgun.'

At the house the Major takes the airgun out of the cupboard. It is a Webley Mk III, very heavy, with a tapered barrel. It is a powerful .22 and is ideal for hunting small game over open sights. At one time it represented the best in British engineering, except that some idiot designed the rails so badly that they lifted off when you tried to mount telescopic sights. Years ago the Major had bought it as a present for his young son, feeling that it was his duty to teach him the manly arts, thinking that perhaps he might grow up to be a soldier, or that one day, if there was yet another war, it would be useful for the sons of England to know how to handle themselves in a fire-fight. The Major had taught his boy how to do rapid fire, how to allow for movement and windage, how to follow through, but now the boy works in the City, pale and sleepless, conjuring money out of thin air, his mouth spewing out American business jargon, driving around in a Porsche instead of a proper car, displaying a kind of energy and merriment that seem entirely artificial and out of character with the teenager that he used to know. The Major strokes the walnut stock of the Webley and thinks of the fantasies he used to entertain on his son's behalf, before the world turned into something that he hadn't realised he had been fighting for. He handles the walnut stock of the Webley and remembers the .303 Lee-Enfield that stayed with him undamaged from the start of the war to its end. He wonders what happened to it.

He takes the airgun out into the field behind the house and is sorry to find that the piteous, oblivious little creature is still there. He realises that he really will have to do his duty. He bends down and strokes the rabbit down the length of its nose. It barely reacts. It occurs to the Major that the animal is so nearly dead that he might just as well leave it to die at its own pace, let it make its own quietus. He remembers Glub Pasha telling him years ago that his Arab troops believed that animals should be given time to think about life while they die, which is why they used to cut their throats with three strokes of a knife. 'Whatever happened to Glub Pasha?' he asks himself.

The Major strokes the rabbit's nose again, and says, 'Little fellow, I want to say how sorry I am for what's ... for what's been done to you. Poor little bugger. I'm so sorry.' He strokes the animal's flank and feels the hard starkness of the ribs.

He straightens up and cocks the underlever of the Webley. He takes a lead pellet from the tin in his pocket, opens the tap of the gun and drops the pellet in. He checks it has gone home properly, and closes the tap. Against his will, but in accordance with his duty, he places the barrel of the gun between and just forward of the rabbit's ears. He steels himself, squeezes the trigger and feels the gun leap in his hands.

At his feet the rabbit has flung itself on to its side, and from its mouth there spurts a small cascade of inconceivably brilliant scarlet blood. Its back legs kick feebly, and, most heart-rendingly of all, so great is the pain of its starvation compared to the pain of its death wound that it continues trying to eat, its jaws moving ceaselessly.

It kicks again, and then the Major makes a mistake. He knows that really it is dead already, that it died instantly, but he wants it to stop kicking and chewing. He reloads the gun and places the gun barrel against the side of the rabbit's head, right against the hideous globe of its left eye socket. He pulls the trigger and then leaps back in horror, because a thick shower of bright white pus has exploded out of its head and spattered his trousers, his jacket, his hands, the barrel of his gun. It had never occurred to him that the swelling had been anything other than a swelling. He walks backwards a few paces, sees that the animal is completely dead, wishes it, perhaps ridiculously, a safe homegoing to wherever it has gone, and walks swiftly back to the house, too upset for thought.

Joan has waited in the kitchen, and she sees him come in, his face white with distress. She puts her hand to his face, and he says in tones of quiet disbelief, 'Its head was full of pus, and it exploded.'

She looks at him as he takes a paper towel and wipes down his clothes and the gun. 'Go and change,' she says. 'I'll put your things in the machine.'

The Major sits at the desk in his study, hands on his knees, looking out of the window at the laurels. A squirrel spirals up the oak tree, and a green woodpecker inspects its crevices for bugs. His clean clothes feel stiff and unyielding. His wife comes in with a cup of tea. It is her own blend, half Tetley tea bag and half Earl Grey. She puts it down carefully on his blotter and asks, 'Are you all right, darling?'

He says, 'It was very upsetting.' He pauses, and

then asks her, 'Did I ever tell you about the German soldier?'

'Which one, darling?'

'When we were sent out to collect the papers from the dead.'

'No, you didn't tell me.'

He continues to look straight out of the window. 'We'd been fighting for three days,' he said. 'We were all exhausted. No sleep. It was bloody hot. It had been hot for weeks. Appalling ... very tough. Bloody hell, actually. Then the Germans withdrew, and my platoon was detailed to gather the papers from the dead. For the Red Cross. Send them back through Switzerland.'

He pauses in order to collect himself. 'I found this body. In a foxhole. He was damned bloody fat, this German. I remember thinking he was too fat to fight, that the Germans must have been damned desperate to go round recruiting anyone as fat as that.

'He had a nice belt, a black leather one, and it so happened that mine was buggered. Broken at the buckle. I was holding my trousers up with a string. Not very soldierly.

'I tried to undo the German's belt, but it was too tight, so I put my foot on his stomach to get some purchase. That was when I found out that he wasn't fat, he was swollen.'

The Major continues to look out at the laurels.

'I vomited. I've seen lots of corpses. They don't seem like people, not even the corpses of your friends. But that was the first one that actually exploded.

'Afterwards we looked through the papers. They were all love letters and pictures of girls. Piles and piles of them. We sat and looked at them and said nothing. He was called Manfred Schneider, the one with the belt. Up until that day I loved killing Germans. It was all I wanted to do. Nothing I'd rather. I had a passion for it. But after that I stopped hating them. After that I only killed for duty.'

Joan places her hand on his shoulder. He looks up at her and she can see that his eyes are glistening with choked-back tears. She strokes his thin grey hair, and kisses him lightly on the top of the head. Discreetly she turns and leaves the room. With his hands on his knees, his cup of tea cooling on the blotter, and his eyes brimming with a lifetime's unsheddable tears, he looks out over the laurels, and remembers. He will never tell anyone, not even Joan, about the mercy killing that is sometimes all one can do for a hideously wounded friend.

# THIS BEAUTIFUL
# HOUSE

I love it at Christmas. I just sit here at the end of the garden on top of the rockery, like a garden gnome. I don't find the stones uncomfortable. I sit here and look at the house. It's very beautiful, I always did think so. I grew up here, and I am still here now, although I spend much of my time out in the garden just looking.

Other people may not think it beautiful, but it's beautiful to me mainly because I always loved it. I loved my childhood here, and I loved the house when I had to go abroad on military service, because it represented everything I was fighting for, and I loved it when I came back to Notwithstanding from Korea, and settled into the life I was born to. Here is the clump of bamboos behind which I used to conceal myself when playing hide-and-seek with my brothers and sister. Further up there on the left is a bird table that I made when I was at school. It's amazing that it hasn't rotted away by now. The lawn isn't very smooth, there's too much couch grass, but we used to set up a putting green on it in the summer, and it ruined my father's scores at the real golf course because he kept hitting the ball a long way past the hole. Here is the big apple tree that was so easy to climb, and produced great Bramleys that my mother made into pies. One year we tried to make cider, but it was very sharp. We had rabbits in the orchard, in a big wire enclosure that was movable. They kept the grass mown if you remembered to move the cage around. Of course they'd escape quite often by burrowing underneath, and they'd go and raid the vegetable patch, but they came when you called them anyway. The cage started life as a chicken run, but we found the pullets too ill-natured. There used to be a modest fruit cage just here as well, and I frequently had to go into it to free the robins and blackbirds that got stuck inside. They would fly about in a silly panic, and didn't know you were trying to be helpful. 'Funny kind of fruit cage,' my father used to say. 'Keeps birds in rather than out.'

The house isn't very old. It's Edwardian, in the Surrey farmhouse style. I remember when the Virginia creeper and the wisteria were planted, and now they're all over the walls. I don't know who the architect was, but it's a very conventional design. Most of the other family houses around here are quite similar. The first people to live in this house came down from the north. I think they were in textiles. Then it belonged to a writer who was quite famous in his time, but now no one's even heard of him. Then it belonged to a retired naval officer and his wife, and then it was ours. I have so many happy memories. I don't ever want to leave.

Inside there are five bedrooms. My parents had the one at the back. Mine was above the kitchen. Every morning the smell of frying eggs and sausages would get me out of bed in a good mood. My room wasn't big, but it was big enough for my model aeroplanes to hang from the ceiling on string, and for my toy soldiers to have decent-sized battles. I had a little cannon that worked on a spring, and you could put ball bearings or matches into it, pull back the lever, release it and mow down the enemy. When I grew up I would find little ball bearings all over the place.

My brother Michael shared a room with my other brother Sebastian. They were twins, but not identical. My sister Catherine had the room opposite my parents, and sometimes I would creep into her room at night with a sheet over my head and give her a fright. Or I'd listen for when she went to the loo, and I'd lie down at the corner of the corridor and grab her ankle as she went past in the dark. It worked every time. Then my mother told me to stop, because it was unnerving being woken up by screaming in the middle of the night. Catherine used to get revenge by leaning over the banisters and spitting on my head when I was underneath in the hallway. It's hard to imagine that she grew up to be so beautiful and refined, and married a baronet.

On the top floor up the back stairs, under the roof, is a lovely big dusty attic. I think it had been fitted out for a servant to live in, because it had a proper little fireplace, and the rafters were all boarded in. I spent hours up there. I fixed a dartboard to the wall, and I threw darts at it, backhand, underarm, over my shoulder, every possible way. I got very good at it. It was one of my party tricks. I used to go up there when I was miserable as well because no one would know I was weeping.

I always liked the bells. You'd press a button on the wall in any room, and it would ring in the pantry, and a little brown semaphore would wave back and forth in a box above the door, and indicate which room you were ringing from. Catherine and I used to push the buttons to make my mother go to the front door only to find nobody there. Once my mother went to the door and when she opened it, the cat was sitting there on the mat in the porch, looking up at her as if he'd pressed it himself. The cat just walked past her into the hallway and my mother was briefly astonished, until she realised that it couldn't possibly have been Tobermory who rang the bell. The cat was named Tobermory after a talking cat in a story that my father read to us once. The moral of the story was that if you can talk, it's better not to tell the truth.

Our phone number was 293, amazing when you consider how long the numbers are nowadays.

I love sitting here at Christmas time, at the end of the garden. I don't feel the cold. I like to sit here because the house looks so wonderful with the Christmas tree behind the French windows. There's a full moon, and I can see everything around me with perfect clarity. The stars are out, and I can never remember which ones are the planets. Perhaps they're the very bright ones. Sebastian used to point them out to me, but I don't know how he knew. I used to point them out to girlfriends when I was being romantic, but I was bluffing. I knew that they didn't know either. The house and the garden and the sky look like something out of a Christmas card, appropriately enough. The only thing missing is snow. I only ever remember one white Christmas, when it snowed as we came out of church, and Catherine was wearing a lilac coat with a hood that had a lining of white rabbit fur that framed her face and made me think that she was the prettiest sister that anyone ever had. Everything is silver and shadow now, except for the Christmas tree, which is glowing with all sorts of different-coloured lights that reflect off the tinsel and the glass balls.

It reminds me of that dreadful night of the fire. We had little candles in those days, little candles that sat on cups that clipped to the branches of the Christmas tree, along with all the tatty taffeta angels that we'd inherited. It looked magical but it wasn't ever a good idea. Trees dry out, and they're full of resin. They go up like a torch.

We all went to midnight Mass, and when we got home we had a nightcap. We talked about plans for Christmas Day. My father used to like to go shooting, but my mother more or less forbad him. She said it wasn't nice to go round bowling over rabbits and blasting birds out of the sky on the day when our Saviour was born to bring peace and harmony to the world. We decided we'd all walk to Abbot's Notwithstanding and back again before lunch, but my mother would have to drop out because someone had to baste the goose. I think she was probably relieved, because she wasn't a great one for unnecessary exercise.

The whole family were there, including the baronet. We liked the baronet. He didn't put on any airs, and he didn't have any side. He had a quiet charm and a confidence. He gave up the army for Catherine's sake, because she didn't want to have to be sent off all over the world at a moment's notice. It was decent of him because he was a Coldstreamer, he was doing well, and he obviously loved it. He and Catherine came down from Cambridgeshire in the Riley to be with us for Christmas. Sebastian and Michael came down from Merton, and I was living at home anyway, because I didn't want to move anywhere else, not unless I married, and anyway I'd found a decent job in Guildford. I paid rent to my mother without telling my father, which seemed the best thing. Knowing her, she spent the money on shoes.

That night, what with us being tired and having a tot of whisky inside us, we forgot to put out the candles on the tree, just as anyone might, but the next thing I knew, I woke up choking. I got out of bed, hacking and coughing, and I groped about in the smoke. But I couldn't find the light switch and there was a terrible pain in my lungs, and I was coughing so much that it was agony. I felt that I was vomiting my lungs up. My eyes stung so badly from the smoke that I couldn't open them, and even so they were still streaming with tears. I remember the pain, the coughing, the stinging in my eyes, and the insuperable fear, the not knowing where I was in the room, the roaring noise, and then it was as if my chest and my brain were full of molten lead, and I must have passed out. I don't really know what happened next.

As I sit here at the end of the garden, on the rockery, looking at the Christmas tree with its electric lights, it's hard to believe that the house was almost gutted. The tree must have set the curtains alight, and so on. Anyway, it's all been repaired, and you'd never know that anything happened. It's part of the wonder of the house. It doesn't die, it just keeps on evolving. The house is alive. It watches over me always, and it's watching me now.

The house may be alive, but my family aren't. They all perished in the fire, from inhaling the smoke, every one of them, including the cat. Even so, it doesn't stop them turning up. Just now my father put his hand on my shoulder, and said, 'Come on, my boy.' Death hasn't changed him at all. He's just as solid, he's still got the same voice and even the same smell of Three Nuns pipe tobacco. He wears the plus fours and long socks and brogues that I used to find so embarrassing and old-fashioned. Every time I sit here, he comes and asks me to leave. I wish he wouldn't. I love him, but he isn't entitled to tell me what to do any more.

They're all here now, as solid and real as when they were alive. There's Catherine and her baronet, hand in hand, and Sebastian and Michael looking at me pityingly. There's even the cat. It's not Tobermory. This one is called Gerald, and he was two cats later. Gerald used to drink from the dripping tap in the bathroom basin, whereas Tobermory would get under the sofa, stick his claws into the hessian underneath, and drag himself along on his back as fast as he could go. Gerald settles on his haunches and looks up at me with interest, as if I were an experiment.

My mother is here too. She reaches out a hand to try and hold mine and says, 'Please, darling, please,' but I take my hand away, not roughly, but gently. I know she loves me, you see, and I don't want to cause her any hurt. She implores me with her eyes, and still holds out her hand.

'Come on, you big fool,' says Sebastian, grinning like a schoolboy, and Michael thumps me on the shoulder with the same old fraternal violence and says, 'Come on, old thing. You've been here quite long enough.'

'I'm watching the house,' I say.

The baronet lights a cigarette, and when he throws the match to the ground, it disappears. 'Look,' he says, 'I know I'm not strictly family and whatnot, only being married in, as it were, but you've got to give it up one of these days, this watching-over-the-house lark.'

'It's really the house watching over me,' I say. 'Anyway, you're all dead.'

'When are you going to understand?' asks Catherine, shaking her head.

'What's wrong with staying here?' I say.

'Please,' says my mother.

After a while they leave, one by one, as they always do. My mother and Catherine give me a gentle kiss on the cheek. It's surprising how you can distinctly feel the kiss of someone who is dead. My father once surprised me by taking my head between his hands and kissing me on the forehead. He would never have done that when he was alive, and he hasn't done it since. Michael and Sebastian subject me to more claps between the shoulder blades. They all turn and wave modestly before they fade away not far from where the bonfire always used to be. Only Gerald stays a little longer. He winds himself around my legs a few times, and reaches up to touch a claw to my hand, as he used to when he suspected that it contained a morsel of Cheddar cheese. Eventually he wanders away after the rest of them.

I don't understand why they keep coming back. I am glad to see them of course, but they're dead. I keep telling them, but they don't seem to be able to take it in. They don't seem to understand why I won't go with them. Perhaps death makes you less perceptive.

Anyway, I am perfectly contented, sitting atop this rockery by moonlight. I love it here. I love this beautiful house, I love the way it holds me as if it had hands and I was cupped inside them. I sit here and it watches over me, I feel absolute happiness, and there's nothing I'd rather do.

# TALKING TO GEORGE

The mist hangs above the paddocks and molehills, and the horses snort and nod their heads, their breath condensing in the cold air.

The girls inhale the scent of leather and saddle cream; their world consists of the creaking of girths, the sweet smell of horses' sweat, the seduction of straw and the clatter of hooves on the cobbles of the yard.

The gardener turns into the drive, his pipe stuck into his mouth, the smoke flaring behind him as the motorbike rattles along with its chair bolted on to the side. He has kept the bike in a secret shed for thirty years and more, and his wife knows nothing about it; it is the mistress and lover he never did have, the secret friend, the last connection with youth. It is to him what the horses are to the girls.

John switches it off and it pre-ignites, reluctant

to stop. 'Bloody thing,' says John to himself, irritated and perplexed.

John twists the key in the lock, and the door creaks, the bottom scraping the floor, and, 'Bloody thing,' says John again.

'Boy not here,' he says, 'gettin' later every day, he is. Never mind, 'snice to have the place to yourself, first thing,' and he takes his provisions from a knapsack and opens a tin. He approaches the corner, tweaking the threads of a web, calling, 'George, George, here, George, I brought you some flies, good boy, look what I've got. Bluebottles, two of 'em, yes, yum yum,' and John leaves the flies for George on his web, turning away to make the tea. The kettle hums, and John hums too '. . . *There'll always be an England, while there's a busy street* . . .' John puts four sugars in his mug, and a drop of milk. He lights his pipe for the umpteenth time and is alerted by the sound of a bicycle being propped against the shed and then falling over as it always seems to do. 'Bloody thing,' says Alan, outside.

'Morning, John,' says Alan, coming in, compensating with cheeriness for his fractional lateness. 'Tea on the brew?'

'Just about boiled. You make it and I'll watch.'

'Is that the baccy you grew yourself?'

John offers his pipe and raises his brows. 'Have a puff. I say it myself, but it's all right.'

Alan is unsure, but he takes the pipe and draws, and tries to restrain his coughs. 'Blimey, it's like cigars,' he exclaims, 'but it's kind of sharp, a bit of a bite in the throat.' He shakes his head, as if in regret, and says, 'Try as I might, I wasn't cut out for the weed.'

'You accustom yourself,' says John, and Alan suggests, 'You could soften it up with honey, you could try brandy,' but 'That's for nancy boys,' says John.

The door scrapes and Sylvie comes in, with a 'Hello, boys. Kettle on? What's a girl got to do for her cup of tea?'

'Hello, Sylv,' say the males, and John's got a question, a provocation, a pertinent enquiry. ''Bout time you got your own kettle, innit? Whoever heard of a stable without a kettle?'

Sylvie knows that John knows that there is a kettle in the stable. 'Don't you want me then?' she mock-protests. 'I'll go away and sulk. Can't a poor girl get a cup of tea any more? You're brutes. And anyway, I'm only coming in to say hello to George,' and she walks across the cracked concrete of the floor, with its patches of ragged matting. Her hips sway without her knowledge, her body speaking the language of enticement without her explicit permission. Alan looks at the hair that flows down her back to her waist, and the hips that are speaking.

'Hello, Georgie boy,' says Sylvie, peering into the web.

207

'Hello, Sylv,' says Alan in a squeaky voice, and then, dropping it down to normal, 'He gets fatter every day. You know, it occurs to me that he's probably female. Aren't the females big, and the males a bit small?'

John blows smoke from his cheeks, and pretends to growl. 'I hope he in't female, 'cause if he is, I'll chuck him out. Females in the potting shed, I don't hold with it.' And here Sylvie puts one hand on her eloquent hip, and pouts in reproof, and John's eyes sparkle. ''Cept for Sylv, of course, and anyway, he can't be female, 'cause what female would put up with a web like that, all covered with dust? She'd be out and at it with a feather duster, spider-sized.'

'You're out of date,' says Sylvie. 'Nowadays we give the duster to the bloke and off we go to karate classes.'

'Females is females,' John asserts. 'You know what I think? I think men are closer to nature. Here we are,' (and he gestures with the stem of his pipe) 'drinking tea with a sodding great web up in the corner, an' we don't care. In fact, we like it. Now, I bet if my missus or your mum came in here and saw George, she'd flip her lid. There's things that women just don't understand. Like spiders, and motorcycles, and beer. And did you ever see a woman shoot a catapult? Course not.' John sucks hard on his pipe. Point proven, but the pipe's gone out.

'I like George,' says Sylv, 'and I like motorbikes.'

Alan supports her, he wants her to smile. 'There's a woman near us who plays cricket, smokes a pipe and shoots squirrels with a twelve-bore.'

'Well, she in't a woman then, is she?' says John, and he strikes a match on the floor. Sylvie and Alan exchange a glance.

'What am I up to today?' asks Alan. 'Weather forecast says fine.'

'The weather forecast in't got a gardening nose. You stick your head out of that door and sniff. It's going to rain, you can smell the crackle and spark.' John can't resist a dig. 'That'll be a good trick to impress the other nobs with when you go to that university.'

'I'm not a nob,' Alan protests, although he knows that he is.

'Course you're a nob ... posh voice, mum and dad a car each, nice big house. Don't get me wrong, I don't care if you are, it's all right wi' me as long as you do your work, but this place' (he waves his pipe) 'is all my life, and for you it's a stop on the way.'

'Well, I'm a nob,' says Sylv, 'and I'd better get to work. See you later, boys. See you, George,' and the men watch her leave, her loquacious body talking of happiness, and the door scrapes, and John says, 'Lovely girl.'

Alan grunts noncommittally, giving himself away, and John smiles to himself. 'Anyway,' he says, 'you jus' carry on digging the veg patch 'til it rains, an' then you can come back in here an' we'll have some tea. I'm going to put some more daffs in the orchard. Seen the dibber? And did I ever tell you the secret of naturalising daffs? What you do is, you broadcast them.'

'Like on the radio,' says Alan, humour seizing his speech. 'This is the BBC Outside Broadcasting Service. Today we are broadcasting daffs.'

'You throw them out,' says John, 'with a back-hand sweep o' the arm, like that. And then you plant them exactly where they fell, see? And when they come up, they look as though they've been there for ever, an' that's how you seed grass an' all. Broadcasting.'

Outside in the damp day, Alan digs energetic-ally, breaking for pauses of thought. A blackbird sings, and Alan is glad to exist. '... It's funny how I like to be here, the open air, the birds, loading up twigs on the long-term compost, and the rest on the short-term compost, admiring the espalier. How many years does it take? It looks so magical, like something out of a Salvador Dali picture, all those branches growing into each other, tree to tree. And John with his sad face, and his big moustache for a tea strainer, acting the old codger. Wheelbarrows and mud and wellington boots and George the spider, and a robin taking the worms from under your spade, forks that make a note when you flick a finger at one of the tangs. The stable girls in their jodhpurs and brown boots, and the big horses. Mr Gull and his white Rolls-Royce. It's like a village all in itself. I wonder what Dad would say if I told him, "Sorry, Dad, I'm not going to university, I'm staying at the stud farm and I'm going to be a gardener all my life." He'd probably say, "How bucolic." Mum would scream the house down, though. No, Dad would probably say, "That's fine for now, but you won't be happy if you don't use your brain," and I'd say, "But Dad, you have to be an encyclopedia to be a gardener," and he'd just shrug and say, "You know what I mean, though." If I was as rich as Mr Gull, I wouldn't have horses. Just the stable girls. That Sylvie is so gorgeous, it hurts. Don't think she's even noticed me, though. When you see her on a horse, it makes you think of things that you wouldn't admit to your mother. It's getting dark, I think it's going to rain.'

The shed door scrapes, and John is there, the wheel of the barrow protesting. 'Hello, George, it's me again. Lifted the onions, thought I'd better afore it rains, and you know what, George? It's about this time I like the best; a bit of dew on the grass of u morning, wasps in the apples, not too hot, not too cold, making sandcastles full o' parsnips and carrots, leaving beans on the stalk for seed, making nice tight onion grappes. It was Harold taught me that. Forty-five years ago. Blimey, all that time working here, man and boy. I wonder how many tons I've barrowed in my time, how many clods I've turned. And poor old Harold, went mad and died, and here I am, same age as him when he went. Makes you think, makes you pause, eh, George? I reckon it was all them garden chemicals. Went yellow, went mad, and died. That's why I went organic. Maybe his missus poisoned him. Old sourpuss. And something else, George; I reckon our Sylvie's taken a shine to our Alan.

'I wouldn't like to tell this to anyone else, but when I look at Sylvie I feel sad. Reminds me of everything I can't have any more. Everything I've lost. Such a lovely girl,' and here John feels the beginnings of tears at the corners of his eyes and cannot know whether it is because he is sad, or whether it is because he is sentimental, or because to him Sylvie is entirely beautiful. 'Better go pick up some damsons,' he decides at last, 'it's the season of jam, returned.'

The door scrapes, and John has gone. The door scrapes once more, and now Sylvie has come to lean on the earthy bench amid the flowerpots and morsels of string, and talk again with George. 'Anyone at home? Hi, George, how's it going? I've got to stop coming in here, I really have. I'm running out of excuses. Do you think I'm being too obvious? I mean, how am I supposed to make him notice me? Do you think he's shy, or am I ugly, or what? And he's off to university soon, and it'll be too late. I've been watching him, he's out on the patch where the lettuce was, digging it over, and throwing the worms to a thrush. I think that's sweet, like John bringing you flies. And, while I'm here, you can tell me why big spiders only come out at apple time. I mean, one minute it's summer, and there aren't any spiders at all, and then the next minute it's autumn, and you walk along the garden path first thing, and you get a face full of web, and you go, "Yikes, aaah," and you flap your arms to get it off, and then your mum says, "Get some tomatoes, love," and you find you can't do it without making half a dozen whopping great spiders homeless . . .'

Out on the vegetable patch John is watching Alan, who is working twice as hard as before, as if to prove something to the older man. 'That's going well,' says John, and Alan sighs and wipes his brow on his sleeve. 'Hard work, though,' he says.

'This idea of yours about burying horseshit one foot deep is all very well, BUT.'

'You're young,' says John. 'Get strong now, it'll never fail you later. Kettle on?'

'Is it time?'

'It's always time,' and so Alan thrusts the fork into the dark earth, and together they go to the shed, where Sylvie is talking to George. She straightens up at the scrape of the door, and Alan says, 'Hi there, Sylv, what's up?'

She turns and smiles, sheepish and sweet. 'I'm skiving,' she says, 'you caught me.'

John is scraping the door, back and forth, back and forth, wondering why with time it hasn't worn to a free movement. 'You any good at carpentry, fixing things?' he asks, and Alan is modest. 'Not so bad. Why?'

'That door's got to be rehung, and while you're at it, I reckon on a new lock. We don't want thieves again.'

'Thieves?' repeats Alan. 'Didn't know we'd had 'em. What did they take?'

'It were twenty year ago,' says John, 'didn't I ever tell? And a right to-do it was, with the police up.'

'But what did they take?'

'They didn't take anything, that's the queer bit. They broke down the door, and it in't never been right since, and then they dunged in the kettle.'

Sylvie gives a little squeak of horror, and Alan wrinkles his nose. 'Dunged in the kettle?' he says. 'Oh my God, that's horrible, I don't believe it, in the kettle? That's foul, it wasn't this kettle, was it? I haven't been drinking from it, have I?'

John savours Alan's disquiet and Sylvie's wide-eyed disgust and then reassures them. 'Oh no, I emptied the muck on the compost, no point in wasting it, and then I boiled the kettle twice, and then I left it with bleach in all night. And then I boiled it every half-hour and kept emptying and refilling it, and then the next day, first thing, I made a cup o' tea, and I sat here in this very same place, just lookin' at it, lookin' and lookin' and lookin', and then I thought, "Here goes," and I raised it up to take a sip. But I couldn't. I just sat here lookin' at that cup o' tea, thinkin' I couldn't do it, and then I threw it in the chrysanthemums. And then I threw away the kettle, but then later on I got the kettle out of the bin again, and I thought, "What a waste," so I stuck it in the hedge. It's still there if you care to take a look. And the next thing I knew it had some robins nestin' in it, with five little speckledy chicks, and I used to take 'em a worm or two, and I'd stick my head in that hedge and I'd chuckle and say, "If only you knew what I know about what's been in that kettle, you little sods wouldn't likely be so perky." And anyway, there's been two broods in that kettle every year for twenty, and I reckon by now it might be all right for brewing with.' John sits back and sucks his pipe, but it has gone out again, and he taps out the dottle on the edge of the bench.

'But who'd do that?' asks Sylvie, tossing the fair hair back from her eyes and over her shoulder, thankful to be part of this conversation, to be in the same shed as Alan and the old man. 'Who'd break in and do a poo in the kettle? I mean, it's a bit pointless, isn't it?'

'We never rightly knew,' says John, 'but I reckon it might have been Harold. The old head gardener afore me. Went mad enough, I reckon, to break in and do one in the kettle. Might have been them chrysanths. Nutty about chrysanths, he was. Had so many he couldn't keep up. Worked all God's hours, he did, and never could manage. It was the strain, see? And all them chemicals, more than likely. And he went potty, and anyway, there's me coming into work one day, and lo and behold, there's Harold's wellies sticking up out of the rain barrel, and I have a look, and there's Harold wearing the wellies, and he's down in the barrel head first. And I pull him out, and I say, "Bloody hell, Harold, what do you think you're a-doing of?" and he says, "I'm trying to drown myself, and now you've gone and buggered it up." Anyway, they bunged him in the loony bin and when I go and see him, there he is, lying in bed, and all around him's vases of his own chrysanths that drove him barmy in the first place.'

Sylvie grows waggish, her eyes sparkle, her voice has a tease in it. She catches Alan's eye and laughs. 'The gardeners here are always mad, it's a tradition.'

John growls, 'Cheeky scallywag,' and then he reflects, 'You know the sad thing? The first time I put that kettle in the hedge, it filled up with water from the rain, and the chicks all drowned stone dead and sodden, poor little beggars, so I cleaned it out and put it back with the spout downwards, so it wouldn't happen no more, and I gave the chicks to the ferret, so's at least they weren't wasted.' John remembers his regret at the death of the chicks, and stuffs his pipe from the greasy pouch he has had since before the war. 'Or it might not've been Harold,' he continues, 'we never rightly knew. But I'll tell you one thing; I said to the police, "You take that manure away and get it analysed, and you'll find out everything there is to know about him who did it. Blood group, what he ate, everything. Do a forensic on it," I says, "and then when a suspect turns up, you wait 'til he manures again, and you match it up, and you've got your man." And the copper, it was Arthur Diss was the bobby back then, he says, "Come off it, John, it in't that serious," and I say, "Listen, son, if someone broke into your cop shop and dunged in your kettle, you'd think it was bloody serious," and he laughs and says, "So I would, so I would, but I'm not takin' that away and havin' it analysed. I've analysed it already and I can tell what it is." Anyway, I don't know who it were, but I've an idea it was an Iranian. One o' them Persian johnnies.'

'An Iranian?' repeats Alan.

John looks at him levelly. 'Haven't you ever wondered why there's tank traps all around this place?'

'Tank traps? You mean those big white pyramids? I thought ... well, I don't know what I thought. I thought they were just there, like trees and fences and things.'

'They're tank traps. It wa'n't that pop star who

put them in. You know, the one I told you about. I grew his mushrooms for him. Always pie-eyed and drugged-up, he was, always getting pinched by the drug squad. Anyway, it wa'n't him. He sold the place to the Shah of Iran, and it was him put in all those tank traps so that no one could drive in from Munstead in his little tank and be a nuisance. I said to him, "Your Majesty, there in't any tanks in Munstead, and none in Notwithstanding neither," and he says, "You can't be too careful." Anyway, he came to a bad end, the poor old sod. Died of cancer. Then it was Mr Gull bought this place, and I've been here all the time providing the house with organic veg and flowers. And anyway, I reckon it was an Iranian who did it, because it was some mohammedanny warrior, see, and he came here to assassinate the Shah. And you know how it is, when you're all agog with nerves, it makes you want to relieve your bowels, and if you're that desperate you've just got to do it in the first place that comes to hand. And I reckon that after he'd done it in the kettle, he was still all agog, and he ran away.'

'Iranian poo in a Christian kettle,' summarises Alan, but John contradicts him. ''Cept I'm not a Christian. God knows what I am. I reckon that when you think about God, He scrambles up your mind a bit, see? And like that you don't ever come to no con-clusion. The thing you got to know about God is that He don't want us to work Him out. He's like MI5.

He's like those folk who do all the benefits. Social security and the like.'

Sylvie has a question, something she has to clarify, and she turns and looks at Alan's face, her eyes betraying her anticipation of loss.

'When are you going to university, Alan? You are going, aren't you? Someone told me you were.'

'Next month,' says Alan. 'I'm going to do English.'

Alan feels uncomfortable about this university business, and John makes matters worse. 'Sounds to me like you speak it already.'

'It'll be literature mostly,' explains Alan, unsure if it really will be and knowing that he won't be able to justify it all to the earthy John, whose practical, organic world makes Milton an anomaly. But John's away on his own tack again.

'You know what I like? I like them Latin names. I read 'em in the evenings, all those words. *Erica tetralix, Gynu sarmentosa, Nepeta mussinii, Dianthus barbatus, Lilium martagon, Fritillaria meleagris, Cornus kousa, Chlorophytum capense, Peristrophe speciosa, Primula denticulata*, that's poetry that is. I like all that foreign stuff. It's like I sometimes tune in on one o' them French radio stations. Don't speak a word o' Froggy, but it's nice to listen. You know the strangest thing I reckon I saw? We had a Frenchman living down the village, oh, about fifteen year ago, next to that Mrs Griffiths, the old sourpuss, and he had an

Alsatian dog, and this dog knew all how to speak French. He knew "dindins" and "come here" and "walkies" and "lie down" and "sit" and "get in your basket" all in Froggy, and I said to Herbert, that was his name (the Frog, not the dog), I said, "Blimey, Herb, your dog's a sodding genius, speaking all that French," and Herbert he jus' laughs and says, "Funny you should say that, 'cause every time I see a dog understanding English, I think, 'La la la la la, what a clever dog.'"'

Alan and Sylvie ponder the cleverness of dogs, and Alan says, pointlessly, 'I could do a thesis on the poetics of plant names.'

'Better than all that "O what a lovely flower" la-di-da soppy stuff,' exclaims John, his face screwed up with the pain of so much lyric verse, and then he declaims: 'I wandered lonely as a silly sod, Saw some daffs, and said, "Thank God I wasn't sittin' on the grass, Them daffs'd grow right up my arse."'

Sylvie and Alan laugh with real surprise and delight, and Sylvie applauds. 'That's brilliant,' she says. 'Did you just make it up?'

John shrugs modestly. 'Always could do rhymes, mostly silly stuff. My missus don't like it, mind, so I don't do it much. Can't do serious ones. Anyway, lad,' (and here he pats his thighs as if encouraging them into motion) 'I'm goin' to plant up the strawberry runners for the greenhouse, and then I'm goin' to prune the climbers. When you've done the diggin', you can net the pond to keep out the leaves, all right?'

Sylvie suddenly recalls. 'My mum says, can we have the windfalls to make scrumpy with?'

'Course she can,' says John, and Sylvie stays in the shed while the men go out and toil. Sylvie is breaking off her split ends and talking to George. 'My God, I'm such a skiver, I'm terrible, really I am. Maybe I should have been a gardener instead of a stable girl and then I wouldn't have a conscience about being in here. The truth is, George, I just like being in here because it's where Alan sometimes is. That's the chair where his bum goes, and I can sneak a look in his dinner box, and he's having honey sandwiches again, that he made himself. And his shoes down in the corner, all abandoned and lonely-looking. Do you think I'm stupid, George? I do. I wish I wasn't so stupid. I mean, sometimes I look at myself in the mirror, like when I'm combing my hair, and suddenly I get a little shock. I think, "Sylvie, you're so ignorant, you just don't know anything, and all you think about is horses and saddle sores and bridles and martingales, and you're nineteen years old, and life is just beginning, really." And I just know that there's a great mountain of life out there somewhere, but I don't know where it is and I don't know how to climb it.' Sylvie goes to the window, whose glass is encrusted with lichen, and she looks at it rather than through it, leaning on the bench, always talking to George. 'I get this feeling sometimes when I'm up on one of the horses, and it's just after dawn, and the mist is lifting up from the grass, and the daddy-long-legs are like little helicopters, and I'm galloping the horse in all that chilliness, and the steam rises up from the horse's neck, and I feel as though I'm flowing and flying, and the horse knows what I'm thinking, and I know what the horse is thinking. His mind is all full of alertness and interest, and there's really nothing in there at all except happiness. Happiness about being a horse, and doing horsey things, like just galloping, and making the world roll underneath you, and looking forward to a bag of pony nuts. And for a few moments I know what it's like to have perfect pleasure, and I feel so happy with the horse's happiness that it makes me want to cry, and the horse's hooves are thudding on the turf with a sound as if the earth is hollow, and the leather's creaking, and there's the musty smell of the horse's sweat, and the horse is nodding its head up and down with the motion of galloping, and I think, "Yes, this is it, this is it, this is what it's all about." And then the moment's over, and I'm just me again, and I've lost all that exhilaration and I don't know when it'll come back, and I feel stupid and silly.' Sylvie picks up one of Alan's shoes, noting the shape that is the ghost of his foot, and says, 'I always wanted to count for something, and I don't think I ever will.

I don't think I'll even be happy. 'Spose I'd better go and do some mucking out.' She puts the shoe down, and shakes her head. 'My God, look at me. When I'm not talking to a horse, I'm talking to a bleeding spider.' The door scrapes as she leaves, and she says to George, 'See you anyway.'

Alan is out on the vegetable patch, digging deep rows and turning dung into the trenches. His wellington boots are clogged with manure and rich earth, and he has a blackbird, a mistle thrush and a robin in attendance. He tosses them worms in turn, but each time they pounce and squabble. Alan is weary, his back and thighs ache from his work, and he is longing for his meagre honey sandwiches. He pauses often, hoping for rain that is too heavy to work in.

John is glad of a young man to break the soil. He has been gathering golden-skinned passion fruit from the house front and the trellises, and now he is back in the shed, talking to George. 'A whole basket,' he gloats. 'What about that, then? Harvest of a good long summer. Bluebottles for you, passion fruit for me, God's in His heaven, all's right with the world. Makes you believe, though, doesn't it? Lookin' at a passion flower. That purple, and that bit o' yellow, and that white. And those tendrils that won't let go. And leaves like dark-green hands. And the funny stamens with wobbly crosspieces on top. Looks as if it's made by Him Above in a good mood. I suppose that if

223

you're a spider, then you think that God is too. That would explain the number of bloody insects, any road. Wonder where Sylvie is. I'll tell you something else, Georgie boy; I reckon he fancies her as much as she fancies him. And another thing. I'm jealous. Sixty-seven year old, and I'm jealous.

'Ridiculous, that's what I am. Don't suppose you think about such things, eh? Build yourself a sticky little web and sit back and reckon that you got it sorted. All right for some.'

A sharp wind springs up, and those outdoors shiver and look up at the sky, which darkens suddenly. Thunder roars overhead. A torrent commences, as if a giant has overturned his bath, and Alan rushes into the shed. John is pleased with himself. 'Said it would rain, didn't I? Was I right? I certainly was.'

'You're always right,' says Alan. 'Bloody weather-men, though. I didn't bring my waterproofs because of them.'

'You're gullible, you are,' says John, still pleased about the accuracy of his prognostications, pleased that he knows a few things that Alan will never know, even if he goes to university. 'Put the kettle on, boy, and make some for Sylv.'

The kettle begins to hum, and Alan ladles tea leaves into the pot, which is so ingrained with tannin that its original cream-coloured interior has become completely brown. Like all respectable gardeners' teapots, it has a chip out of the tip of the spout, and the lid has broken in half and been glued back together.

'I think I could mend that door,' says Alan. 'The pins through the hinges are worn out. I could probably replace them with sawn-off six-inch nails.'

John is smoking his pipe and enjoying the feeling of being warm and safe inside while outside the world is drowning. 'Bright lad,' he says, 'but mind you don't go disturbing George.'

'One of the threads goes to the back of that hinge,' says Alan, scrutinising a long thread of gossamer that glistens with dust. 'Christ,' he exclaims, instinctively ducking as the thunder crashes directly overhead. He opens the door to observe the deluge, and the lightning crackles again. The thunder unrolls instant-aneously, and Alan is excited. 'What a corker. Cor, did you see that? Right overhead. It's amazing, the rain's actually bouncing on the ground.'

John is being knowing again, as is his right as an older man, and a countryman. 'When it rains like this, we get a flood. I told that pop star and the Shah of Iran, and I've told Mr Gull 'n' all, I said, "We need a gulley along the drive, 'cause it's clay here, and the water sits and sits before it soaks away." Anyway, that pop star feller only knew how to say "Far out". No, I lie, sometimes he said, "Heavy, man, heavy." He died in the end, did I tell you? Choked on his own vomit, so they say, somewhere in America. Anyway, the

Shah just says, "We'll do it, God willing," and then his country got all political, 'cause things were happening over there, see? And Mr Gull just says, "I'm considering it," and while he's considering it, we get wet.'

'Hi, boys,' cries Sylvie exuberantly, as she lunges in through the doorway, her hair lank and dark with water, which is also dripping from her eyelashes and the end of her nose, which has gone pink about the edges of her nostrils. 'God, it's raining cats and dogs, horses and donkeys, giraffes and elephants. I'm absobloodylutely soaked. Shelter, you've got to give me shelter. If I try for the stable I'll drown.'

'Sorry, Sylvie,' teases Alan, 'John doesn't hold with women in the potting shed.' He pretends to be about to push her back out into the rain.

Sylvie takes her long hair in her hands and wrings out the water. 'He's an old sweetie, really, except that he deceives his wife.'

John's eyebrows jerk upwards. 'You little scamp. I never did.'

'You did too. You told me yourself you've had that motorcycle and sidecar for thirty years, and your wife doesn't know. Seriously, Alan, he keeps it in someone else's shed, and his wife thinks he comes to work on the bus. He's got no principles at all.'

John rolls up his newspaper and takes a playful swipe at Sylvie's head. 'I won't be trusting you with any more secrets. Rapscallion. Anyway, a man needs secrets from his wife. Keeps him normal, keeps him sane. It's privacy.'

Spontaneously, Sylvie plants a kiss on the top of John's head, and he beams with embarrassment, pride and pleasure. She says, 'I used to come in here when I was a kid, and he'd sit me on his knee and tell me stories.'

'You used to pull my moustache and say, "Is it real? Is it real?" There's water in the kettle, new boiled, by the way. D'you still take four sugars?'

Sylvie reproves him. 'Oh John, I gave that up five years ago.'

A small white paw hooks around the bottom of the door, attempting to open it, and Alan says, 'It's Rover.'

'Oh poor pussycat,' says Sylvie, 'I'll let her in. She's soaked, poor little thing, she's pathetic.'

The cat is bedraggled, and frightened of the thunder. She is shivering and miaowing silently, her jaws opening and closing with poignant eloquence. John leans down and heaves her on to his knee, where he dries her with sacking. The cat purrs, and John explains, 'She likes that, she does.' The cat settles, drawing warmth from John's thighs, and all of them sit in agreeable stillness, lulled by the purring, by the sounds of the rain, and the sipping of tea.

'This is nice,' says Sylvie, at last, 'all together in

the shed, safe and warm.' A stray thought occurs to her, as stray thoughts do. 'I've been meaning to ask, what do you boys do when you need a wee? I mean, you never use the stable loo, do you?'

John looks at her a little mischievously. 'Compost heap. No point in wasting it. Nitrogen, see?' and Alan adds, 'It was one of John's conditions of employment when I came up looking for a job.'

'There's water coming under the door,' observes Sylvie, nodding her head towards a puddle by the threshold.

'Might have to sit on the table. Can't stand wet feet,' grumbles John. 'My old man, he got trench foot in the war, the first one, and he always told me, "Don't never let your feet get wet. They'll go white and spongy, and then the meat falls off." It's like when you leave a piece of chicken in a bowl of water. Bloody horrible.'

A whimsical idea occurs to Sylvie. 'Does this shed float? I mean, we could be like Noah's Ark. With the cat and everything.'

'And George,' adds John, in the spirit of fairness.

'It's really bucketing,' says Alan, shivering with that delicious threat of wild weather in such a domesticated land.

'It's setting in all day,' asserts John.

'What'll we do?' demands Sylvie. 'I swear we're all going to drown.'

'We'll do what we always do,' decides John.

'We'll drink tea, and then we'll wash the green rims from off the top of the flowerpots.'

Alan groans. He suffers from the sudden and extreme weariness of the young man who is about to have to do something that bores him to death. This is worse than having to clean his room or put on a tie for the arrival of guests. 'Let's do "I wish",' proposes Alan. 'Let's say exactly what we'd rather be doing. Who's going to start? Sylvie?'

She scowls at him sweetly. 'I'm not starting. I'd feel stupid. Anyway, it was your idea.'

Alan pauses, and sighs. 'I wish it was snowing instead of raining, and I was tobogganing down the seventeenth hole on the golf course, the one that's almost vertical, with the snow hissing under the runners, and I'm steering by sticking my welly into the snow, and my cheeks are so cold that they ache above the bone, and there's all the excitement of wondering if I can avoid the oak tree, and then I crash into the ditch on purpose, and just lie there spread-eagled, and one of my sisters comes up and drops a great big armful of snow on top of my head. You feel so happy.' He sips at his tea, affected by his own vision. 'But what really happens is that suddenly you're just terribly cold and wet, and your mittens are so soaked that your fingers freeze, and you wish you'd never come out. Have you noticed how snow smells when it's clogged up into ice on your mittens?'

Sylvie is struck unaccountably with gloom. 'Do you ever get that feeling that you wish you were someone else?'

Alan looks at her sitting with her chin in her hands, and answers, 'All the time.'

'Me too,' she says. 'What about you, John?' and John tells them, 'I don't want to be no one else. I just want something to happen. I don't want to be a tree no more.' He catches their puzzled expressions, and explains. 'You take a sapling. It's the first autumn, and the tree goes, "Blimey, that's interesting, all me leaves've dropped off." And then it's spring, and the tree goes, "Well, stone me, all me leaves is comin' back." And then he gets his first bird's nest, and he goes, "Well, in't that a pleasure, to be so useful?" But then it's fifty years later, and it's all the same. He loses his leaves, and he thinks, "Oh, that again," and then the leaves come back, and he goes, "Surprise, surprise, I don't think," and then he's got a dozen bloody birds' nests, and he goes, "The little sods." Well … I've got like that. Over and over and over and over and over and over, same thing each day as I did last year on the same day. Every Thursday, I get home and the missus has done a cheese pie, and she says, "Cheese pie all right, love?" and I say, "Lovely," and every Tuesday it's macaroni, and every Sunday the daughter rings up and says, "'Ello, Dad, how are you?" and I say, "Not so bad. How's yourself?" and I just feel like I want to jump off a high place into a lake, and feel that cold water cleaning out the dust. I got dust where my brain is. I got dust in my eyes. I got dust in my mouth. Just dust everywhere, an' I'm getting old, I know I am, and I look back and think, "What? What? What?" And I think, "What happened, and why wasn't you looking? You're going to your grave, John, and you might as well not ever have lived." You know what? I reckon I chewed on life, and never tasted it at all.'

Alan is speechless; he has never heard John, or anyone older than himself, come to that, acknowledging their own despair. Sylvie is stirred, she has tears in her eyes, and she protests, 'Oh John. Why don't you look at these gardens? How many other people have kept one place so beautiful for so long?' She comes over and hugs him, kissing him on the cheek. He is touched but embarrassed, and he pats her on the upper arm. 'You're a sweet girl, Sylvie,' he says. 'You brighten things up. Do me a favour. Stay sweet. When I'm dead I want to lie in my grave and think about you being sweet, and wishing I'd been young at the same time as you.'

Sylvie pulls a disavowing face. 'I don't want to be sweet. I want to be fierce.' She raises her two hands like forepaws, and growls.

John laughs. 'You couldn't help it if you tried. You're sweet, and that's that. Always were.' John tips the dregs of his tea into a pot of cyclamen, and says suddenly, with impatience in his tone, 'I'll tell you what I really wish. I wish you two would get a move on and go out and do something.' He looks up, pleased by their confounded expressions. He says to Sylvie, 'He's been meaning to ask you out.'

Alan exclaims, 'I haven't. I mean –' and John interrupts, still addressing the girl. 'He watches for you when you ride past, and he says, "Shall I go to the stable and barrow the manure?" and he hangs about doing it slowly, in case you turn up. I've seen.'

'You're an old sod,' moans Alan, hiding his face in his hands.

'Is it true then?' demands Sylvie, thrilled by this turn of events, but also alarmed.

'Course it is,' confirms John, with an upward motion of his arm.

'The rain's stopping,' says Alan, his face still hidden in his hands.

'Don't go changing the subject,' says John. 'It's true, what I said, it's true, isn't it?'

'Yes, it's true,' admits Alan, his ears reddening even more. 'It is true. I'm sorry.'

'Sorry?' repeats Sylvie, thinking that this is a peculiar choice of word, but John turns his eye on her. 'As for you, little miss, you're just as bad. You could've run for the stable, 'stead of runnin' in here. In fact I saw you running over here from the stable, and you got wet when you needn't. In my opinion, and if you want my advice, you two should get something sorted out.' He turns and puts his hand to the doorknob. 'I'm going out. Got to see what the rain's done. Come on, puss, idle cat never caught quick mouse,' and John heaves the door open, sploshing out into the wet world, followed hesitantly by the cat. 'See you, George,' he calls.

Sylvie and Alan are shamefaced; they are both nervous. There is a sense in which their situation was more comfortable when each was just a reverie for the other. Now they are going to have to begin the awkward process of becoming flesh and spirit. Alan looks up at her briefly, and she smiles a little encouragement. She feels her mouth become somewhat dry, and her heart is like a moth. 'What do you normally do on a first date?' he asks.

Sylvie shrugs. 'Flicks, I suppose.'

'Saturday?'

Sylvie remembers her mother's advice about not making it too easy, and replies, 'Friday.'

'What shall we see?' asks Alan, caught between a man's duty to be decisive, and a man's duty to defer to a woman's desires.

'Let's look in the paper,' says Sylvie, who has more common sense than he does. She stands up and places her mug on the potting bench. 'Listen,' she says, 'I'll be back in a mo. I want to go and give John a big hug.'

'Why?' asks Alan, genuinely mystified, and also, much to his own surprise, a fraction jealous.

'Because,' calls Sylvie over her shoulder as she strides away.

Alan blows air through his lips to make them flap together, and then distorts them into a shape that reflects his trepidation. 'Well, George,' he says, collecting the mugs together, and addressing the impassive and discreet spider, 'I suppose I ought to be thrilled, but, between you and me, I'm bloody terrified. I'm going to make a mess, I know I am.' He pauses for reflection, and continues. 'It'll be the usual disaster. Mum won't lend me the car, I'll be late even though I started early, because I'll get stuck behind a tractor on Vann Lane, and I'll be all in a sweat, and I'll have spilt the aftershave so I pong like a hyacinth, and I'll have forgotten to get any money out of the bank. No, the cash machine'll pack up and swallow my card, so I'll have to borrow the money from Sylvie and promise to pay it back, and the film'll be bloody awful, and then afterwards I'll spill red wine all over the tablecloth and Sylvie's white jeans, and then I'll drink too much, and when I drop her off I'll try to kiss her and she'll get angry, or else I won't try to kiss her when she'd hoped that I would, and I'll go home all miserable, and then I won't be able to face her when I come into work, and she'll tell John and all the stable girls what happened.'

Outside the rain resumes, and Alan is comforted by its tattoo upon the tarred felt of the roof. He hears John returning, and quickly confides to George, 'No, I'm not. I'm not going to mess it up, I'm really not.' A thought occurs to him. 'I don't suppose that John and Sylvie would let me.'

The door scrapes as John comes in. He removes his crumpled hat and shakes the drops of water to the floor. 'Still here?' he asks rhetorically.

Alan is moved to say something, he is not even sure what it is until it emerges from his mouth. 'John, before Sylvie gets back, I just want to say ... even though it's a while before I go ... I want to say it's been a pleasure ... the gardens ... working here with you ... all that. I'll be sorry to go to university. Thanks for everything.'

John looks at him for a long moment, and sighs. 'I've worked here all my life,' he says at last, 'this is all it's ever been.' John feels resentful, he wants to say that for Alan this has been merely a picturesque adventure among the peasants, but he does not know exactly how to say it, and in any case he knows that it is only half the truth. The truth is that they have come to be fond of each other, and have learned mutual respect. John says, 'I suppose you'll be needing a job in the holidays. Come back any time.'

Alan smiles and offers John his hand, as if sealing a deal. 'Just try and keep me away,' he says, and John feels a moment of vindication that moves him, but which he cannot entirely explain. 'Let's bring in the tomato plants,' he says, 'I've got a trick to show you that Harold showed me afore his marbles rolled away. What you do is, you bring 'em in, the whole plants, and strip the leaves, and you tie 'em together and hang 'em with the roots upwards, right? And then the ones that are green just carry on ripening, and now and then you chuck out the ones that've gone off. And that way you get your red tomatoes 'til November, and you don't have your missus making bloody green-tomato chutney and putting it in your sarnies every morning.'

The two men walk away together, finding their intimacy, as Britons do, not in words, but in the common labour of their hands.

# THE AUSPICIOUS MEETING
# OF THE FIRST MEMBER
# OF THE FAMOUS
# NOTWITHSTANDING WIND
# QUARTET WITH THE FOURTH

Now that the children were all at the tiny school on the side of the hill near the turning to the church, Jenny Farhoumand began to search for a part-time job. She was in Palmer's music shop in Godalming, looking through the tray of oboe reeds for the stiffer ones, when, quite out of the blue, she was inspired to ask one of the two old ladies who ran it whether or not they needed any help in the mornings.

As it happened they did, and Jenny immediately began to look forward to happy hours browsing through all the sheet music, and teaching herself how to play some of the instruments that were hanging off the walls.

It didn't work out quite like that, however. She had not reckoned with Record Corner being just nearby, up near Mr Garland the dentist, and she spent all her wages every Wednesday in the classical section.

In addition, the shop was really very busy, mostly with young people trying out the guitars. Barnes & Mullins were supplying some surprisingly good cheap ones from Spain, and her heart was constantly in her mouth as the youngsters took them down, knocked them against chairs and then strummed rather too aggressively.

They had a standardised repertoire, it seemed, and she quickly learned to recognise the tunes. They all knew the first few bars of something called 'Stairway to Heaven', they all knew a song called 'The Streets of London', another one called 'The Last Thing on my Mind', and another one called 'Suzanne'. Those who were reasonable players all knew a tune called 'Anji', which could be played in lots of different ways while always sounding the same, and there was another called 'Anonymous Spanish Romance'. Everybody could play the first part in E minor, but then they ground to a halt as soon as it went into E major. She grew to expect it, and would inwardly wince as the E major part drew nearer. Still, people ordered copies by the hundred. The youngsters were inclined to buy little things, which were really not much use, such as castanets, because that was all they could afford. They bought the cheapest guitar strings, and then had to come back for more when they broke shortly afterwards.

One morning Jenny was in the shop, shaking her

head and smiling. She had just seen the General go by, without his trousers on, accompanied by a policeman. The General was talking animatedly about going to buy a cricket ball, and the policeman was humouring him as he guided him by the arm. He was such a sweet old man, but he was losing his marbles. She reminded herself to take him a pot of marmalade.

Shortly afterwards a woman in her thirties came in with a clarinet for sale. It was a nice one, a Buffet RC, and it was in good condition. Jenny laid it out on the desk and checked that everything was working. She squinted at the pads, looked at the mouthpiece with its little tooth marks, and then put it back into its case.

'I can't really offer you a price,' she said, 'because I don't own the shop. Can you leave it with us? Give me your phone number, and we can arrange for you to come in.'

The woman seemed flustered. 'Oh, I was really hoping to sell it today. I do need the money, you see. It's quite urgent.'

Jenny nodded sympathetically. 'I'm not the buyer, I wouldn't be allowed. I'll ring you as soon as I know, I promise.'

As soon as the woman had gone, Jenny picked up the telephone and dialled directory enquiries. Stamped on the clarinet she had found the words 'Property of the Inner London Education Authority'.

Three hours later, and by now seething with rage, Jenny had still not managed to locate anybody in the Inner London Education Authority who knew anything at all about how they acquired or disposed of musical instruments. She had been passed from one person to another, rung dozens of different numbers, and been told, 'Oh, that's not our department. Why don't you try so-and-so? Hang on, I'll see if I can find the number.' Then she'd hear her interlocutor calling out to the other members of the office, 'Anyone know so-and-so's number? Anyone know who does musical instruments?'

Jenny gave up, and listened to a young fellow with huge sideburns and curly long hair fumbling his way through 'Für Elise' on one of the Spanish guitars. He was the one who always broke his D string and had to come in for another one. Last time she'd persuaded him to buy two. More often than not he appeared with a large, patient golden retriever that lay down and sighed until his young master had tried out all the guitars that he couldn't afford. When he had finished the little bit of Beethoven, she said, 'You don't know what a relief that is. If I hear "Stairway to Heaven" one more time, I'll scream.'

The young man smiled. 'Lucky you warned me. I was going to play that next.'

Just then the policeman, having disposed of the General, strolled past the window of the shop, and

Jenny ran out and buttonholed him. He came in and looked at the clarinet, with its stamp.

'It's a good one, is it?' he asked. 'Expensive?'

'Yes,' said Jenny, 'these are worth a lot. They're very sought after.'

'Well, madam, you should ring this customer up, and tell her that you can't buy it without a receipt, and she'll have to come in and fetch it away if she hasn't got one. You let me know when she's coming, and I'll be here to ask a few questions, or one of my colleagues will.'

Jenny took his name and number, and duly rang the vendor, who seemed quite distressed. 'Oh no,' she said. 'Oh no. I don't think I've still got the receipt. I got it last year, and then I never played it. I've no idea where the receipt is.'

'Well, I'm sorry, madam, you'll have to come in and get it. We can't buy instruments without one. Have you any idea when you can come by?'

'Well, I have an appointment for the optician's tomorrow at twelve, so I can come at about half past. Is that all right?'

'That'll be absolutely fine,' said Jenny. She put down the phone and then picked it up again, leaving a message for the policeman at the station. The young man played the first bar of 'Stairway to Heaven', and Jenny put her fingers in her ears. 'Only joking,' he said, putting the guitar back on the wall.

'I suppose you want a D string,' said Jenny.

'A whole set this time,' he said. 'I'm feeling rich.'

The following morning the policeman was in the shop, and the clarinet was on the counter when the woman came in. She looked at the policeman, and then at Jenny. The policeman said, 'Is this the lady concerned?' and Jenny nodded and said, 'Yes.'

The policeman addressed her. 'Madam, I have reason to believe that you may be in possession of stolen property, namely this here clarinet, and that you may be committing an offence by trying to sell it.'

The woman's reaction was surprising. She began to laugh.

'Madam, this is serious,' said the policeman. 'This is no laughing matter.'

'It is! It is!' said the woman, sitting down abruptly on the stool normally occupied by guitarists. She snorted with laughter, and began to fumble in her handbag.

'Madam, you must stop laughing,' said the policeman.

The woman said, 'You think it's me? Me selling stolen property? Me? Me? Oh that's rich! Oh dearie me, how funny.' She sat and giggled, fumbling in her bag until she brought out a note. 'I found the receipt,' she said, handing it over.

Jenny took it and handed it to the policeman. Together they looked at it. It read: 'One Buffet RC clarinet, sold at auction.' At the top of the notepaper was stamped 'Guildford Police Auction'.

'Oh Christ on a bicycle,' said the policeman.

After the policeman had gone, Jenny apologised to the woman, and they laughed about the incident together.

'The look on his face!' said Jenny. 'It was priceless! His ears went red!'

'Does this mean I can sell the clarinet?' asked the woman. 'Only, I bought it last year, thinking I was going to make the effort, but I never got round to it, and now this wonderfully good flute has come up. I need the money. I couldn't bear it if someone else got the flute. It was designed by Marcel Moyse. It's got funny little platforms all over it, to rest your fingers on.'

'You're a flautist?' asked Jenny. 'Are you local? Are you mad, and do you play out of tune and breathe in the wrong places? Do you have much spare time? Do you play with anyone? Have you got children? I'm Jenny, by the way. I'm an oboist.'

'An oboist? And you're asking me if I'm mad?'

'Look, it's lunchtime. I'm off in a minute. Why don't we go and have a baked potato at Fleur's?'

'Just steer me away from Record Corner,' said the woman.

'Oh, me too,' said Jenny, 'don't let me go near it,' and they hid their faces in their hands as they passed the Lloyds Bank at the corner of Pound Lane.

# SILLY BUGGER (1)

It is spring, when the Surrey countryside is burgeoning extravagantly with new life. There had seemed to be almost no wood pigeons during the winter, but now, unaccountably, there are entire flocks of them in the fruit trees and on the lawn. The tumescent grass grows up behind the mower even as it mows. The cat brings in two baby rabbits a day, and crunches them down like carrots, head first. By the end of the day only two cotton tails and two green bags are left, but the cat is still demanding its usual ration of Felix and biscuits. The pheasants that have survived the last season's holocaust strut ridiculously in the orchard, the males engaging in combat, while the females wait to be covered. The voice of the turtle is heard again in the land, but for the last time, because the turtle doves will not come again in subsequent years. They are exterminated pointlessly but systematically by the Maltese while en route from Africa.

The fruit trees clothe themselves in frothy pinks and whites, as if for a wedding with the summer. Bluebells burst from the floor of the woodland, and nettles and Jack-by-the-hedge overwhelm the ditches. The air is heavy with the rich whorehouse smell of lilac. Flies come out of hibernation in the window frames, and desiccate on sills.

Amid this grotesque natural prodigality, death pokes about with a stick. A young sparrowhawk lies dead at the edge of the field. Robert picks it up and thinks it is the most beautiful thing he has seen since the day that he landed the Girt Pike. A thrush falls from its nest and expires in the brambles below. A barely fledged pigeon falls directly in front of a foxhole. Two moorhens disappear from the village pond. The road is scarlet with gory pancakes that had once been rabbit kittens and hedgehogs. A baby fox is lost, and the Major slows down carefully, as does Polly Wantage, but not long afterwards it is run down by one of the nuns from the convent, whose mind is obliviously on higher things. The hedging and ditching man offers her the consolation of his philosophy, and promises that he will bury the little corpse, but after she has driven on he picks it up by the tail and swings it into the trees behind Mrs Mac's house, where it is gourmandised by rats. The General's dog, Bella, finds the body and rolls in it, so that she has to be exiled to the garden shed until the stench wears off.

Spring, ambiguous equally in beauty and horror, bears in on Robert. Everyone knows that he can't help looking after young or wounded birds, and he and his Uncle Dick have even knocked up a little bird hospital in the garden, made of one-by-two and chicken wire. So it is that John the gardener, who works on the Shah of Iran's stud farm in Munstead and who lives in one of the other council houses near the Institute of Oceanography, comes round one evening, cupping something black and fluffy in his hands.

'The dog brought this in,' he says to the young boy. 'I put it back out so 'at its mother could come for it, but then the dog brought it back in again, and I thought it might be yours.'

Robert is puzzled. 'Why would it be mine?'

John says, 'Well, it is now, boy.' He advances it, and Robert takes it carefully. It is a young rook, with a full-sized head, a small body and a very short stumpy tail. 'It's half fledged,' says John. 'I reckon you should be able to do something with it. It's not scared at all. Good sign, that is.'

'I had a pet jackdaw once,' says Robert.

'Same idea, this is,' says John, 'except different.'

'Thank you,' says Robert, and takes the bird indoors.

'Oh, not another one,' says his mother insincerely, glancing up from the sink, where she is scrubbing the green rings off the flowerpots.

'I've never had a rook before,' says Robert, in self-justification.

'Must be from the elms behind the water tower,' says his mother. The water tower is a notorious local landmark. It is distinctly phallic, especially now that it has been painted pink. Nearby are elms that have been a rookery for a hundred years. 'Maybe you should take it back there and let the mother find it.'

'I've tried that with birds lots of times,' says Robert, 'and they always die. The RSPB only tell you to do that 'cause they don't want everyone turning up with little birds for them to look after. I don't think they care about birds at all.'

His mother has heard this speech before, and she shrugs. She suspects that he might be right. Robert has successfully brought up quite a few birds over the years, but he did once kill a thrush by feeding it too many worms. Uncle Dick says that some little birds don't naturally know when to stop. Rooks do, though. They eat more and more slowly and hesitantly, and then stop.

Uncle Dick has spent fifteen years in London, and now he talks like a Londoner, but he has come home to Notwithstanding because of 'something to do with a woman'. He enjoys being back home, especially the evenings gossiping and drinking beer with barley-wine chasers in the Chiddingfold Ex-Servicemen's Club, which does not seem to have any connection with the services at all. For all anyone knows, it might have some ex-servicemen among its members. It has two distinct classes of clientele, the older men who sit at the bar and booze for hour after hour, and the younger people of both sexes who like to dance and fancy each other. Abba's 'Dancing Queen' gets played several times a night in the hall at the side. There is a lovely dark-haired Polish girl who dances to it and fills every boy's heart with longing.

Uncle Dick works at the West Surrey Golf Club, where there is a special hut for the artisans, in compensation for not being allowed in the clubhouse, and he spends all day happily driving around on large mowers, except when it's raining, when he sits in the hut smoking roll-ups, eating Rich Tea biscuits, and drinking large cups of strong coldish milky tea with four sugars. He sells all the lost balls he finds to Bob French, the club professional, who sells them on to the members, so that occasionally, for a small consideration, a golfer is fondly reunited with a Dunlop Warwick or a Spalding Top Flite that had been presumed missing for ever. The ones that are too cut up for resale, Uncle Dick gives to Robert, who dismantles them, adding the strange squashy bags in the middle to his unusual collection. Just now Uncle

Dick is spending most of his spare time constructing a proper golf green on the lawn of Mr Royston Chittock, a recent arrival from London who is planning to spend his retirement in the village. 'Now there's a genuine silly bugger for you,' says Uncle Dick, whenever the subject of the newcomer crops up.

Uncle Dick is enthusiastic about the new rook. He and Robert are on their hands and knees in the hallway, gazing down at it in the log basket, where it sits in the middle of the heap of long grass that Robert has torn from the verge side. The little bird is perfectly calm, exuding dignity and self-importance. Its disproportionately large head, hunched into its shiny black feathers, combined with its pert insouciance, create an impression that is very appealing. 'Sweet, isn't it?' calls out Robert's mother from the kitchen.

'It's got eyes like Elizabeth Taylor,' says Uncle Dick. 'They're violet.'

It is true; the bird really does have wonderfully violet eyes. 'Let's call it Lizzie, then,' says Robert's mother, but Robert demurs. 'It might be a boy.' In any case, Robert has a private superstition that you shouldn't name a baby bird immediately. If you do, it always dies.

'How do you know if it's a boy or a girl?' asks Uncle Dick.

'Wait and see if it lays eggs,' calls Robert's mother from the kitchen.

'Nah, you know what I mean, before that.'

'I asked the vet once,' says Robert, 'and he said that the only way to tell is to cut them open and take a look.'

'Got a Stanley knife, love?' jests Uncle Dick, and Robert pretends to punch him in the arm.

The older man and the boy gaze down at the serene little bird with broad, soppy smiles on their faces, and then, quite suddenly, it emits a squawk so loud and alarming that the two leap backwards, as shocked as if they had been punched in the face. 'Bleedin' 'eck,' says Uncle Dick. 'That gave me shock an' a narf.' The fledgling emits another disproportionate squawk, and Dick says, 'Noisy bugger. Must be hungry.'

Robert goes into the kitchen and mashes up bread, milk and Felix. It is his standard corvid mix. He rolls it into slushy balls, comes back and kneels down. The moment that the bird opens its beak to squawk again, Robert pushes a food ball right down its throat with his forefinger. It feels very warm inside the bird. Surprised by this sudden invasion of food and finger, an expression of stupid wonder appears on its face. Then it yells and gapes again, and Robert pushes more food into it. He is fascinated by the tongue, which is sharp-tipped, and hinged in the middle, with a backward-pointing spike at either side of the hinge. 'Lethal tongue,' says Dick. 'It's to stop the prey getting out,' says Robert knowingly. Robert knows that rooks are really birds of prey, even though it never says so in the bird books. He once saw one flying low, chasing a small rat across the village green, and then seizing it and killing it in a trice by stabbing it through the eyes. It won't be long before Lizzie takes to keeping an eye on the cat, and stealing its mice by swooping on them when they are being tortured on the lawn, leaving the cat baffled and perplexed. Lizzie and the cat will be fascinated and repelled by each other. Each would like to kill the other, but they keep a respectful distance, except when the cat is asleep, when Lizzie hops up to it, pecks it smartly in the haunch, and then skips away gleefully.

The rook does end up being called Lizzie. It much prefers men and attacks women, tugging at their hair and earrings, pecking furiously at the rings on their fingers, and even at their eyes. She has a very feminine air about her too. When she is a year old she will try to mate with Robert's fingers, her soft feathers trembling ethereally in the palm of his hand.

Uncle Dick says, 'Don't get too fond of it, lad. Birds is like women, they always bugger off in the end. You've just got to enjoy them while they're there.' Robert already knows this. Members of the crow family will stay all summer, but they always leave in autumn. He has been bereaved before, and it makes no difference how much you love them, or they you.

Uncle Dick says, 'Let's teach it to say something,'

and every time he sees Lizzie he says, 'Silly bugger, silly bugger, silly bugger.'

'You could teach it something nice,' reproves Robert's mother, and Dick says, 'Silly bugger's probably more useful, innit.'

Lizzie passes through the stages of her infancy and youth. Robert makes her a little contraption out of twigs, and on it she learns to perch. Robert knows that if you don't give them a perch they get sore backsides from sitting in their own waste. She learns to hop out of the log basket, and, just like a toddler, begins to empty the waste-paper baskets, tear things up, upset ornaments and excrete randomly. She clambers up Robert's body, her wings beating, pricking him through his clothing with her sharp little claws, and spends most of her time sitting on his shoulder, rearranging tufts of his hair and murmuring strange, soft, guttural endearments in his ear. He wears a Breton sailor's cap, in those days known as a 'Donovan hat', for those occasions when she prefers to be on top of his head, and an old tea towel for when she'd rather be on his shoulder. Uncle Dick chucks her under the chin, and says, 'Silly bugger, silly bugger.'

To Robert she always reacts like a fledgling. Even after she has successfully pulled her first worm from the lawn, she still greets him with a gaping maw, quivering wings and vociferous affirmations of hunger. She is always in attendance when Robert's mother is in the vegetable patch, demanding bugs and heaving at the laces of her clodhoppers. No one's laces are safe from being tugged undone.

Later Robert makes her a little open-sided house with a grown-up perch in it, which he winds with string for better grip, and he installs it in a lilac bush with its back to the prevailing wind. Lizzie takes up residence, sleeping there at night with her head tucked under her wing. Robert goes out every night to say goodnight to her, and she rewards him with contented sleepy noises.

Robert used to teach birds to fly by sitting them on an outstretched arm and running, or by pushing them off. It didn't work very well, because birds never see the point of flying until they have actually tried it, so now he takes the bird between his hands, and tosses it into the air like someone launching a racing pigeon. Uncle Dick showed him how to do it a couple of years ago, calling it 'moonlaunch' and saying, 'It always works, boy. Toss 'em up, and they can't help flapping.' At first it causes Lizzie much comical alarm, and she protests indignantly, since hopping has been perfectly satisfactory so far, but she flaps her wings by instinct, and it is only a few days before she is flying tentatively round the house and returning to Robert's shoulder, panting from the effort and very pleased with herself. They carry on playing moon-launch long after she has learned to fly. He chases her about the lawn while she takes evasive action, and then he scoops her up and hurls her into the air. She croaks with mock indignation, and then returns for more. Uncle Dick loves to watch it, and says, 'Wish I had a camera.' One day in summer, when the family is having lunch in their tiny garden on a Saturday, she takes a few beakfuls of Blue Nun from Robert's mother's glass, and puts on a comic display of inebriated flying that culminates in her landing unintentionally in a tureen of soup on the garden table. They drink the soup anyway, since she is generally a fairly clean bird, and she hasn't pooed in it. She loves showing off to visitors, and performs aerobatics all over the garden for their benefit. She hurtles round and round the house, and the family start to refer to it as 'Lizzie's fly-past'. On days of high wind she flings herself about at altitude, and Robert concludes that rooks really do enjoy flying, because they definitely do it when they don't need to.

Lizzie loves the games that are common to intelligent animals. She plays peekaboo, and chasing and being chased. Most of all she enjoys keepaway and ambushing. She takes nuts and bolts from Robert when he is working on his bicycle, and deposits them on the roof, so that Uncle Dick has to borrow a ladder from John the gardener to get them back down again. Lizzie goes up behind him, tugging at the cuffs of his trousers from the rung below. She particularly

likes to make barefooted people dance by pecking at
their toes, most especially if the toenails are painted.
Dick sees the playful affection that has grown up
between bird and boy, and reminds him once again
that 'Birds is like women, they always bugger off in
the end, so don't get too attached. She can't go before
she's said "silly bugger", though.'

In fact Lizzie has learned to say something else.
The first time it happens is when Robert goes out as
usual to call her from her lilac tree, first thing in the
morning. He is spooked to hear his own voice, his
own special sing-song bird-calling voice, cooing 'Come
on, come on' from the middle of the tree. It turns out
that Lizzie really does only say it when she wants him
to come on. This involves a huge physical and intellectual exertion on her part, her whole body shaking
with the effort, the feathers on her head fluffing up
like a crest. Uncle Dick is disappointed. 'I'll get her
to say "silly bugger" in the end, if it flippin' kills me,'
he says, and he redoubles his efforts while Lizzie eyes
him suspiciously from her perch, trying to stab him
in the eye if he gets too close. It's one of her golden
rules that all that glisters must be pecked. It is also a
rule that anything that is new, or that might annoy
the humans, must be pecked. Robert accidentally
breaks a window with a cricket ball, and when Uncle
Dick replaces it, Lizzie systematically removes the
putty and eats it. She does it so many times that

finally Uncle Dick rigs up an apparatus made of wires to keep her away. She sways and rocks on the wires, balance being almost impossible, but manages to peck the putty out anyway, and Uncle Dick finally cuts strips from a metal tape measure, and sticks them down on to the putty. Lizzie is perplexed, and pecks at the steel strip until she realises the futility of it, whereupon she goes off to stab at the cat, where it sleeps on the lawn. Then she sets off the mole traps by tugging at the chains on the mechanism.

One day Lizzie takes the bait in a rat trap. It smashes across the base of her beak, and she stands for a second, paralysed by pain and shock, with her head pinned down. Fortunately Robert is in the kitchen, and he rushes to release her, his heart thumping with horror and dismay. He feels terrible, because it was he who set up the trap in the first place, ever since he'd seen a rat preening itself in the electricity box above the fridge. Lizzie stands perfectly still, blood seeping out of the cracks in her beak, and Robert sees that she has long fractures and splits running along the entire length of it. His first thought is that she will have to be put down, and his eyes fill with tears of guilt.

He scoops her up and takes her outdoors, but then brings her back inside. There is no one about, and no one to turn to. He puts her down again on the kitchen table, and goes to the telephone in the hallway. He searches desperately inside the spiral-bound telephone book, where finally he comes across the number of Mr Lakin in Farncombe, which his mother has entered under V for vet. The receptionist takes mercy on him because of the panic in his voice, and Mr Lakin talks him through. He tells Robert to look at Lizzie head on, and see if her face is symmetrical. He asks Robert if he knows what 'symmetrical' means. Fortunately Robert has recently learned it in maths. It is one of those words that makes you feel intelligent when you use it.

Robert takes Lizzie in his hands, and she croaks forlornly. He scrutinises her carefully and then goes back to the telephone. 'Her head is still symmetrical,' he tells the vet, adding, 'and she's not bleeding very much any more.'

'Well,' says Mr Lakin, 'she is almost certainly all right then. It means that nothing important has been broken.'

'What about her beak?' asks Robert. 'It's all split.'

'Beaks mend themselves,' says Mr Lakin.

'Do they?' says Robert, sceptically. He has heard that beaks are made of the same kind of stuff as hair and fingernails, so surely they couldn't mend themselves, not until they grow out?

'You'll be surprised,' says Mr Lakin. 'They really do. She won't do much pecking until it doesn't hurt any more, but she'll be able to pick up food and swallow it. The only thing is, a bird can die of shock. You've got to keep it warm, and try to comfort it as much as possible. A drink of water or milk is a good idea as well, but not too much.'

Robert says, 'Thank you,' and the vet says, 'If it takes a turn for the worse, just bring it in.' Robert says 'Thank you' again, even though Uncle Dick isn't there with his car, and the bus from Lane End takes an hour. He worries that Lizzie would be dead by the time they arrive.

He sits all evening with her cupped in his hands against his chest, talking to her and putting her up to his face. He loves her dry toasty smell, especially on the top of her head. The thought of her dying fills him with grief, and he tries to let hope get the upper hand, because now that his mother has come back from Hascombe he doesn't want her seeing him cry.

In the morning Lizzie is in good spirits, and accepts gifts of grapes and cheese, but it is some weeks before she resumes the mischievous and violent pecking which is her main enjoyment in life. Robert worries for ages that when Mr Lakin's bill arrives, he might not have enough pocket money to pay for it, but no bill ever does. Mr Lakin has several pro bono cases a year of little boys with accident-prone pet corvids, often including incidents with rat traps, and in any case he doesn't charge for advice.

Lizzie reaches sexual maturity, and the lovable

feathers at the base of her beak fall out in manifest-
ation of it. Her violet eyes fade. She looks a lot less
pretty now that she is a full-grown rook, but her
feathers are glossy and iridescent. She has taught
herself how to ant, utilising the ants that live in the
crevices of the crazy paving, and two or three times
a day she bathes joyously in a bucket that has been
left to catch the overflow of one of the gutters. She
stands on the edge of the bucket, and then hops in,
splashing with delight. She hops out, shakes herself,
and then skips back in again. Visitors watch her
with pleasure sparkling in their eyes, and they say to
Robert, 'Whoever would have guessed that a bird
could be so much fun?' and 'When you grow up I
expect you'll be a vet.'

It is autumn, and Uncle Dick warns Robert that
soon Lizzie will leave home and go to find some rooks
to live with. That's what they always do, they can't
help it, that's nature for you, it doesn't mean that they
don't love you. Lizzie goes for walks with Robert and
he holds her on his wrist and reaches up into elder
bushes so that she can devour the berries. She loves
them so much that she yells with pleasure in between
each beakful. The lilac excrement that ensues is so
acid that it removes patches of black paint from Uncle
Dick's Ford Prefect.

Every evening Lizzie meets Robert at the bus
stop when he comes back from school. The moment

that he gets off at Lane End, she lands on his shoulder and murmurs hoarse endearments as she rearranges the hair about his ears. The boys are envious because he seems like a wizard, and the girls are fascinated and repelled. Lizzie stabs anyone who reaches up a finger to pet her, and she is particularly infuriated by fingers that wear rings. Robert feels set apart, privileged, because he has a bird that meets him at the bus stop and comes home with him on his shoulder, even if occasionally she flies away and back again when their progress seems too slow.

It is autumn, and then winter, and Lizzie has still not left home. She sleeps in the lilac bush, her head under her wing, her feathers dusted with frost, and every day she follows her routine, confounded only by the ice on her bucket, which Robert has to remove so that she can bathe. He is astounded by her immunity to cold and high winds. Uncle Dick professes astonishment that Lizzie is still there, he says that he has never before heard of a rook that stayed after autumn, and neither has anyone else, and he is still determined that one day she will learn to say 'silly bugger'. He says it to her repeatedly, and she just ruffles her feathers and replies 'Come on' in Robert's voice.

The following spring Lizzie starts turning up with another rook, who remains at a sensible distance while she receives her grapes and cheese, or accompanies

Robert home from school. Robert is glad that she has found a friend, but worries that he will take her away.

There is no sign of this, however, and she is her usual ebullient and affectionate self, until, suddenly, she has gone altogether.

There has been no slow detachment, no gradual growing apart, no chance to become reconciled or resigned, no chance of farewell. The little shelter in the lilac is deserted, the bucket is disused, there is no more need to buy a bunch of grapes every week. Now they won't need so much Cheddar either.

Robert and Uncle Dick sit side by side on the doorstep at the weekend, and Uncle Dick says, 'Well, I did warn you, son. They're like women, they always bugger off sooner or later. Don't matter how nice you are.'

Robert doesn't believe him. He thinks that the bond between them was something special, that Lizzie wouldn't just disappear all of a sudden. Even so, he can see that Uncle Dick is right. She probably went away with her friend to make eggs. That's what Uncle Dick says. 'It's the call of the wild, son.'

Uncle Dick puts his hand on Robert's shoulder as he stands up. 'Sorry, son,' he says, and as he walks away he adds, 'Did I tell you, son? Couple of days ago I thought I heard her say "silly bugger". I wasn't sure, though.'

Robert goes up the lane and turns right into the

woods behind the Institute of Oceanography. By the pink water tower he stands under the elms and looks up at the rooks. They are squabbling over nest sites, and repairing old ones. He sits on a stump amid the ferns of bracken until dark, convinced that Lizzie couldn't be up there making eggs. He would recognise her voice if she was there, and in any case she would come down the moment she knew he was there. He sits there until dark. He thinks of what Uncle Dick says about women. 'You can find a really special one, son, and then she goes and breaks your heart, and then one day you realise that you're glad you had her, and all right, you'll miss her for ever, but that's that. You don't have to grieve no more.'

Robert listens to the sleepy noises of the rooks above him in the dark, and because there is no one there except the birds, he allows himself to cry silently for a while. Eventually, when the cold sets in and the dew starts to settle, he stands up stiffly, rubs his eyes on his sleeve and starts for home. Once again, spring is about to hurl new life into the world, and soon there will be new birds to look after in his garden hospital. No doubt it will never be the same again, but, as Uncle Dick says, 'You carry on, son. You got your memories, so that's what you do. Life's a bugger, but you look straight ahead, and you bleedin' well carry on.'

# SILLY BUGGER (2)

Royston Chittock was bought out by his partners for quite a handsome sum. They had been saying flattering things to him, such as 'You've put so much into the business, old boy, isn't it time you had some life for yourself?' and 'You deserve a rest, old boy, all work and no play, and so forth.' But really it was because they could not bear to work with him any more. He was the kind of colleague who gets bees in his bonnet. He would become obsessed by trivial matters, and it had become worse and worse as time went by. Finally they had decided to try and buy him out after he had spent six months worrying aloud about whether or not the banisters on the staircase up to the office were the right height. He was getting the secretaries to walk up- and downstairs several times a day, in order to compare their opinions. He was asking clients about it instead of discussing business, and he was taking up far too much time on the topic at meetings. His previous obsession had been to do with the properties of manila envelopes, and before that he had been worrying about the likelihood of an airliner falling on the office while on the way to Heathrow.

Blessed with a huge lump sum, and the relieved good wishes of his former colleagues, Royston Chittock sold his house in Dover House Road, Putney, and moved southwards down the A3 to Notwithstanding, a village where he knew nobody, and with which he had no prior connection. It was a short train journey from there to London, a fact which was of value to him because, like anyone who has been a Londoner for any length of time, he was profoundly attached to the delusion that London is the centre of the universe. He found a modest house near the sign which said 'Best Kept Village 1953' and planned to spend a long and comfortable retirement golfing, gardening, and collecting and dealing in stamps. There was very little that he didn't know about the philately of Japan and the former colonies. It was an ill-omened time to move. The evening after his arrival, the Horse and Groom and the Seven Stars in Guildford were blown up, killing five youngsters and injuring sixty-five.

His new house was named Mole End Cottage, and with good reason. When the estate agent from Messenger May Baverstock had pointed out to him that because the house backed on to a large meadow, there was a problem with moles in the garden, he had not been particularly concerned. He had no plans to play croquet, and it occurred to him that soil from molehills might be ideal as a potting medium. He looked benevolently upon the three dozen heaps of upturned earth, and reflected that one could live with moles easily enough. 'Live and let live, that's what I say,' he repeated to himself whenever the topic popped into his mind.

Out in the garden Royston Chittock trimmed the hedges neatly, installed edging to the beds, created a modest rockery, spread pea shingle on the paths and planted a miniature ornamental cherry. He put a small bird table in front of the kitchen window, and a bird bath in the middle of the flower bed. The lawn he left to the moles, until winter had passed, and the difficulty of mowing it began to irritate him.

The fact was that you couldn't mow unless you flattened the molehills by spreading them around, in which case you ended up with squashed muddy discs, or you shovelled the spoil into a barrow and dumped it elsewhere. Royston Chittock chose the latter course, reasoning that he could use it all on the rose beds.

He had bought a second-hand Suffolk Punch cylinder mower in good condition, and with this trusty machine he created immaculate stripes up and down the lawn. On one weekend he would mow lateral stripes, and on the next he would mow longitudinal ones. It all looked very smart, until, on following mornings he would look out of his bedroom window and see new heaps of soil dotted evenly all over its surface. He could live with it, he decided. Yes, of course, he really could live with it. Live and let live.

He noticed when mowing that if the ground was the slightest bit damp, his feet would quite often sink into the surface. He would fetch soil from the rose bed to pack into the little declivity. Once or twice he nearly sprained an ankle. 'Bloody moles,' he began to say to himself, but of course he could live with them really.

Within a year Royston Chittock had succeeded in becoming a member of the West Surrey Golf Club, because an unusually large number of elderly members had recently been translated to the Great Nineteenth Hole in the Sky, and he had managed to get himself proposed by a member from whom he had bought a collection of stamps from British Guiana for a deliberately overgenerous sum.

The problem with golf, of course, is that it very quickly becomes an obsession. One is inevitably hooked from the first moment that one does a beautiful drive straight up the middle of the fairway, or sinks a twenty-five-foot putt on a roller-coaster green. Mr Chittock was not exactly a beginner, since he had trifled with the game for years, as a necessary part of his business life, but this course was very different from the overcrowded ones in the orbit of London. It was old, the holes were long and well thought out, it was heavily wooded, there were not too many people on it, and above all it was a course that required some intelligence and subtlety from the player. It was the ideal course for someone such as himself, thought Royston Chittock.

The first hole sloped gently upward, and had an interesting ridge across the middle. The second was a par three with an elevated green surrounded by bunkers. It was on this hole, on his first round of golf as a full member, that Mr Chittock lofted a beautiful shot into the air, saw it describe an aesthetically perfect arc, saw it descend elegantly and discreetly, saw it run as if with intent, saw it strike the flagpole, skip into the air, hover a moment and descend into the hole.

A hole-in-one; Chittock was almost too thrilled to play on. Even so, he managed five pars and two birdies thereafter, and his head began to buzz with the notion of entering and winning tournaments. He was sure he could do it, even though he had scored ten on the sixth hole because of slicing into trees, heavy rough and a bunker, and then doing three putts.

When he got home Chittock wrapped his ace golf ball in a duster and placed it reverently in his sock drawer. He took it out several times a day to caress it and sniff its lovely aroma of gutta-percha. Because he now could not stop thinking about golf, he mitigated the resultant insomnia by taking the sacred ball to bed with him. He would never actually use it again, because of its totemic power. From its nest in the sock drawer it would emanate concentric success-waves that Chittock felt he could pick up on his internal antennae as he played.

He had to all intents and purposes discovered the meaning of life, or at least the meaning of his own. He played all day, every day, even using a red ball in the snow, once scoring an eagle on a par five because the ball skidded for miles on a patch of ice, and ended up two feet from the hole on a temporary green.

It inevitably occurs to golfers that it might be a good idea to practise their putting at home. They begin on the carpet in the drawing room or the hallway, but of course the ball goes too fast, so that when they get to the course they find that their putts stop short. Then they try the lawn, and realise that the grass is too coarse, so that when they get to a real green, they hit the ball a long way past the cup.

The old professional at Wentworth, Tom Haliburton, used to say that one drives for pleasure and putts for money. Royston Chittock knew very well that matches are won on the green and not on the tee, and he was interested in winning every club competition that he could, so he kept his handicap artificially high, and decided to dedicate himself to the study of putting. Like so many golfers before him, Royston Chittock decided that the only solution was to make a proper green on his own lawn, one that could be kept closely mown, and weeded and rolled. Fortunately one of the greenkeepers who worked at the West Surrey lived in Cherryhurst, the row of council houses near the Institute of Oceanography. His name was Dick, he talked like a Londoner, and he lived with young Robert's mother. Robert referred to him as 'Uncle Dick', but most people were fairly certain that he wasn't that kind of uncle.

For a very substantial sum Mr Chittock engaged Uncle Dick to make him a putting green in his spare time, and so it was that one afternoon he came round to Mole End Cottage in his black Ford Prefect in order to survey the garden and work out the best plan for a green.

'You'll have to get rid of these moles, squire,' said Dick, as they walked the grass. 'They'll make a right mess of everything if you don't. Wouldn't even be worth starting.'

'Is that difficult?' asked Mr Chittock.

'It can take bleedin' years,' said Uncle Dick. 'The buggers keep coming back. You kill one batch of them, and that just makes accommodation for some more little buggers to move in. Drives you barmy. Best bet would be to get the moleman.'

'Is it difficult? I mean to get rid of them oneself?'

'You can get the traps in Scats,' said Uncle Dick. 'You get three of them, and I'll show you how to do it.'

Accordingly, Royston Chittock went to Scats, a great barn of a place on the outskirts of Godalming, where one could wonder at and acquire all sorts of implements and contraptions whose uses were known only to farmers and those who kept horses. Unable to identify a mole trap, Mr Chittock enlisted the help of a comely seventeen-year-old assistant with the kind of thighs that could make a shire horse wince.

He came away with three gadgets that worked like doubled scissors on springs, with a sort of a tongue on a chain that would release the jaws of the trap if a mole moved it. In his kitchen at home, Royston Chittock discovered quite soon that the tongue also caused the trap to snap sharply and painfully shut if one poked it with an enquiring finger.

When Uncle Dick returned two days later, with young Robert's pet rook perched on his shoulder, he found Mr Chittock standing in the middle of the lawn gazing forlornly around at his molehills. He looked up and said, 'Well, I've put the traps in the molehills, but I haven't caught any.'

Uncle Dick took off his cap and scratched his head. He sighed and said, 'You don't put them in the molehills, sir.'

'Oh, don't you? Where else would they go?'

'It's like this, sir; the hills is at the end of side tunnels, and they scrape the spoil out of the main tunnels an' up the side tunnels, just to get rid of it. They don't come back, and if they do, they're always pushing some soil in front of'em, and what gets caught is the little bit of earth they're pushing. You don't hardly ever catch 'em by just sticking those things in the hills like that.'

'Oh dear, what am I supposed to do then?'

'You stick 'em in the main tunnels, sir. Here, I'll show you.' Uncle Dick pulled the traps out of the hills, and walked about very slowly, scrutinising the ground beneath him. Finally he stopped. 'Here we are,' he said, pressing down with his foot. 'See that, sir? The ground gives just there, so there's a tunnel right underneath. If you'd fetch me a trowel, I'll show you what's to do.'

Mr Chittock went to his potting shed and returned with a gleaming stainless-steel trowel that had clearly seen little service, and Uncle Dick knelt down and cut a neat square out of the turf. He excavated the hole a little, and put his hand in to investigate 'Right,' he said, 'the tunnel goes straight through there, so I'll put the trap in.' He set it carefully, and inserted it into the hole. Then he fetched a couple of handfuls of long grass and packed them loosely around the trap, sprinkling a little soil on top. He took a twig and stuck it into the ground

273

beside the trap, saying, 'Just to show where it is. It's easy to trample 'em accidentally, like.' He took the remaining two traps and recommenced his careful walking about. 'Now look at this, sir,' he said. 'That's a very, very small molehill, sir. That's what I call a house-keeping hill. The tunnel goes right beside that, so you take a dig in it and find out which side the tunnel goes. Then you dig it out a bit more and set the trap as usual. And one more thing: moles are dead good smellers, so you don't wash your hands with soap. In fact, it's best to wear your gardening gloves or do some gardening first, so your fingers don't pong of anything but soil.'

The next morning Mr Chittock found that two of the traps had been sprung. One was empty and the other came out of the ground with a large tube of dark-brown velvet mole in it. The jaws had clamped across its chest and neck, and its nose was bright red. Chittock felt a pang of guilty triumph. It was the first mole that he had ever actually seen, and he was fascinated by the big bony paddles fore and aft, the marvellously smooth close fur and the sharp little canine teeth, immaculately white.

Royston Chittock became fairly good at setting the traps, and he caught his quarry a good 50 per cent of the time. On each occasion that he caught a mole, he would clear the hills off the lawn, tip the soil on to the rose beds, and visualise all over again what it would be like to have a perfect lawn that was good enough to putt on. He might even install a bunker so that he could practise chipping out of it.

Inevitably there would be new molehills within five days. 'Like I said,' Uncle Dick informed him, 'you should call in the moleman. As long as there's moles in that meadow out there you're going to get them coming back in here.'

So the moleman was summoned. Joshuah Entincknapp was a man in his sixties of stout peasant build. He was fond of saying that 'Moles 'ave only got feet, they 'aven't got legs'. He dressed in hobnail boots, corduroy trousers and a thick cotton shirt closed at the collar by a tatty old green woollen tie. Beneath his shaggy tweed jacket he sported a waistcoat of his own manufacture, consisting of precisely one hundred mole skins. There had been a time when he'd supplied a local furrier with best skins at sixpence each, and it had taken seven hundred skins to make a fine lady's coat that would sell for forty guineas. He'd stretch the skins dry by nailing them to a board with one nail through the snout and one through each foot, so you wouldn't damage the skin itself. Nowadays there wasn't much of a market for them.

The most striking feature of the moleman's appearance was the lack of his right eye, which did not have even a glass substitute in the socket. This loss had been brought about by a Rhode Island Red pullet when he was a toddler, his parents having left him in the chicken coop, under the illusion that he would be safe in there while they painted the kitchen. It felt odd to look at his face, depending upon whether one focused on the concave empty socket, or on the bright dark eye that gazed ironically from the other.

Joshuah Entincknapp had heard from Uncle Dick that Mr Chittock was something of a townie out of his depth in the countryside, and he therefore made a point of speaking slowly and carefully to him, to compensate for his backwardness. 'Well,' he explained, 'Dick yonder was quite right. You can trap as many as you like in this garden o' yours, but they'll still be slippin' in from that meadow, and I don't reckon you'll ever catch up with yourself. No you won't. And what's worse, this garden o' yours, it's like a main road, you got those moles passing through all the time when they're going somewhere else, 'cause those moles don't like to get too crowded, they like to live on their own, they do, so they got their own living quarters, and they don't let no other moles in, and they also got these main roads that they share and share alike, and they use them roads to get from place to place, and it so 'appens you've got something like a Kingston Bypass going through 'ere, so you've got residents and you've got passers-through. Do you follow me, sir?'

'Oh Lord,' said Mr Chittock, 'isn't there anything you can do?' He began to fear that he never would have a lawn good enough to putt on.

'Well, it so 'appens that there is, but it all depends.'

'Depends? Depends on what?'

'Cats, sir. Do you 'appen to like cats?'

Royston Chittock gave the matter a moment's thought. 'Well, I can't say I've ever known many. I've never had one. I've known one or two, to pat on the head, so to speak. Why do you ask?'

''Cause I got a cat and I hire 'im out, sir, but I'm warning you he's expensive. He's the best moling cat in Surrey, sir.'

'A moling cat?'

'Yes, sir, a moling cat. You see, cats are specialists, sir. You get cats who only do birds, and you even get cats that only do pigeons. You get cats that do rabbits and voles, but they won't touch birds and mice. You even get cats that do frogs and nothing but. It so 'appens that there's occasional cats that do nothing but moles, and it so 'appens that I've got one. But he's expensive, sir.'

'How much is he, then?'

'Fifty pounds a week, sir, plus livin' expenses, and I get the moles for the skins.'

'Fifty pounds a week? That's an awful lot. Really, fifty pounds a week?'

'Best moler in Surrey, sir. He'll clear that meadow 'til there's not one left. He's guaranteed.'

'Really, it's too much, Mr Entincknapp. I think I'll persist with the traps.'

Mr Entincknapp shrugged. 'As you wish, sir, but you know where I am if you change your mind. Mind you, there's other things you can do.'

'Really?'

'You can dig a trench all around this garden o' yours, three feet deep, and that'll put 'em off. But it'll cost a lot more'n fifty pound, and it won't help your trees much. Or you can pour diesel down the tunnels. They hate that. Or I once knew a gentleman who just laid the garden to concrete.'

'Really? Concrete?'

'He was that desperate, sir. But he liked his concrete, sir. He came from Croydon, and that's what he was used to. "Mr Entincknapp," he says to me, "no more bloody moles and no more bloody mowing," and I says to him, "Just you wait 'til it's summertime, it'll be so bloody hot out in this garden o' yours, you won't be able to stand it, you're gonta bake like a bloody steak and kidney pie," and it so 'appens I was right about that one. It was south-facing, and it got so bloody hot it peeled the paint off his windows. Served him right, silly bugger.'

Royston Chittock persisted with his traps, but after the passage of another month it seemed that there really was to be no end to the invasions of his garden, and there never was going to be a nice lawn good enough to putt on.

So it was that one day Mr Joshuah Entincknapp

arrived with a basket containing one very large, short-haired, amber-eyed, smoky-blue cat with a huge head, an uneven moustache, bristling whiskers, smart white dickie and white spats.

It was released in the drawing room, and introduced to its host. 'Mr Chittock, sir, this is Sergeant Corker. Corker, this is Mr Chittock.'

'Pleased to meet you, Sergeant,' said Chittock, bending slightly at the waist, as he looked down at the cat. The cat gazed back with the kind of expression one reserves for those who are beneath serious notice.

'Sergeant Corker likes to sleep in an armchair,' said the moleman. 'He likes to come in and out through the window, so you'll have to leave one open, and he only eats Felix. I've brought you his bowl, and he doesn't like to eat out of anything else.'

'Oh, do I have to feed him? Doesn't he eat the moles?'

'No, sir, he only catches 'em. You'll find he has a very generous nature, sir.'

'A generous nature?'

'Yes, indeed, sir, you'll see what I mean soon enough.'

The moleman scooped Sergeant Corker up into his arms, and the two men went out into the garden. Over the fence, Mr Entincknapp displayed the meadow of molehills to the cat, and a kind of quivering excitement came over it. Its eyes seemed to be popping out of its head with eagerness, and it was clearly straining upon the start in the moleman's arms. 'You get to work, then, Corky,' said the moleman, allowing it to leap down. The cat twisted through the pickets of the fence, and trotted out into the meadow. 'You probably won't see much of him,' said Mr Entincknapp.

Every morning and evening Sergeant Corker reported in for his Felix, and every now and then Mr Chittock had to resign himself to reading his newspaper in his second-favourite armchair. In truth he rather liked having the cat around. It was quite a responsive and friendly animal, purring gratifyingly when addressed or caressed, and chirruping and rubbing up against his legs when on the cadge. It had a very focused and tranquil attitude and somehow made the house seem more complete. Out in the meadow it would sit upright, patient and motionless amid the molehills like a feline heron. Often Sergeant Corker could be seen sitting companionably with Troodos, the Barkwells' cat, a specialist in voles.

Most amazingly, Sergeant Corker brought in dozens of moles, mauing triumphantly as he trotted up the garden path to lay them out carefully in rows on the mat at the back door, like collections of fat furry sausages, which the moleman would collect every evening. Mr Chittock began to feel positively disturbed by such monumental carnage. He felt guilty that so many innocent deaths were being laid to his account, and left for him as gifts. Nonetheless, he did not call a halt to the slaughter, and after two weeks the number of the dead began rapidly to diminish.

After eighteen days, it seemed apparent that Sergeant Corker had completely cleared the meadow. He now took on a bored and restless mien, prowling about, moaning softly, and swinging his head and tail with frustration like a caged jaguar. He spent less time in the meadow, knowing that it was not worth his while to stalk there, and finally, at the expiry of three weeks, Mr Joshuah Entincknapp arrived to take him away in his basket, but not before he had had a falling-out with Mr Chittock.

The latter gave him a manila envelope containing one hundred and twenty-nine pounds, with that sum clearly marked on the outside.

'One hundred and twenty-nine, sir?' said Mr Entincknapp. 'It's supposed to be one hundred and fifty, sir. Fifty pounds a week, sir, and you've had him for three weeks.'

'Indeed, my good man,' replied Royston Chittock, 'but for the last three days he hasn't done any work. He didn't catch any at all. So I owe you for eighteen days, not for three weeks.'

The moleman was stunned. 'Eighteen days, sir? Why, sir, he didn't get any more because there weren't any. You agreed three weeks, sir, so you did, and it's three weeks you've had him for, and that's one hundred and fifty pounds.'

'I'm sorry, Mr Entincknapp, but that's my last word. I have rounded it up, you know. Strictly speaking it should be one hundred and twenty-eight point five seven one four two eight pounds, that's to six decimal places, and I have rounded it up to one hundred and twenty-nine pounds.' He looked imperiously at the moleman and said, 'You are excused.'

'Oh, I'm excused, am I?' replied Mr Entincknapp. 'Well, sir, that's very big of you. Excused, eh?'

As he started to leave with Sergeant Corker, he turned and said, 'Did you know, sir, that round here "chittock" is an old word for "magpie"?'

'No I didn't. How very interesting.'

Mr Entincknapp opened the garden gate, and said, 'A very appropriate name, sir. Magpies are bloody thieves, so they are.' Thereupon he left, without a backward glance, his single eye glowing with anger and contempt.

Mr Chittock felt sad afterwards in his empty house, and thought about getting a cat of his own.

There had not been a molehill on the lawn for over a week, and Uncle Dick therefore returned in his spare time in order to make the lawn lovely enough to putt on.

Mr Chittock had not realised that the creation

of a putting green is no simple matter, and neither is it cheap. 'How long will it take?' he asked the green-keeper. 'A couple of weeks?'

Uncle Dick looked at him as if he were mad, and said, 'It'll take a good year, sir, unless you don't mind a bodge.'

Chittock was astonished. 'A year? A whole year? How can that possibly be?'

Dick explained. 'I don't mean a whole year of me being here workin', I mean a year before it's fit to play on without makin' a sorry mess of it. It's got to settle, and the grass has got to get contented. First thing is, this is clay soil. It's heavy stuff, so we'll have to dig out a couple of feet for drainage, and fill it up with shingle, unless you'd rather be sloshing about in mud. Then we got to put a few pipes with holes in when we build it up.'

'Build it up?' echoed Mr Chittock, who had hitherto been thinking of a green that was at lawn level.

Well, sir, do you want the green raised, with nice curves and little difficult bits, and a bunker to chip out of like a proper realistic green that's just like the real McCoy? 'Cause if you do, you'll need to build it up.'

The idea appealed to Mr Chittock, who pictured himself holding aloft a series of trophies. 'Very well,' he said, 'but can you make it behave just exactly like the ones at the West Surrey?'

'Yes, I can, sir, but in the end everything depends on the maintenance.'

Chittock stroked his chin with his hand and said, 'Perhaps you'd like to do the maintenance?'

'I'm sure we can come to an accommodation,' said the greenkeeper. 'I expect young Robert would mow it for you. It's the mowing and rolling that matters mostly, and putting down poison for the worms, and I can come and sort out the spiking and feeding and everything else.'

Royston Chittock volunteered to help Uncle Dick with the labouring, having entertained romantic ideas about the dignity of labour and the benefits of fresh air and fitness, but after one hour he had aching muscles and blisters on his hands. He told Uncle Dick that he had urgent paperwork to attend to, and left him smiling knowingly to himself as he removed and stacked the turves.

Dick set about cutting cubes of clay out of the ground. It was just the right time of year for it, because the ground was neither baked hard, as it is in summer, nor sodden and glutinous as it is in winter. Even so, it was very hard work, complicated by the roots of a may tree nearby, and Dick almost regretted not having ordered in a small earth mover. His reason for not having done so was that he was being paid by the hour, and couldn't see the point of hurrying anyway. He was happy to dig out the hole over several visits, as long as it didn't rain too much and turn into a quagmire. He reflected more than once that it would have made an ideal garden pond if it were puddled. The clay was just right, smooth and almost yellow, unalloyed by dirt and stones. It occurred to him that he might be able to sell any surplus to the brick factory.

As the days went by the hole grew larger and the heap of spoil turned into a small hill. Then one day a lorry came from Godalming, reversed across the lawn, leaving tracks four inches deep and emptied several yards of shingle into the hole. Uncle Dick built a kind of wall of clay around it, and laid irrigation pipes out from the centre in a fan. Then another lorry came from Godalming with a load of medium shingle, followed by another a few days later with a load of coarse soil, followed by another loaded with medium soil.

Uncle Dick spent some frustrating hours with his client, who hummed and havered over precisely what contours he wanted. Several times he arrived at something that was simultaneously beautiful, practical and challenging, only to have Mr Chittock come out and say, 'I was just looking at it from the landing window, and I thought, "What if we just ..."' and then he would explain that he wanted something quite different to what had been previously specified. In the end, taking account of Mr Chittock's endlessly retelling the story of his ace on the second hole at the West Surrey, Uncle Dick proposed that they reproduce the contours of that particular green, in commemoration of the historic feat. The ploy worked, although the new green would have to be very considerably smaller, and the bunkers proportionally less horrifying.

A lorry containing several yards of sieved topsoil arrived from Hurtmore, and reversed across the ever deepening tracks in the lawn. Uncle Dick raked it for hours to get it into shape, and six inches deep. When this was done to his satisfaction, he knocked on the door of the house and informed Mr Royston Chittock that, although he would be back from time to time, in order to get rid of any weeds, and to roll it, there would be a six-month wait before the next step.

'Six months!' exclaimed Chittock. 'Six months! Really, this is preposterous! Six months!'

'You let it settle before you seed it,' said Uncle Dick imperturbably. 'That's the best way to do it. If you want it done badly, I'm sure there's those that might oblige.'

A certain hostility had arisen between the two men over the previous weeks. It was not just because of Mr Chittock's frequent changes of mind. It was because the latter's urban suspiciousness led him to cavil constantly about payment, both for labour and materials. He all but accused Uncle Dick of slacking when he wasn't looking, and of over-ordering shingle so that he could sell some of it on. Uncle Dick had become more and more irritated and curt with his client, and that had only made things worse. By now he had also heard the moleman's story about the short-changing of Sergeant Corker, and, after initial disbelief, had come to share his disdain for the displaced townsman.

Uncle Dick turned up once a week to see how the ground was settling, sometimes with young Robert's pet rook, Lizzie, in attendance. Ever since the bird had learned to fly, she had taken to dropping out of the sky on to the shoulders of those she knew, so that she would meet Robert when he alighted from the bus upon returning from school, or, with a jubilant squawk, crash-land in his mother's shopping basket when she was walking home from the Cricket Green Stores, in the hope that it might contain cheese or grapes. If Lizzie spotted Uncle Dick, whether at the golf course or elsewhere, she would land on his shoulder, murmur sweet nothings in his ear, and set about tidying up the tufts of hair that protruded about his ears from beneath his cap. When he was working on Mr Chittock's new green, she sat in the hawthorn tree, raising and lowering the feathers on the top of her head as she watched out for worms or leatherjackets. Uncle Dick would stop and stroke her under the chin, repeating 'silly bugger, silly bugger'. Mimicking young Robert's voice, she would reply, 'Come on, come on.'

The six months passed, and Uncle Dick raked the green, sowed it with fescue bent and rolled it. He was confident that the birds would leave it alone, because the seeds had been treated with something to make them taste horrible, and he was confident that there wouldn't be any worm casts either, because he had dosed the ground with the same poison that they used at the West Surrey.

Mr Royston Chittock came out of the house and said, 'How long before I can use it, then, my good man?'

Uncle Dick was irritated by the patronising cheeriness that Chittock sometimes liked to affect, but he replied truthfully, 'Six months, sir. And in the meantime you've got to get yourself a little mower with a very fine adjustment, and get those blades sharpened absolutely perfect. Your Suffolk Punch is a damn fine machine, but it's too big and clumsy for a green. If you're interested, sir, I expect young Robert would come and mow for you.'

'Six months?' repeated Chittock. 'Another six months? Really, I had no idea it would all take so long.'

'Well, I'm sorry to say that it does, sir, and there's no point in hurrying. I did tell you it would take a year. You wouldn't take a bird out of the oven afore it's done, and you shouldn't use a green 'til it's good and ready.'

In the six months that passed, Royston Chittock worked hard at his golf and managed to win the Stableford competition and the Major Whitworth Men's Memorial Medal. There were some murmurings in the clubhouse, and he received a joint letter from the men's captain and the secretary requesting that he submit new cards, since he had consistently been playing far better than his handicap suggested. The letter congratulated him politely upon the extraordinary progress that he had obviously made with his game.

At last the time expired and Mr Royston Chittock had a beautiful green ready to use, a perfect miniature of the second at the West Surrey. Uncle Dick, supervised by Lizzie from her perch in the hawthorn tree, had given it the final mow, cut the first hole and installed a new white cup. Mr Chittock was thrilled.

His delight did not extend to rewarding Uncle Dick with a large tip, however. Instead he disputed the final account, and paid for four hours' less work than the greenkeeper had actually done, saying, 'Come, come, my good man, I'm not a fool. I've kept a record of when you've been here and for how long, and one can't help noticing that your propensity for stopping and drinking tea has recently become greatly exaggerated.'

Uncle Dick looked at him long and cold and pocketed the brown envelope, saying, 'Well then, Mr

Chittock, sir, if you intend to cheat me after all I've done for you, and in my spare time too, don't ask me for any help if things go wrong.'

'Cheat you? Really, this is an outrage! Cheat you? How dare you accuse me of such a thing?'

'I speak as I see,' replied Uncle Dick, and he departed with his head high and Lizzie wobbling on his shoulder. That evening he telephoned Mr Joshuah Entincknapp.

They met up in the Merry Harriers, a pub that for years had advertised itself with cheerful irony as purveying 'warm beer and lousy food'. From its ceiling there was suspended an impressive collection of chamber pots, but perhaps its most appealing feature was a very large and amiable long-haired Alsatian dog named Beulah, whose hobby was collecting stones. This hound had several heaps of them in the garden, and had quite worn down the tips of its canine teeth.

Over a pint or two of mild and a game of darts, Uncle Dick and the one-eyed moleman discussed how to get even with that bloody Mr Royston Chittock.

A week later Royston Chittock rose joyfully at eight in order to go out and do some early-morning putting. Tomorrow he would practise those frightening three-footers that had ended the career of Peter Alliss, but today he was going to do some long curving putts. It would be beautiful.

Upon looking out of the window his eyes practically bulged out of his head. He felt as if he would faint and sat down on the bed for a few moments. Then he went back to the window. It was all too true, and it was just as he feared. There was a large molehill on his new green.

He ran outside, clutched his hands to his temples, and went to fetch his spade and barrow. He scraped up the molehill and emptied the spoil on to his rose bed. That morning he putted with a heavy heart, and very badly, glancing frequently at the crumbs of spoil that disfigured his perfect green.

The next morning there were two molehills, and the morning after that there were three. On the fourth day there were four molehills, and on the sixth there were six. On the seventh day the moles rested, but on the following Monday there was one. Swallowing his pride, he telephoned Uncle Dick in the evening.

'It can't be moles,' said Dick, 'moles can't get through all that gravel, and anyway, they go after the worms, and there aren't any worms in that green on account of the poisoning I gave 'em.'

'It is moles,' insisted Mr Chittock. 'Really, there are seven molehills.'

'Can't be moles, sir,' said Uncle Dick, 'maybe it's marmots,' and he put the phone down. He stood by the telephone in the hallway, and a smile began to spread across his face, which soon turned into a happy grin. That evening he was laughing so much and so randomly that at dinner time he accidentally sprayed Robert and his mother with tea. He had to go out into the garden to calm down, but was still wiping the tears from his eyes at bedtime. Robert's mother said, 'There's nothing more annoying than not knowing what the joke is,' and Uncle Dick said, 'I'll tell you, love, I'll tell you, I promise. Jus' wait 'til I can speak, won't you?'

Royston Chittock telephoned Mr Joshuah Entincknapp. 'It can't be moles, sir. Moles couldn't cope with all that gravel, and anyway, it's worms they're after, and there ain't worms in that green on account of all the poison.'

'But it is moles,' protested Mr Chittock.

'Can't be, sir.'

Mr Chittock was confounded. 'Well, could I hire Sergeant Corker for a week, just in case?'

'No, sir.'

'No?'

'No.'

'My dear fellow, why not?'

'Because you hired him last time for three weeks and you paid for eighteen days. So he isn't available to the likes of you, sir, and in any case he's busy.'

'Busy?'

'He's clearing the moles out at Feathercombe, sir, and that's a big place. And after that he's doing the manor house. One thing I can suggest, sir: do you have a shotgun licence?'

'A shotgun licence? No. Why?'

'Well, I wouldn't dig into that green to put in traps, sir, because you don't want to disturb that surface more than you have to after all the hard work that's gone into it, but one thing you can do, sir, is stand on that green with a shotgun, and when you see that earth heaving, you blast it one. Never fails, sir. I wish you good day, sir.'

Mr Entincknapp put the phone down, and began to chuckle. He chuckled so much all through the evening that Mrs Entincknapp thought that he must be losing his wits. All he could say was, 'Tell you later, love, tell you later.' He was still chortling and spluttering at night when she was trying to get to sleep, so she made him go and sleep on the settee in the living room. In the morning, at dawn, he went to the golf course, and he and Uncle Dick filled another sack with tilth from the molehills at the bottom of the dip in the seventeenth fairway. On the way to Mr Chittock's house they laughed so much that Uncle Dick had to pull into the side near the pound in order to recover.

Mr Royston Chittock set about acquiring the shotgun licence. He collected the form from Godalming Police Station, filled it in, obtained references from the Reverend Freemantle and his former solicitor in London, and awaited the arrival of the firearms officer.

This gentleman gravely inspected the gun cabinet that had been bolted to the wall in the cupboard under the stairs, and equally gravely questioned Mr Chittock. He wanted to know what the gun would be for. It was for pest control, said Mr Chittock, truthfully, adding mendaciously that he also wanted to take up clay-pigeon shooting, and that a friend in Scotland had invited him up for the Glorious Twelfth.

'Have you any experience of shooting?' asked the officer, whose real mission was to find out over a cup of tea whether or not the applicant might be mad or dangerous or suicidal, and Mr Chittock said, 'Oh yes. I've used one before when I was young, and I also learned to fire a .303.' He did not explain that the shotgun in question had been a garden gun, used by little boys to scare finches away from fruit blossom, and that he had fired it once, unsuccessfully, at a hedge sparrow, nor that the .303 had been for firing blanks in the school cadet force. The firearms officer said, 'Even so, if I were you, sir, I would have a couple of lessons.'

Mr Chittock read two books about shotguns and shooting, and when the licence came through, he drove to Guildford and bought a double-barrelled side-by-side boxlock twelve-bore in Jeffries. It was a St Etienne Robuste, a nice simple gun that would appeal to a farmer rather than a gentleman, had Mr Chittock known it. He told the assistant that he needed it for pigeon shooting, and came away with two boxes of pretty red Eley cartridges, loaded with the usual ounce of number six shot. The forms had been filled in, and Mr Chittock was fully equipped for killing moles.

Chittock never noticed that the number of new molehills depended upon the day of the week, or that there were none at all on Sundays. After he had cleared them up, he spent hours every day standing on his new green with his new shotgun, waiting for the earth to heave. He stood and waited 'til his legs ached and his mind was numb.

From time to time Uncle Dick or Mr Joshuah Entincknapp, or sometimes both of them together, would crawl into the ditch and watch him through the bottom of the laurel hedge. If they were together, it was always difficult to suppress their delight. They would nudge each other, saying, 'Silly bugger, look at that silly bloody bugger, we really got him hobbled, didn't we?'

Mr Chittock wondered if his lack of success was anything to do with being too noisy, or even smelling wrong. He took to wearing his unwashed gardening trousers, and bought an old tweed jacket and hat at the White Elephant shop, leaving them on the compost heap overnight. It didn't work and Mr Chittock continued to spend hours every day, stock-still with his shotgun growing ever heavier on his arm, in a state that approached nearer and nearer to absolute despair, just waiting for the moles.

One day Uncle Dick was hiding in the ditch, watching Mr Chittock, when Lizzie turned up. She had spotted him somehow, even through the canopy of an oak tree, and she descended noisily on to his shoulder with a small cry of joy. Nowadays she often had a wild rook with her, who kept a safe distance, and this companion settled into the oak above to keep an eye on his betrothed. 'Bugger off! Bugger off, Lizzie,' whispered Uncle Dick, fearing discovery, and brushing her legs from beneath him to get her off his shoulder.

Lizzie protested, but took off into the hawthorn tree above the new green. There she sidled along the branch until she was a few feet away from Mr Chittock as he stood forlornly with his new shotgun, waiting for the moles. She examined him with interest, raising and lowering the feathers on the top of her head from the effort of concentration, and suddenly all those months of Uncle Dick's assiduous elocution lessons paid off. In the latter's unmistakable tones, she said, 'Silly bugger.'

Royston Chittock looked up abruptly, and the bird repeated 'Silly bugger', fluttering her wings and bobbing her tail on account of the extreme intellectual effort.

Chittock, his heart so full of rage and frustration that he had to take it out on something, raised the new gun, and fired. Nothing happened because he had forgotten to slip the safety catch. No animal likes to have even a stick pointed at it, so Lizzie skipped to another branch and craned her head in agitation. Chittock slipped the safety catch, and fired again, almost at point-blank.

He had not expected the kick to be so great, and, because the gun had been badly seated in his shoulder, he bruised his cheekbone on the stock. Holding the gun in his left hand, and with his right to his cheek, he looked down at the dying bird, its beak opening and closing, its scarlet blood darkening on the fine grass, its body almost shredded because of the close range of the shot. He was quite unprepared for Uncle Dick's bursting through the hedge like a berserker.

Mr Royston Chittock sold his new shotgun and his house with its immaculate green, and moved back to Putney, where he continued to play below his handicap at Wimbledon Park, and the Duke's and Prince's Course at Richmond. He tried to forget the humiliation and ridicule that he had incurred in Notwithstanding, as Uncle Dick had denounced him, called him every foul name he could think of, and informed him that there hadn't been any moles and they'd just been paying him back for being a stuck-up stupid thieving bastard. The interview had ended with Chittock on his hands and knees, as Uncle Dick's hand clamped the back of his neck and his face was rubbed back and forth in the blood on the green. Then Uncle Dick had picked up the shotgun and fired the second barrel into the beautiful turf, saying, 'Repair it yourself, pillock.'

He wrapped Lizzie's mangled body in a piece of sacking from the back of his Prefect, took it away and buried it sadly on the golf course. He wished he had been able to tell Robert the circumstances of her wonderful linguistic advance, but he judged it better to keep silence and let the youngster think that she had simply disappeared, because birds are like women, and that's what birds inevitably do.

# THE BROKEN HEART

'The thing is, Mr Oak, that there's so much new money splashing about these days.'

'New money? What's that then? What's new about it?' Obadiah 'Jack' Oak hawks up a good gobbet of phlegm, curls his tongue into a blowpipe and ejects it. The projectile describes a graceful arc into the fireplace, where it comes to lie, shining and frothy, on the bed of ash. The young man winces. 'Well, there are lots of people who have money now who never had it before, and lots of people who did have money who now have so much that they're just looking desperately for things to spend it on. To invest in. Fine wines, or classic cars for example. That Triumph Herald of yours is probably worth more than a thousand just now.'

'Got it for fifty pound,' says Jack. 'It's clapped out, that is. Not worth nothing.'

'Believe me, there are people who'll pay a thousand.'

'They're mad, then,' replies Jack. Jack has the peasant's natural reservations about young smart alecs. This one can't be more than twenty-two years old, he has a new suit, shiny shoes, an elegant haircut, and his hands and nails are so clean that Jack suspects him of being 'you know, like, one o' them, like that', which is his way of saying a homosexual. He also has the accent of someone trying to appear posher than he is. Jack is suspicious of anyone who aims above his station. He has been obdurately and solidly himself since he was young, and cannot conceive of either wanting or trying to become someone else. 'So what are you then?' Jack asks again.

'An estate agent,' repeats the youngster. 'I work for Slipsters in Haslemere, and I help arrange the sale of properties.'

'An' you say someone's offrin' two hundred thousand for this?' He looks around his living room, at the flaked and mottled paint, the nicotine-stained ceiling, the missing floorboard and the cobwebbed, rotted window frames. 'They're mad then.' A new suspicion strikes him. 'Are you 'avin' me on?'

'No, Mr Oak.' The young man tries to look suitably grave and trustworthy.

Jack Oak furrows his brow and says, 'But I never said this place was for sale.'

'As I explained, Mr Oak, my client saw this house and enquired about its status at the village shop. I mean no offence, but he thought it might have been abandoned. He asked me to approach you and offer you two hundred thousand for it, in case you should consider selling. I know this is a somewhat unusual way of doing things, but he does like it very much.'

'He likes it two hundred thousand's worth,' observes Jack Oak.

It is the late 1980s and Mrs Thatcher has changed the entire consciousness of the country. She has profoundly inconvenienced and confounded the left by winning a popular war against a fascist government. An energised Great Britain has finally come to understand that it is not high talk but money that makes all things possible. Bright young people are making fortunes in the City, and are not ashamed to be thought vulgar or greedy. People who used to put their money in the post office are speculating boldly. The trade unions are rapidly declining. The government is beginning to rake in wonderful tax returns while lowering the rate. The word 'yuppie' has come into common currency, and people are playing with other acronyms. The present favourites are 'dinky', which means 'double income, no kids', and 'lombard', which means 'lots of money but a real dick'. Socialism is about to be reborn as conservatism with a winsome smile.

The property-owning democracy is on its way, and the estate agent from Slipsters in Haslemere has pointed out to Jack Oak that just now all the money is going into houses. The prices have rocketed, most particularly in London, and in the south, in those places that are on the commuter routes. Commentators talk of the phenomenon in tones that clearly imply that there is a strong element of insanity in it all. Some Jeremiahs are seeing lemmings everywhere, and predicting a crash. Some people on low fixed incomes are realising that they will never be able to buy. In the countryside young people cannot buy houses in their native villages because weekenders are putting the prices out of reach, and they are leaving for rented accommodation in towns. Village shops and post offices are losing their weekday clientele and closing down. The social fabric of the countryside is distorting. Some people who cannot afford mortgages are buying houses anyway, on the gamble that they'll recoup their outlay many times over when they sell, and now someone wants to buy Jack Oak's cottage, because it is ideally situated on the cricket green of a marvellously pretty village on the Portsmouth line to London. It will be fabulous for weekends, it only needs stripping out completely, and a new roof, and an indoor lavatory and a bathroom, and one day it can be resold at a substantial profit, if only Jack Oak will sell. Ever since old Walter died, Jack has been the village's last peasant, with his lips like kippers, his thick yellow nails, his rolling Surrey accent, his aroma of a thousand types of rustic decay and his eyes as round as dinner plates. He is the seventh generation of his family to occupy the little house on the green, and his daughter, Jessie, is the eighth.

She has been listening to the young man with careful attention, and, after he goes, leaving a business card that she secretes in her purse, she sets to work on her father. She is the only child of a wife long gone (run off with someone from the travelling fair on the green, so they say), and in the whole world there is no one but his daughter that Jack Oak loves. She comes over and kneels on the floor in front of him, placing her hands on his knees. 'Da,' she says, in a wheedling tone of voice that reminds him of his little girl when that was what she was, 'Da, two hundred thousand!'

'I like this place,' says Jack. 'This is where I was born, and this is where I'll die.'

'But Da, two hundred thousand! We can go west. Somerset, Cornwall. I've been there. It's right nice. We can get a place twice the size and have money over. An' you don't work no more, anyway, and I can get a job, I know I can. Two hundred thousand, Da!'

'I don't know anyone but 'ere.'

'But Da, who's left here?'

'None to 'ave a drink with,' agrees her father.

'It's all goin' posh. Just think, Da, we'd be set up for life, both of us. No more worries!'

He looks at her strangely. 'I ain't got no worries.'

'Oh Da, you know what I mean!'

'Turn the telly on,' he says. 'I wanta watch something.'

'I'll turn it on if you promise to think about it. Promise?'

'Course I promise. I was goin' to think about it anyways.' He rolls himself a thin cigarette and sniffs it before he lights it. He reckons the sniffing is better than the puffing. He thinks about how some people are trying to stop the little boys from fishing in the village pond, in case someone falls in, and how they don't let you throw sticks into it for your dog any more in case it frightens the ducks. He spits contemptuously into the fire. The place soon won't be worth living in, that's for sure.

So it is that not three months hence Jack and his daughter are completing the melancholy task of dismantling two centuries of settled family life. Into boxes go rabbit snares and mole traps, his father's pipes, the horseshoe from above the door, glass jars of assorted nails and screws, tobacco tins full of brass washers, a seized-up revolver that his father brought back from the First World War and never handed in, a wooden quiver of African arrows that came back with his grandfather from Tanganyika, tattered Bibles and hymnals, faded photographs and samplers from the walls, and penknives with broken blades. Jessie tries to throw things away, to burn them, saying, 'But Da, we won't need this! What do yer want this for, Da?' and he replies, 'It's mine, and I want it, that's what.' When she says, 'But Da, we can get new things now,' he replies, 'Ain't nothing wrong with the old one.'

Jessie has been having terrible misgivings recently. Her father has even tried to dig up every shrub in the garden so that they can be planted at their new place. He has emptied the contents of the compost heap into sacks, has filled more sacks with the best soil from the vegetable patch. Jessie had been hoping to move out with two days' hire of a man and van, but all this junk and soil and shrubbery is spoiling her plans, and besides, it's very embarrassing. The man with the van has taken to smirking. Her father has assumed the air of someone resolutely making businesslike preparations in the face of imminent death. He is saying things like 'Well, it don't really matter any more. Don't reckon I'll be long for the world any road. Reckon you might as well enjoy the money, that's what I say, 'cause it won't be much use to me when I'm dead an' under.'

Out of consideration for her father, Jessie has resisted going for the kind of house she really craves, something clean and new on a smart housing estate, and has found a pleasant cottage for next to nothing in the village of Herodsfoot, near Bodmin. She is sure that he could be happy there. The house is very like the one they are leaving, with a decent-sized vegetable patch and a blue front door. It has one more room, and an inside lavatory, and it doesn't really need much decorating. She has had to take charge of everything, because Jack's mind goes into a spin when he has to concentrate on things like deeds and contracts. He signs the documents that she places before him, and says, 'Might be signin' my life away, for all I knows.'

On the morning of their leaving Jack hands over the key to the estate agent, and sits in the passenger seat of his Triumph Herald. He looks resolutely forward, at nothing. He is too choked to drive or to speak. He refuses to be unmanned by weeping, and he feels a portion of himself shutting off. Jessie starts the engine and squeezes his hand comfortingly before she puts the car into gear. 'It's a sad day, isn't it, Dad?' she says, and he does not reply. She has taken lots of photographs of the old house, and plans to frame some of the best ones for the walls of the new one. She combines a sort of pre-emptive nostalgia with a contradictory sense of bright new beginnings. She is optimistic but she feels tears prickling in the corners of her eyes. 'Goodbye, old home,' she says, and then starts the car off down Malthouse Lane. They pass the hedging and ditching man, who is examining a freshly excavated workman's boot. They pass the house where the General used to live, and which is now fitfully occupied at weekends by a couple from London who have already complained about the noise of chickens from over the road, and the crack of shotguns in the Hurst. They want horses banned from parts of the common because they chew up the footpaths, and they want to stop the teenage boys roaring around the tracks on old motorbikes. They want a fence round the village pond so that their child won't fall in.

'Goodbye, Notwithstanding,' calls Jessie, waving to the trees on Busses Common. 'We still love you. Goodbye, you good old place.' She wipes her eyes on her sleeve, and drives on.

Two months later Mrs Griffiths is mightily surprised to find Jack Oak standing at his usual post in the village shop, having bought his customary pack of cigarette papers. He hawks up phlegm, and remembers to swallow it.

'Artnoon,' says Jack, as usual. 'Turned out nice again. Looks like rain, though.'

'Mr Oak!' cries Mrs Griffiths. 'Why, I thought I must have seen a ghost! What brings you back to these parts?'

'Jus' visitin',' says Jack. 'Jus' visitin'.'

Mrs Griffiths says, 'I thought I saw your car outside.' She has improved in recent months. She has become sociable and talkative, has joined the Conservative Association, and collects money for the RSPCA and the donkey refuge. She has tried going to church but is horrified by how undignified and informal the services have become during her many decades of absenteeism, and so she has given up again. She has finally got round to writing a true-life romance, and it has been published by Mills & Boon under the name of Sophia D'Arcy de Vere. She is bursting with pleasure and pride, but can't think of anyone she'd dare tell, in case they should read it and come across the steamy scenes.

'How long are you staying?' she asks.

'Back tonight,' replies Jack. 'Got nowhere to stay round here no more.'

'How do you like your new house?' enquires Mrs Griffiths.

'It's all right,' says Jack, with a shrug.

'It's nice, is it?'

''S'all right.'

'Nice people? Have you made friends yet?'

'Ain't got round to it,' says Jack.

'Nice village?'

'Nice enough, if you like it.'

Mrs Griffiths tries a new tack. 'Have you met the people in your old house? They're terribly nice. Not here much, though. They've made some terrific improvements already.'

'Weren't nothing wrong with it in the first place,' says Jack, with an edge of bitterness in his voice. 'Can't see what they want to go changing it for. They ain't got the right.'

Mrs Griffiths and the lady behind the counter exchange significant glances. They are both thinking 'Poor old Jack'. Mrs Griffiths notices that Jack is much thinner and greyer than he was. He is still stinking and filthy, but his health is clearly worse, and he has a forlorn and vanquished air.

Over the next few weeks Mrs Griffiths encounters Jack more frequently. When he has finished in the shop he walks straight across the middle of the cricket pitch, and stands outside his old house with his hands in his pockets, just looking at it. One day the new owners see him and assume that he is a vagabond up to no good. The young man comes out, and Mrs Griffiths arrives just in time to set him right, to prevent him from calling the police, and to prevent Jack from telling him to bugger off. The young man is nonetheless afraid that Jack Oak might frighten the children, and he glowers at him every time he sees him standing immobile outside, like the trunk of a ruined apple tree, with his hands in his pockets, just looking and looking and looking at his old house.

The situation becomes steadily sadder and more absurd and Mrs Griffiths thinks about calling the social services. Instead she manages to trace Jessie in

309

the West Country, and Jessie says she's tried to stop him, to talk him out of it, but she can't. Jessie says that she's at her wits' end, but he always comes back and maybe he'll stop eventually.

On one occasion Mrs Griffiths comes to the village shop early and realises that Jack must have been there all night, finding him asleep in his Triumph Herald with nothing but a rug to cover him, and one day in January she calls round at his old cottage in order to collect for the donkey refuge and to ask if the new owners are intending to vote Conservative. There is a hoar frost, the twigs are thick with glistening rime, she is well wrapped up, and she walks carefully so as not to wintle on the rimy Bargate stones of the path. She feels fresh and renewed on freezing mornings like this.

As she goes up the path something snags the corner of her vision, and she turns her head quickly. There is a small garden shed on the left-hand side, up against the front hedge, and from the threshold protrudes a pair of old muddy brown boots with much-mended laces. She runs over, sure that she recognises them, and she puts her hand to her mouth in horror. 'Oh Jack!' she cries. 'Jack!' even though she has never addressed him by his first name during the sixty years of their entire acquaintance. She goes down on her knees and pulls back the crisp and stiffened rug from his face, 'Oh Jack, oh Jack,' she wails, and puts her hands to her cheeks and weeps in high-pitched little sobs. His hair is sparkling white and rigid with hoar frost, and his face is open-mouthed and grey. His teeth are like tombstones, his sightless eyes are round like dinner plates, but he has an arresting and horrible beauty.

They arrange for Obadiah Oak, known to everyone as Jack, to be buried in St Peter's church-yard instead of the one in his parish in the west. Jessie tells everyone at the funeral that she will never forgive herself, but people reassure her that she really did think she was acting for the best. The coroner establishes that it was misadventure, that he died specifically of hypothermia. Mrs Griffiths and the residents of longer standing, however, know perfectly well what it was that killed him.

# THE DEATH OF
# MISS AGATHA FEAKES

Miss Agatha Feakes summons her menagerie of animals. 'Chuffy chuffy chuffy chuffy!' she calls. It is her last day on this earth, but she does not know it yet, and the morning starts in its usual fashion. No one knows why she calls 'Chuffy chuffy chuffy chuffy' rather than the actual names of her dogs and cats, but the village has grown accustomed to it, and only the little children, whose minds have not got used to anything, wonder about it any more. Her voice is like the call of the cuckoo, mellow and tuneful, with a touch both of mournfulness and optimism. Like the cuckoo, her call carries for miles across the fields and coppices, and there is indeed a real cuckoo that roosts in the Hurst, who cranes his neck in curiosity and surprise whenever Miss Agatha Feakes calls her animals at seven o'clock in the morning.

Unlike the cuckoo, which is shy, as if it were ashamed of its own ways and would prefer to pass itself off as a wood pigeon, Miss Feakes is outgoing and conspicuous, even though she lives without human company. She had a lodger for a while, who conducted a lurid affair with the ever-obliging postman, but now she contents herself with the companionship of rabbits, chickens, goats, cats, Labradors, West Highland terriers and a jackdaw that she rescued when it was a fledgling. She does not need an alarm clock any more because the jackdaw thinks that it can sing, and joins in with the morning chorus. She wears a brown peaked cap because the bird sometimes sits upon her head and was never house-trained.

Miss Feakes feeds them all. The small dogs yap, bouncing up and down like quaint Victorian toys, and the slavering Labradors put their front paws up on the wooden table whose surface about the edges has been scoured by claws for forty years. The cats adorn the centre of the table and the shelves where plates used to be, otherwise entwining themselves about her legs, which are wound permanently, not only with cats but also with flesh-coloured elasticated bandage, reminding the village's old soldiers of the inexplicable puttees that they used to have to wear in the old days.

One of these old soldiers is the postman. He originally arrived as the batman to the General who used to own the house next door. He is thin, and very fit from cycling in all weathers. Even in winter the skin on his face and neck is golden brown, like old waxed pine, and he wears brightly polished army boots that he has maintained ever since the 1950s. He tells the children that his bicycle clips are for catching the change that falls through the holes in his pockets. He whistles when he arrives at the gate, and the dogs come to collect the biscuits with which he has befriended them, and which, for the purposes of his correspondence with the Inland Revenue, he considers to be a legitimate business expense. He leaves Miss Feakes's house until last, because she expects to give him a cup of tea.

He hates having to drink it, but he is soft-hearted. 'Do you think the weather'll hold up?' he asks her, as he surveys the grimy newspapers that serve in the place of carpets. Miss Feakes would not dream of taking a tabloid paper because the sheets are not big enough, and so she takes the *Daily Telegraph*, of whose editorial outlook she approves. In the evenings she reads about the cricket and falls asleep over the crossword.

'The forecast's always wrong,' she says, as usual. 'I know all about the weather from watching my animals.'

'Animals can foretell earthquakes,' says the postman, 'so I hear tell.'

He looks at his cup of tea. There is a decade of

tannin stain about the rim, and an oily film floating on the top. The tea tastes of cats. Some of them are not very domesticated and the whole house reeks of warm tom's urine, of wet dogs, of decaying newspaper, of dust. The house exhales a stupefying halitosis. It is so nauseating that no one can stay in there for longer than twenty minutes, and accordingly the postman rises to leave, his cup of tea unfinished. Today he will buy Miss Feakes a present. It will be a potted hyacinth, whose powerful scent of aunts and grandmothers might improve the atmosphere of the house, and he will find Miss Feakes's discarded body in the kitchen when he comes to give it to her in the morning. After the burial he will go to the graveyard on his own, and plant the hyacinth in her grave, so that even death might not defeat his good intentions. Nearby the yew tree that was originally planted to secure longbows for the King's army, beneath a mother-of-pearl sky that is reeling and drunken with rooks, he will take off his cap and gaze down upon the new-turned earth, and then, like a true Briton, he will restrain his tears as he paces out his grief along the rutty track that leads to the hill. He will see the deep green of the dog's mercury, and, above the busy noise of Mr Hamden's tractor, he will be spooked by the cuckoo that sounds like Miss Agatha Feakes calling her dogs.

But Miss Feakes is not yet dead, and she conducts her day exactly as if she will live for ever. She sits in her armchair, and, one by one, she defleas her cats. They sit expectantly, according to the daily ritual, and they jump, purring, into her lap. She combs the fleas from their necks, stroking against the lie of the fur, and then she does their flanks and haunches. She fluffs up the fur of the long-haired ones, and gives them whimsical hairstyles which she then pats flat again, so as not to compromise their dignity. When she does their bellies, they go wild-eyed and silly, and sometimes they embrace her wrists with their front paws, biting at her fingers from sheer pleasure. Miss Feakes extracts the fleas from between the tines of the comb and drops them into a cereal bowl that is full of scalding water. They struggle a little, and die. She likes to poke at them with a forefinger, so that they sink to the bottom and drown more quickly. Miss Feakes keeps all the fur from her combings, and puts it in carrier bags, because one day she is intending to have it spun, and then she can knit herself the softest and most personal cardigan in the history of the world. Sometimes she thinks that it might make more sense simply to use it for stuffing cushions, but really it wouldn't be the same.

When she has finished with the cats, Miss Feakes decides to go shopping. She has the same car that she has had since before the war. It is a grey 1927 Swift four-seat open tourer, with black mudguards and running boards, and a high steering wheel. The car is lovingly maintained for free by the two teetotal brothers at the garage, but at present the hood is falling apart and she has contrived to lose the wooden dash-board, exposing all the wiring. Therefore she takes it out only when her animals have not forecast rain. With long pins she secures a hat that, like her car, was flamboyant in her youth, and heaves at the starter handle. She has been feeling a little weak and woozy recently, and between each effort she pauses for breath and leans on the car, one hand on the top of the radi-ator for support. After so much time with the one car she has the knack of starting it, though, and it knocks into life and settles down into a steady tick. The car has a crash gearbox, but Miss Feakes is a maestro in the art of the double declutch, and the gears grate only when she surprises it into first. At the end of her drive she honks the rubber bulb of the horn several times, so that people will know that she is coming, and she will not have to lose precious momentum by using the brakes or changing down. In the village there are forty-two reckless drivers. Forty-one of them are nuns from the convent on the hill, who have altogether too much faith in the protective power of the Blessed Virgin, and the other is Miss Agatha Feakes, who today is going to Scats Farm Shop in Godalming in order to buy worming tablets, feed for her goats and chickens, a blade for her bowsaw and a new pair of wellington boots. Miss Feakes cannot easily reach her feet any more, but she has toenails like chisels, which

destroy the toes of one pair of wellington boots every
six months. She reminds herself daily to ask the doctor
to cut them for her, but when it comes to the crunch
she prefers to forswear the indignity. It is bad enough
that he unwraps and rewraps her bandages, inspecting
her varicose veins that are always in danger of ulcer-
ation. Twenty years ago he suggested an operation, but
she said, 'And who is going to look after my animals?
I have responsibilities, you know,' and so he never
suggested it again. Miss Feakes takes her creatures very
seriously; she has agreed with the vet that he can
purchase her house in advance of her death in return
for free treatment during her lifetime.

Miss Feakes returns from Scats. She passes the
hedging and ditching man, who is examining the rusty
remains of a shovel that he lost there ten years before.
Once home she unloads the sacks of feed herself,
heaving them into the shed and depositing them
among the tatty collection of rakes and forks and
faghooks. Miss Feakes always leaves the door of the
shed open in summer so that the same family of
swallows can breed in the top left-hand corner, and
today she goes up on tiptoe to see inside, because the
chicks are chirping, but she feels a little dizzy and
decides to go in for a cup of tea, well deserved. Outside
the kitchen her ancient car creaks as it cools down,
and one of her cats wrests the last warmth from the
engine by perching on the bonnet.

Miss Feakes is fortified by her tea and digestives, and in the company of her Labradors goes out into the Hurst. She has established that if she collects one fallen branch every week, and saws it up, she will accrue enough logs to see her through the winter. She has no other source of heating and would not have been able to afford the fuel even if she had. The oaks and beeches are kind to her, and she seldom has to wander far, but she likes birch logs best because they split so well. Miss Feakes likes to watch the flames of her fire because sometimes one sees a turquoise flame of unearthly beauty, so one can even look forward to winter.

On the way to the Hurst she meets a neighbour. 'Hello, Aggy, how are you?' asks Joan, and Miss Feakes replies, 'Orfy ell,' because she had not expected to meet anyone and has not inserted her teeth. Her favourite qualifier is 'awfully' and so Joan knows that Agatha is awfully well. 'Lovely day,' says Joan, and Agatha agrees, 'Orfy ice.'

Now Agatha is in the Hurst, the twigs breaking beneath her feet, and the pigeons calling. Her dogs put up an iridescent cock pheasant, who cries petulantly and whirrs away across the field. From the distance come the sounds of tennis, the hollow clonk of croquet balls. A boy called Peter is shooting a tin can with an air rifle, and the pellets zip as the can skips and clatters along a gravel path. Overhead the whoosh of a hot-air balloon from the club in Godalming sets her dogs barking, and Fred, the hippy-haired mechanic from Alfold Crossways, putters towards Hascombe in his home-made motorised hang-glider, which one day he will fly illegally to Ireland, where he will fall in love, never to return.

Miss Feakes finds a newly fallen limb of beech, but it is caught up in brambles, and she hacks at its twigs to disentangle it. She has a billhook that she uses for this, which she also uses to split kindling. In the 1960s she used to imagine that the kindling was Harold Wilson, who was an 'awfully horrid little man'. In this village only one person votes Labour, and only one person votes Liberal. The Liberal is considered a madman, and the Labourite a potential traitor. He owns the pub, however, and therefore has to be endured. Miss Feakes has voted Conservative ever since 1945, out of gratitude and respect for Winston Churchill.

Miss Feakes huffs and puffs as she drags the limb home. The dogs prance and growl, darting at the other end of it with their jaws, tugging at it, indulging some heroic doggy fantasy comprehensible only to their own simple imagination. The wood scrapes and bounces on the stones of the track, and Miss Feakes feels an unaccustomed weariness. It is as if her legs are becoming churlish. 'Come on, old girl,' she thinks to herself. She believes that old people live longer if they make no concessions to age, and in any case she thinks of herself no differently now than when she was eighteen, and strong and striking.

At the gate Agatha hears the telephone ringing, drops the branch and runs for the back door. Without taking her muddy wellingtons off, she pushes the door open, darts into the kitchen to fetch her teeth and dashes into the hall. Agatha is terribly excited, because nobody telephones her in the normal run of things. She is pleased that somebody wants to talk with her, she wonders who it is, she feels her heart jump with anticipation, and then she realises that the telephone wasn't ringing. 'Oh fire and fiddlesticks,' she says, 'it's that bird again,' for there is a starling in the village that has learned to imitate the telephone, and it flies from oak to oak along with its flock, causing young girls to think that at last he's phoned, causing widows to think that a child has called, causing the Rector to dread that it might be the rural Dean.

Agatha plonks herself down on the second step of the stair. She feels disappointed, and a little sick from all the rushing and hoping. She thinks that, since she's got her teeth in, she might as well phone someone herself. She tries to invent pretexts that she hasn't used before, and then she rings Joan. 'Oh hello, Joan,' she says, her voice full of cheeriness, 'awfully nice to see you this morning. I just wanted to tell you that I saw some awfully cheap spades in Scats, and I thought, "I must

tell Joan." Didn't Peter break yours? If I remember rightly
... Oh, you got another one ... well, never mind. Why
don't you pop round later and we'll have tea? I've got
some lovely digestives. It would be awfully nice.'

In the house next door, Joan's heart sinks into her
shoes. She is making fudge for the Women's Institute,
she is trying to listen to a soap opera on the radio, and
she remembers all too vividly that Agatha's tea tastes
of tomcat's water. She is sweating and uncomfortable,
unsure whether or not it's because of the menopause
or because of the effort of stirring the huge saucepan
of boiling goo. 'Oh Aggy,' she says, 'you must come
round here, I'm sure it's my turn. About five o'clock?'
Joan is fond of Agatha, and even secretly admires her
magnificent disregard for housework. Joan suspects that
if she were to be widowed and live to a solitary old age,
then she would end up just like Agatha too. Joan thinks
it remarkable that Agatha's abundant halo of snowy hair
is usually immaculate.

Agatha is thrilled to be popping next door later,
and it is with renewed verve that she fetches two chairs
from the kitchen and uses them to help her saw the
log. Her new blade cuts sweetly, and she ensures that
the sawdust falls on to newspaper so that she can use
it as litter for the hamster. Waste not, want not.
Thinking of the hamster inspires her to fetch it from
its cage and let it run around her body, up one arm,
across the backs of her shoulders and down the other

arm. She puts it in the pocket of her cardigan and it falls asleep. Agatha fetches a deckchair and decides to have a doze in the garden, so that she will be feeling as fresh as possible at teatime.

She catches the delicious pre-war smell of Joan's roses wafting in from the garden next door, and is lulled by the rattle and whine of a lawnmower in the middle distance. Her jackdaw flops out of the drawing-room window, and waddles portentously out into the middle of the lawn. It croaks from time to time, talking to itself about nothing in particular, peering between the blades of grass in the hope of interesting snacks, and then it menaces one of the cats, who regards it with aristocratic disdain and coolly parades away into the rhododendrons. A huge heron flaps slowly overhead, its belly laden with expensive goldfish from the big new pond constructed by the nouveau riche couple who moved in recently because it was so convenient for London. A light aircraft crosses the sun, casting a fleeting shadow upon Agatha and her house, and she is suddenly reminded of when the beautiful young men used to do victory rolls directly above, not a hundred feet in the air, teasing the tips of the oaks, and she could see them clearly in their cockpits, with their white silk scarves, and goggles, and leather headgear. She used to jump up and down, and wave, and they would smile and wave with one hand as their wondrous and romantic machines swept them back to Dunsfold aerodrome after another successful defence of country and king, the exhaust at the sides of their engine nacelles spitting bravado and orange flame. And that was how she got to know some of the handsome airmen, because they all turned up one summer evening in a three-tonner, and, with the aid of a ukelele, serenaded her from the gate, and then vaulted over it and invited themselves to tea, saying that they simply couldn't resist coming to visit the beautiful girl who always waved to them when they were flying home from seeing off the Hun. One day, on her birthday, two of them flew overhead in a Gypsy Moth and dropped roses and then landed in the field behind, so that the cows panicked, and they came in and invited her to a dance at the mess. Agatha smiles in her sleep, remembering that she spent three days bullying the Rector's daughter into teaching her how to waltz.

Agatha goes to tea with Joan at five o'clock precisely and Joan notices that there is a little piece of bramble in Agatha's hair, but she doesn't say anything. They talk about how the village isn't what it was. There's no one to run the village shop, and weekenders and commuters are snapping up the houses so that local people, born and bred, can't afford to live in their own community. The girls' cricket team is up to full complement, but the men's is two players short, and Agatha says that she'd play in it herself if she were younger. 'I used to bowl an awfully good googly.

'Did you know that Polly Wantage used to play for England?'

'Gracious,' says Joan, 'did she?' Joan is surprised that one can live in a village for so many years, and yet know others so slenderly.

'She was quite the spin bowler,' says Agatha. 'Wonderful leg break.'

Joan tries to imagine Polly playing cricket but she sees Polly only as she is now, apparelled like a man, in plus fours, hairy tweed jacket and deerstalker hat, prowling the woods in unrelenting pursuit of squirrels. The children say that she eats them, but this has never been proved. Polly lives in a large house in the woods at the end of a muddy track that is almost impassable in winter. She shares it with her lifelong companion, a secretive woman who wears fine dresses and lorgnettes and is rumoured to be an artist, but hardly anyone has ever seen her. Everybody suspects that Polly and her companion might be more than friends, but nobody has said so openly. Polly once scored a century against Australia. She is the kind of character who belongs to this soil and these people, in the same manner that the bracken belongs on Busses Common, and it is unwarranted for others to pry into details.

Agatha goes home and calls her menagerie. 'Chuffy chuffy chuffy chuffy!' She arranges the bowls about the floor, on top of the newspaper, and decides that she will spend the evening knitting another grey cardigan. Agatha is not fat, but she has pendulous breasts and can't be bothered with brassieres. She knits vast and shapeless grey cardigans that she mistakenly thinks will disguise their fascinating motion, and she wears each one until it disintegrates. She sits in her armchair in the living room, with the windows open so that she can hear the linnets sing, and her needles click together. 'Shoo shoo,' she says to the cats who come to tug at her wool.

Outside in the Hurst, Polly Wantage is shooting squirrels. The twelve-bore cracks, the dogs of the village are set to barking, and Agatha hears the little pellets pattering down through the leaves like the first drops of rain. Agatha deprecates this slaughter of innocent creatures, and she tuts about it to herself, but she pardons it because she thinks that Polly Wantage must be slightly dotty.

At eight o'clock Agatha decides to have supper, and goes to make a pot of tea. She arranges four digestive biscuits on a plate, which she will eat slowly in order to make them last.

She feels a sharp ache in her left arm, and then a blow from a sledgehammer seems to strike her from within. She gasps and falls to her knees. She has never known such bone-breaking pain in her whole life, and she is bewildered, breathless and astonished. She puts her hands to the floor and crawls a little way, but then lets herself collapse slowly sideways among the animals' dishes. She smells newsprint, mud, Kitekat and Chappie, and closes her eyes in agony and resignation.

Peace descends upon her like a mother's hand, and she has the feeling that she is flying away over the fields. Below is the stumpy tower of St Peter's Church on the hill, and, twenty miles away, the sparkling angel on the summit of Guildford Cathedral flashes a scintilla of golden light. She is higher than the rooks, and finds herself in a vast and empty space. She looks about expectantly, thinking that someone is coming to meet her, but there is no one at all. Not even her father, who spent his life behind a newspaper and a pall of pipe smoke, nor even her mother, who lived her life as if it were a penance.

There is no one to meet Miss Agatha Feakes. But then she looks down and sees that there are hundreds of animals; there are cats and rabbits, goats and hens, guinea pigs and dogs. She is shocked to realise that she knows all their names, all their likes and dislikes, all their whimsies. It strikes her as wondrous that her life must have been so abundant in affection.

She is about to pick up the first rabbit that she had when she was six years old, but she becomes aware that someone is coalescing out of the light. He is tall and slim, he is dressed in RAF service dress, and he has his peaked cap under his right arm. On the left breast of his tunic he wears the purple and white diagonal stripes of the Distinguished Flying Cross, and the red and white diagonal stripes of the Air Force Cross. She is about to shake hands, but he leans forward and kisses her softly on the cheek. Surprised, she puts her hand to her cheek, and smells Sunlight Soap, brilliantine and eau de cologne. Casually he removes the morning's brambles from her hair, and says, 'Hello, old thing.'

'Alec?' she asks, incredulous. 'Alec?'

Flight Lieutenant Alec Montrose raises a quizzical eyebrow and runs an elegant forefinger along his thin black moustache. He smiles, and Agatha's lips tremble at the memory. 'When I heard you'd been killed,' she says, 'I was most awfully upset. I cried buckets and buckets, for weeks and weeks. I wrapped the ring in tissue and I put it in my jewellery box, and every now and then I take it out and look.'

Alec bends down and places his cap rakishly on the head of a sleeping Labrador. When he straightens up he puts his right hand on her left hip, and says, 'My dance, I think.' Out in the ether Victor Sylvester's band strikes up their favourite tune. He draws her close and she lays her head on his shoulder. It is as if he is taking away all the accumulated weariness of life; it empties out of her like water from a jug.

In the arms of Alec Montrose, Agatha waltzes

and whirls away on lightened feet, and, far below, the village in which she was born and nourished, and into whose soil her body will melt away, prepares itself for the night.

# AFTERWORD

There was a long period during which I persuaded myself into believing that my childhood was a rural idyll. Upon reflection I realised that in fact I spent the greater part of my youth at boarding schools. My public school was admittedly in beautiful countryside, and I spent much time working for a local farmer, or walking on the local estate and sunbathing naked in its bracken when I should have been doing sports. The estate had a gibbet, hung with the ragged corpses of multitudes of vermin, and this is presumably how its gamekeepers proved their worth. I did partially fail to grow up middle class because I had exclusively working-class jobs at first, but all this is not quite the same as growing up wearing smocks and clogs, surrounded by geese and dozens of siblings, fetching pails of warm milk, and eating dishes made of the green and chewy parts of wild animals.

My village in southern Surrey was many years past the era of rural idyll. The centuries of 'idyll' were in any case a period of ignorance, disease, servitude, bone-numbing cold, relentless hard work, perinatal death and extreme penury. People died not of old age, but of being worn out. The idyllic moments must have been all the more precious, and all the more memorable, for their rarity. What was really special about those times was that everyone knew everyone else. Villages were proper communities, with all that that entails in terms of social support. These days, although a small core of sociable and helpful types is always to be found, village families often live in complete isolation from each other, buttonholed by their television and computer screens, and getting in their cars to go and see their friends elsewhere. There are people in villages today who don't know their neighbours at all, and would rather go shopping than to the village fete. Psychologically speaking, they are townies.

The villages of these islands were transformed progressively by the mechanisation of farming, rural de-industrialisation, the train, the bicycle and the motor car. In our village we no longer had just a few families who had intermarried for generations. The youngsters grew up and left, as I did, and families moved in not least because it was on the Portsmouth line to London.

Every morning bowler-hatted, pinstriped gentlemen
with their furled umbrellas strode to the station up New
Road, all of them looking like Major Thompson. In
the early 1950s my village won the Best Kept Village
competition, a sure sign that it was no longer a func-
tioning place of work, but had become simply a lovely
spot to live in. The lord of the manor wasn't some bluff
old gentleman with a hunter and two Labradors, but
an expert on Handel. There was no farrier, no blacksmith, no limeburner, no wheelwright, no cartwright,
no bodger making chair parts in the woods. The
butchers, bakers, grocers, cobblers, confectioners and
saddlers had all gone. There was a Malthouse Lane,
but the malthouse had become a farm. You still found
hops growing in the hedgerows. No one kept a pig in
their yard with the intention of cutting its throat in
the autumn, and no one was obliged to live off rabbits.
Poachers no longer poached out of necessity, because
you could get very cheap chicken in the new
Godalming Waitrose. The glass trade that had made
nearby Chiddingfold world-famous had long since
collapsed, on a whim of King James I. In Chilworth
the vast gunpowder factories had disappeared after
the Great War, and the ironmakers had vanished some
time in the late eighteenth century, although there is
plenty of ironstone left. The only specialist manufac-
turers in the area made walking sticks. I remember
just two old men who had the proper Surrey accent,

which has probably gone altogether by now. They used the strong postvocalic R that you still find in Dorset. There was 'for'ard' for 'forward', 'to'n' for 'to him or them', 'hosses' for 'horses', 'they' for 'them', 'twas' for 'it was', 'mos' for 'most', 'ye' for 'you' in the accusative, 'they was' for 'they were', 'ha' for 'had' when using the pluperfect. There were a few dialect words still left, and, according to Eric Parker, 'Joe Bassetts' had been the name for cockchafer grubs. I imagine that the dialect never was studied systematically, and is now almost lost for ever. At the beginning of the twentieth century, George Bourne noted down the speech of his gardener, Bettesworth, and anyone who is curious to know how Surrey spoke should take a look at his *Bettesworth Book*, and *Memoirs of a Surrey Labourer*. I worked for some months with a gardener who talked exactly like him.

There was a coal merchant and a brick factory. There was still a village shop, and a village pond, and a cricket green. There was still a rectory with a proper rector in it. There was still a pub, whose ceiling was decorated with a collection of chamber pots, and which to this day advertises its fare as 'warm beer, lousy food'. They had a dog called Beulah, who had rounded canine teeth because his hobby was collecting large pebbles. Most reassuringly, there was still an affable village policeman who got about on a bicycle, and a permanently suntanned village postman who kept his boots polished like the old soldier he was and wore clips around the bottom of his trousers.

In one corner of the green was a scrapyard and travelling fair run by a family who were referred to as 'the gypsies'. There was a time when it was proposed to set up another gypsy site at a place called Cuckoo Corner, and our gypsies joined in the protest against it, on the grounds that the new gypsies would probably be a lower class of gypsy who would give them all a bad name. Ours had a small pack of genial Alsatians that were almost unrecognisable as any breed because of their caking of mud and oil. Without the scrapyard I would never have managed to keep my Morris Minor going. They had a cleaning machine so powerful that it took the paint off my motorcycle. At the top of the hill was a school for delicate children. It was run by nuns whose suicidal driving was widely notorious. It had originally been built as a private house by a famous astronomer, who added an observatory, and was the first person in the village to have a car. There were still some small farms. One year I worked on the potato harvest, driving a tractor and trailer alongside the harvester. I had an accident with it, of course. I once helped to dismantle a chicken battery, and fell into the fragrant slurry pit at one end. My shoes were not allowed in the house thereafter, and neither were my trousers after I had worked on a pig farm.

Below the convent was common land, containing

a sandpit which must have been the remains of a small quarry and steep paths which were ideal for tobogganing. I have lovely memories of racing my mother and the dog down the hill, whooping with delight. My mother had huge furry mittens that I used to press to my cheek, and sometimes she went out on our walks with a trowel and a small sack so that she could collect the horse droppings for her roses. In those days the common was deep in flourishing bracken, which was ideal for hideouts. It was also ideal for courting couples, but it has now been reverted to heath by a new generation of eco-purists. Beyond, through a pinewood, was Sweetwater Lake, ringed by rhododendrons, still and silent, where I poached in vain for the rumoured trout, until I was caught by Colonel Redhead, who let me off because I had a proper fishing rod and hadn't broken off any branches. Behind the gypsies' scrapyard, extending all the way to Chiddingfold, was the Hurst, a very old wood full of mysterious pools and hummocks. It had a disused road that reminded me of Kipling's poem, except that it has never disappeared.

And now I begin to realise why, despite my better judgement, I cannot help looking back on it all as a rural idyll. The old social structure had gone, along with the old trades, but the countryside was intact. Because we had an inflexible family rule that the dog must be walked daily, I was out in the woods and fields every single day that I was at home. I discovered all sorts of secret places that will remain secret. I know where the bluebells and kingcups are. There is a sandpit where, infected yet baulked by the spirit of Wordsworth, I wrote my first bad poems while the dog sighed with boredom next to me. The Hurst was muddy and bewildering, but I got to know every inch of it. I know where the wild strawberries are.

Initially I decided to call this village Notwithstanding because for a long time I felt that it had not withstood. I was quite wrong about that. I had been disgusted by someone telling me not to throw sticks into the pond for the dog because it might frighten the ducks, and by some newcomer protesting about the calling of cockerels in the morning, and so I had begun to think that all was lost.

However, there really are one or two old families left. The village still looks exactly the same; there is still the Cricket Green Stores, a pond, a school, a pub, a disused pound, a village hall, cricket on the green. The cricketers still wear whites. The villagers planted trees to celebrate the millennium, the same as every other village. After all these years of accumulating the stories herein, I have grown fond of the name. It reminds me of the strange names of other English villages, and, after all, anyone who wishes to know the real name can work it out.

What has not withstood is the population. Most

of the people I knew are dead, because I was young then.

I was at a *salon du livre* in Pau a few years ago, when I met a French artist called Jacques. He told me that he adored Britain, because it was so exotic. I was dumbfounded and asked him what he meant. He replied that if he went to Germany, or France, or Belgium, or Holland, they all seemed the same. But *'La Grande Bretagne, c'est un asile immense.'* On reflection I realised that I had set so many of my novels and stories abroad, because custom had prevented me from seeing how exotic my own country is. Britain really is an immense lunatic asylum. That is one of the things that distinguishes us among the nations. We have a very flexible conception of normality. We are rigid and formal in some ways, but we believe in the right to eccentricity, as long as the eccentricities are large enough. We are not so tolerant of small ones. Woe betide you if you hold your knife incorrectly, but good luck to you if you wear a loin-cloth and live up a tree.

I began to write these stories, only to be flummoxed by Tim Pears, who, in 1993, and very much under the influence of the same Latin American writers who had influenced me, published *In the Place of Fallen Leaves*. It is a beautiful book, set in the English countryside, which will one day be considered a classic. I wrote to him saying something like

'A pox upon you, varlet, you've written the book I was just about to write', and he replied, 'I'll keep England if you keep abroad.' In the front of my copy he wrote: 'To Louis, fortunately busy abroad.' I have stuck to this agreement until now, and I hope that Tim forgives me for breaking it at last. His book obliged me to approach mine differently, but I hope that it is worthy to be somewhere near his on the shelf.

These days I live in a village in Norfolk, a place where there was only recently a man who lived in the woods with his animals. There is someone else who is a crack shot with a shotgun even though he has only one arm. This village is closer to its past. The dialect and accent just about survive. The names on the graves and war memorials are the names of families who still live here. I hope that one day my son and daughter will feel the same way about their childhood village in Norfolk as I do about mine in Surrey. In these stories I celebrate the quirky people I remember: the belligerent spinsters, the naked generals, the fudge-makers, the people who talked to spiders. I have not written what did happen, but what might or could or should have happened, and at one point I have ventured into a more distant past. Some of the stories I heard turned out to be false, as village rumours often are, but I kept them anyway. The moment I began to write I found that my instinct for fiction rapidly overwhelmed my respect for the truth, so that this village might be any village at all. Either way, the literary truth lies not in the details, but in the flavour.

The invisible background, of course, remains precisely that. I mean the imminent prospect of nuclear annihilation, the industrial strife, the inflation, the class warfare, the threat of petrol rationing, the terrorist bombs and the destructive 'generation gap' which meant that children no longer wanted to be like their parents, and parents felt hurt and bewildered. Literary writing then, as now, was almost entirely metropolitan. I don't mourn these things, any more than I mourn the discontinuation of death by appendicitis. I mourn the people, and I mourn my lost youth, which I entirely wasted through not having enough fun.

I have refused to romanticise the countryside in the sentimental way that seems obligatory in England. After all, the first things that strike you upon coming back from living in a town for any number of years, is the truly shocking amount of roadkill, and the late-winter horror of myxomatosis. Those who grow up loving the countryside do so in the same way as they grow to love their parents. I have aimed to capture the feeling of the times, and I do so remembering not so much the village as those who have been translated into the graveyard of St Peter's Church, and would otherwise have been forgotten. May they not rest, but live. Inter alia: Mrs Booth, Martin Carroe,

Connie and Cecil Chapman, the Churchills, Rev. Elton and Eileen, Molly Gabb, John the Gardener, Bernard Grillo, Sybil Harcourt-Clark, Alan Harper, Joan Herman, Mrs Hopkins, Molly Hyde, Lavander, Dr Strang McClay, Alan, Douglas and Brenda Maclachlan, Major John Major, Mrs Marriage, General Martin and Jean, Beetle and Tony Nation, the Nicholls, Mary Parker (memoirist of the village, and fellow Morris Minor driver), Peggy, Mrs Robertson (who once spent several days in the bath), Dicken and Ruth Steele, Trotty and Ted Sutton, Rev. David Thompson, Jack Thorn, Buzz Walford, Dennis Wieler, Beryl Williams, Yeoli and Kit Wilson. And Eric Parker, soldier, village patriot, indefatigably enthusiastic naturalist, and literary father of the village. I wish I had known him.

'Archie and the Birds': *Punch* (March 1997)
'Obadiah Oak, Mrs Griffiths and the Carol Singers':
      *Country Life* (November/December 1996)
'Archie and the Woman': *Independent* (15 August 1998)
'The Girt Pike': *London Magazine* (July–August 2002)
'Mrs Mac': *Daily Telegraph* (27 December 1997)
A version of 'All My Everlasting Love': *Waterstone's Diary* (1997)
'The Happy Death of the General': *Sunday Times* (8 July 2001)

'Rabbit': *New Writing 10* (Picador, March 2001)
'This Beautiful House': *The Times* (18 December 2004)
'The Broken Heart': *Saga Magazine* (January 2003)
'The Death of Miss Agatha Feakes': broadcast on BBC
     Radio 4 (1996)